MARINA GIRL

Heather Joy Hampton

To order additional copies of this book, contact:
Xlibris Corporation
1-888-795-4274
www.Xlibris.com
Orders@Xlibris.com
92453

CONTENTS

If you are not too long, I will wait for you all my life.

—Oscar Wilde

ACKNOWLEDGEMENTS

Embracing and publishing this book has been the hardest thing I have ever done. Pulling 75,000 words out of your ass is a tough thing to do. Pulling 75,000 words out of your heart is even more painful, like kidney stones, if kidney stones were emotional lumps scraping through veins down to my fingers tapping away at a laptop for two years.

My parents stood by and encouraged me in ways I can't quite understand until I have children of my own someday. Their faith in God pushed me through the darkest times of my life. Their belief and trust gave me strength. Their patience gave me courage when all I wanted to do was to be done with everything. I want to thank both of them for believing in me, for believing in each other, and for loving each other and teaching me what lifelong commitment is all about. Both of your have hearts bigger than you know, and I love both of you more than words can say.

I want to give big juicy smooch of thankfulness to all of my friends and family who supported and encouraged me along the way: Cliff and Melanie, Michael and Lauren, David and Danya, Aunt Patti, Uncle John, Aunt

Sherri, Uncle Danny, Aunt Arlene, Uncle George, Aunt Lorraine, Uncle Bill, Nana and Papa, Ke'ston, Kynleigh, Deven, Lyle, Camille, Amanda, Joe, Lia, Dev, Nicole, Adam, Matt, Annie, Dan, Mira, Steve, Jenn and many others.

To all of the magnificent people I encountered in San Francisco: every single one of you touched my heart and I will forever remember my time in San Francisco as my "good old days" especially the moments I enjoyed with the lovely ladies I had the pleasure and honor of sharing a home with. This book couldn't have been possible without the encouragement and support of my Pacific Heights Gentleman. You will always be my Mr. T.

I would also like to thank the Xlibris staff, Sal Sessa for the author photography, and Livia Hajovsky for the illustrations (and also for being my Mom).

—H.J.H.

MARINA GIRL'S LEXICON OF TERMS AND ABBREVIATIONS

30Sexpress: Marina neighborhood bus line that runs down Chestnut Street during rush hour, delivering Marina girls and guys into the Financial District after being vertically spooned by fellow riders.

bennie: Friend with *bow-chick-a-bow-wow benefits*, otherwise known as a booty call

cash 'n' prizes: Lady's assets. Breasts are the cash winnings and lady parts are the prize, as in a game show where someone wins cash and prizes

code yellow: Urine, pee-pee, tinkle, what you whisper to your friend at a quiet establishment or house party when you need to pee

code brown: Poop, number two, what you tell your roommates after pooping and making a stink

competitive dating: Dating someone because your friends are impressed by his job, car, apartment, looks, etc.

dart board dating: Sporadic dating pattern most often identified by dating individuals of drastic lifestyles, appearance, religions, occupations, locations, and personalities in the hopes of eventually figuring out the mate best suited for you

Dateway: The infamous Marina grocery store nicknamed Dateway for its reputation as the unofficial best place for the heterosexual white bread crowd to cruise for dates. The Marina Dateway is not a place to grab a gallon of milk in your pajamas. It is also not a place to gossip about Marina dudes, for there is a 22 percent chance your cart will bump into them midbreath. Nor is it a place to purchase supersized tampons (or any size of tampons for that matter), laxatives, or hemorrhoid cream (even if it is for under-eye circles). You better cross the Golden Gate Bridge to plug the vagessa or cure a code brown.

Depressica: Malaise of a melancholy Marina girl diagnosed by bunny slippers in the afternoon and oversized sunglasses worn indoors to disguise smeared mascara from last night. *Code red-elevated status would be Jessica Depressica.*

DOB: Dirty old bastards. If a Peter Pan is over the age of forty and still frolicking on Striped Shirt Alley with twenty-three-year-old Marina girls, he's a dirty old bastard.

douche bag pic: A guy who has a shirtless picture he took of himself in the bathroom mirror.

expiration dating: Dating someone knowing that the end of the relationship is in sight, normally due to moving or differing lifestyles.

fat butt skinny legs: Double-pleated khaki pants situated on a middle-aged man body with a bit of a paunch that make his legs look skinny and his butt look fat.

field of dreams: Creating a positive environment conducive to finding a boyfriend. Best example would be trashing all the stuffed animals, twin mattress, lace bedspreads, and hot pink comforters a.k.a. "If you build it, he will come."

Freegan: Person who adopts an alternative lifestyle as an urban forager based on limited participation in the conventional economy and minimal consumption of resources. In other words, they make you feel like an asshole by digging through your trash and eating the leftovers you just threw out.

gaysian: A homosexual man who is Asian.

good jeans: Jeans that may or may not be designer, but they make your booty look like two scoops of ice cream.

hairspiration: Being inspired by your haircut/color to do things you normally would not do

husbands: Guys that are dating in the hopes of finding that special someone to share the rest of their life with, or at least a girl that fits all their must-have requirements.

jelly: Being jealous.

just-add-water boyfriend: Meeting a guy and immediately falling in love with the idea of him without falling in love with him

liquid courage: Two glasses into an evening when you are drunk enough to lower your inhibitions but not too drunk to make an ass out of yourself. Also, see *hairspiration*.

little piggies: Toes, normally used in conversations surrounding getting a pedicure, or needing a pedicure.

man-child: Twenty-three-year-old recent college graduate making a six-figure salary and not a lick of sense about what to do with it.

mini: A potentially long-term relationship that fizzles within three months. Causes of minideaths include weird bedroom preferences, concealed drug habits, Peter Pan anti-relationship virus, and sudden intimacy death syndrome (see SIDS).

missed connection: craigslist online posting when you have a "moment" with a stranger across the room but do not exchange info: "Looking for the sweet piece of ass wearing a terry cloth jumpsuit. I was wearing a popped collared shirt and seersucker shorts at Betelnut last Sunday. Hit me up if you're single."

Pacific Heights Gentleman: A particular breed of men, usually rehabilitated former Marina Peter Pans, who live in the Pacific Heights neighborhood next to the Marina.

paper for numbers: Toilet paper for your number 1 and number 2, usually said under your breath when your roommate says "What else do we need to get?" while standing in the middle of Dateway. "Ummm, we need paper for our numbers. Ya know number 1 and number 2."

pecan and walnuts: *Man parts,* usually used in derogatory terms.

Peter Pan syndrome: Marina dudes, SoMa studs, Richmond players who live a stunted adolescent existence fueled by vodka red bulls and filled with high-end electronics and outdoor sporting gear. Their boyish good looks and charming personalities thinly disguise a layer of selfish whimsy, most often exhibited by a refusal to entertain the concept of growing up. The opportunity cost of committing to a Marina girl, or any woman for that matter, is far outweighed by doing whatever the hell they want whenever the hell they want. They just want to be boys forever! The Peter Pans of the Marina are clouded in an air of righteousness. They mock certain immature behaviors and then concoct their own theories for behaving identically as the lecherous people they fancy themselves to be superior to.

sausage factory: Location, usually a drinking establishment, filled with men.

sudden intimacy death syndrome (SIDS): Acronym used to explain the unexplainable situation where a relationship, usually a mini, dissolves overnight without explanation.

Striped Shirt Alley: Union Street/Fillmore Street, also known as fraternity row or the Bermuda Triangle

two-buck-chuck: Some winemaker down in the Central Valley of Southern California got the brilliant idea one day to buy up a bunch of failing wineries, combine them, and mass-produce popular varietals of wine on the cheap to be sold at Trader Joe's grocery store for only a $1.99 a bottle under the name Charles Shaw.

vagessa: Lady parts, downstairs, va-jay-jay, peek-a-choo, kooffee, okay fine I'll say it, vagina.

MARINA GIRL

CHAPTER ONE

TWANGY FRESH MEAT

Be yourself; everyone else is already taken.

—**Oscar Wilde**

TWO DOZEN "S'CUSE me" and "sorry" apologies were met with blank stares without a grasp of the Southern manners version of the English language as I navigated the metal tote-your-crap-rent-a-cart with a mind of its own through the San Francisco International Airport baggage claim and over to the cab stand. After four hours of antsy thumb twiddling, stale peanut munching, and grueling turbulences, I was ready to start my new life in San Francisco.

"Mornin'! Can I get a lift into the city?" I said as I wheeled my metal cart to the taxi at the front of the cab stand. The ninety-pound cab driver wearing a newsboy cap peeked over a newspaper and looked me up and down.

"No worries, I gotcha," she said, popping her gum as she reached for one of my suitcases.

"That's okay, I have it." I whiffed, blowing a lock of hair out of my face, lifting the oversized suitcase.

"Workin' for the tip somehow, ya know? I'm Chelsea." She took the suitcase out of my hands and slid it into the trunk. Chelsea mastered the art of invisible makeup and casual stylishness in a scruffy yet feminine way I could not quite understand, while half-heartedly loading the rest of my luggage into the trunk of her cab.

"Pleased to meet you, I'm Olivia." I sunk down into the crackled imitation leather back seat of the taxi cab and blotted my forehead with a handkerchief. It was fifty-five degrees outside, yet I had a flop of sweat that mirrored a point guard at the free throw line.

"So Olivia, where are ya headed to in the city?" Two-bit Chelsea with the trendy hat asked as she pulled out a notepad.

"Can you take me to Jackson and Davis, please?"

"Well well well, fresh meat, I see, you new in town? I can tell from the twang. No worries, you'll lose that accent soon enough." Chelsea decided as she jotted in her notepad and smacked it shut.

"What if I don't want to lose my accent?"

"Oh shit, lady, you're gonna lose it quick. Unless you enjoy people thinking you're inbred, but whatever, Bee-younce-eeah is on!" Chelsea turned up the volume and sang along to the music blaring from her taxi's janky speakers, twisting her head back and forth to the beat.

It all started with a phone call from the vice president of the architectural firm where I worked, after he heard through the corporate rumor mill I was willing to relocate for the right opportunity when I was notified my group was downsizing. Mr. Vice President made me an offer I couldn't refuse to relocate to San Francisco, so suddenly my twangy Texas world was turned inside out.

I had been living in the uptown neighborhood of Dallas and nursing a serious case of cabin fever due to living within thirty miles of my parents

HEATHER JOY HAMPTON

all my life combined by a tumultuous breakup with a very bad boyfriend. Plus, frankly, I was bored as hell. So when the call came, I was easily transportable and ready to get the heck out of Big D.

Within three days, I was flying to San Francisco for an interview with a few of the California high-ranking honchos. Those smart motherfuckers knew what they were doing by letting me spend a weekend all expenses paid: the city simply seduced me. Wandering through Chinatown back to my hotel room, the California street cable car's bell caught my attention in one of those definitive moments in time as a lanky tourist hung off a vertical grab bar to capture a photo of the Bay Bridge as the cable car careened down the steep incline. I cupped my hands around my eyes to block the sun as I watched the tourist's excited reactions. In that moment, I decided to move to San Francisco. I spent the rest of the weekend attempting to find an apartment and melted off three pounds walking up and down the steep hills of San Francisco.

"I found an apartment. It's a small studio, but it's a few blocks away from work and seemed safe," I said as I gasped at my first glimpse of the Golden Gate Bridge at the Powell-Hyde cable car turnaround, which minutes before catapulted me from Union Square to Fisherman's Wharf.

"Well, ummm, where are you right now?" my dad asked.

"I'm waiting for a cable car to take me back to my hotel," I said, taking a picture of the bridge from a distance.

"Wait, hold on a second, baby—Peanut, quit dribbling that ball!—I swear your brother is driving me crazy. Now, what is a cable car?"

"I'll show you pictures when I get back to Texas."

"So I guess this means that you are really moving then . . ."

"Yep, this will be home, Dad."

Growing up in hotter-than-hell Texas, there are only two seasons: summer and "the other one." Texans spend six months out of the year in sweltering triple-digit heat and the rest of the time in a dysfunctional, spastic relationship with the evening news meteorologist. Forty-degree temperature changes, torrential flooding, tornadoes, and ice storms were the norm October through April, so the foggy, mild climate of Northern California was a welcome change.

I always desired to live in a more urban environment like Manhattan, but the rat race of New York City was too daunting. San Francisco's seven by seven miles of steep hills, gingerbread Victorian painted ladies, and ocean adjacent location was the remedy to cure my cabin fever. My alabaster complexion that produced the nickname Snowflake in high school was also looking forward to the year-round sixty-two-degree weather.

I enjoyed my easy existence in my Texas bubble where everything was inexpensive, men were chivalrous and tall, and football was the primary religion. It was also all I knew, so I questioned if I liked Texas solely because it was familiar. My last couple of weeks in Dallas had a mellow routine of spending most weekends watching football at my favorite bar across the street from my apartment on McKinney Avenue and grabbing burritos as big as my forearm at one of the thirty Tex-Mex restaurants within a three-mile radius of my apartment. My soon-to-be San Francisco life was a postcard in my head of the glistening Golden Gate Bridge, shopping in Union Square at the five-story Macy's department store, and sipping pinot noir in tiny wine bars.

One cloudy December morning, exactly eleven days after the phone call that rocked my world, movers packed all my earthly belongings, crammed them into a big truck that lumbered down the tree-lined street I lived on in the uptown neighborhood of Dallas, and changed my life forever. Those carefully packed suitcases held two weeks' worth of suits, shoes, toiletries, Christmas presents, bedding, and other items I would need to get by while sleeping on the floor of my studio apartment until the movers delivered everything else.

Two-bits Chelsea switched on the hazard lights and clicked the taxi meter as I paused for a moment to calculate a tip for someone that lifted more than her body weight in luggage (minus the inbred comment) in front of my new high-rise residence in the Financial District of San Francisco. Habib the doorman (fancy, huh?) emerged from the double doors with a wheelie cart I only thought hotels used to help carry my junk into my five-hundred-square-foot studio with a view of the Bay Bridge.

"Hold on, let me put my bag down and find my wallet." I smiled to Habib as I fished through my purse while he unloaded my suitcases.

"Pardon?"

"I'm supposed to tip you, right?" Habib tsk-tsked, turned on one of his wing-tipped heels, and walked back to the elevator muttering under his breath in whatever language they speak where his people come from.

Twenty minutes later, my toiletries were neatly lined up in the bathroom vanity, suits hung in the closet, and seven pairs of shoes stacked in the closet cubby holes. I kicked off my shoes and sat down on the carpet, looked around, wondering where I would hang pictures. Even empty, the apartment felt claustrophobic. I walked toward the big patio and slid the sliding glass door open. It was half the size of my apartment in Texas, twice the rent, but totally worth it I decided as I gazed out onto the Bay Bridge in the distance.

Becoming a Marina girl didn't occur immediately. The stereotype of a Marina girl was a label initially unknown to me when I moved to San Francisco, but I instantly connected with that version of the San Francisco social scenery. As I walked through the crowded Financial District that afternoon for the first time, in my cheap turtleneck and cowboy boots, I found myself swimming in one of those definitive moments in life that grab you by the back of the neck, wishing I was one of the stylish and hurried Marina girls scurrying down Market Street to the Pine Street 30Sexpress bus stop. Each of the two dozen or so Marina girls was uniquely fresh, chic, and effortlessly dressed versus other San Francisco residents who appeared to have gotten dressed in the dark out of the dirty clothes bin. Those girls represented every reason I moved to San Francisco, a city that is a seductress to so many, welcoming every vice and delicacy in exchange for a steep cost of living.

Many come to San Francisco to be themselves, to escape from others, to chase whimsical fantasies, to taste the juice of societal freedom that so many parts of the country frowned upon. I wanted an adventure. I wanted to discover what I was made of. I wanted to live a life that was full of personal growth and unique experiences and accomplish more than I ever dreamed of. I wanted my life to be everything and nothing like I expected so when the opportunity presented itself to move to this quirky, topsy-turvy, glamorous, sparkling city by the bay I jumped at the change to turn my life upside down.

The dead bolt of my front door made a whack sound as I shut it after the movers finally left. "Okay, let's get this party started," I said out loud as I clapped my hands together in excitement. I turned around and bumped my head into the stack of boxes in front of me. I looked around the stack and only saw another stack. I squeezed between the two stacks into another stack. The entire apartment was filled floor to ceiling with moving boxes. *What if I needed to pee?* I thought as I bit my bottom lip. There were too many boxes in the way.

By sundown, most of the boxes were finally unpacked. I was making progress, but it wasn't pretty. I spent the rest of my New Year's Eve unpacking and playing furniture *Tetris*, rearranging everything to get it to somehow fit. My shoes had nowhere else to go but in the kitchen cupboard.

From a distance, I heard fireworks and stepped out onto my balcony to watch the kaleidoscope of sparkling bursts dance across the night sky. The twinkling white lights of the Bay Bridge off in the distance reminded me of the white lights wrapped around my parent's Christmas tree. I blinked to release a chubby tear and realized there wasn't a single person to softly wipe it away. I was all on my own from now on.

CHAPTER TWO

BRAGASAURUS

Life is just one damn thing after another.
—Elbert Hubbard

B RIGHT AND EARLY the next morning, I woke up with a food hangover from the Chinese takeout stinking up my pint-size refrigerator and decided now was the time to get up close and personal with nonperishable food. I walked across the street over to the tiniest grocery store I had ever shopped in and quickly loaded up on shaved turkey lunchmeat, a loaf of whole wheat bread, head of lettuce, jar of mayonnaise, and a two liter of diet soda into my handheld shopping basket.

It was New Year's Day, and I assumed most of my new neighbors were nursing hangovers instead of grocery shopping, which made the store feel a bit less claustrophobic. I walked down the adult beverage aisle toward the checkout stand and stopped dead in my tracks. Gin, scotch, bourbon—oh my! Score one for San Francisco! I could get big girl booze at the grocery store.

I headed toward the express lane with a pleasant smirk that quickly turned into a wide-eyed WTF nose flare from the code yellow stench reeking in front of me in line. He was wearing a dusty black wool coat of the variety I had only seen in period films . . . and a *top hat.* His face was lined with soot and weariness from living on the streets. He paid for his cheap booze in change and skulked away. I felt guilty for calling him Benjamin Franklin in my head.

"That will be $21.07."

"Really? Are you sure?" I asked, mentally recalculating the prices of the items in my basket. Everything seemed expensive, but I was buying the basics to make a sandwich. Alrighty then . . .

"How's the unpacking going, sweetie?" My mom's voice boomed as I balanced the phone between my shoulder and ear as I unpacked groceries.

"Mom, I bought just a few things to make a sandwich, and it cost me over twenty bucks!"

"Well, did you buy the good cheese?"

"No, just the basics," I grumbled, shutting the cabinet door with a whack, the sound reverberating in the perfect square box I now called home.

"Wine?"

"Nope, but you can buy liquor at the grocery store *on Sundays.*"

"You're in a different world now, baby, get used to it."

MARINA GIRL

Even the homeless man dropping a stinky code brown on the sidewalk couldn't muster my excitement for starting a new job in downtown San Francisco. I felt oh so very cosmopolitan wearing my new pair of knee-high suede boots as I walked in through the glass doors to the twentieth floor of a high rise situated on a bustling Market Street corner in the Financial District.

"So here's your space, only temporary, mind you." Henry Wadsworth said, clearing his throat as he showed me into a windowless room filled with rolls of site plans and carefully labeled boxes. The scuffed particle board desk he motioned towards was scattered with hand-me-down office supplies, and a desk chair missing an armrest. I was a well-compensated indentured architect thanks to the iron-clad relocation agreement I signed, which stipulated all expenses incurred to ship my silly self to San Francisco would need to be repaid if I decided to jump ship.

"Olga didn't approve of the new office space improvements, so we're here until whenever." Henry Wadsworth said, reacting to my eyes surveying the room. My new boss, Olga, was a disheveled German woman with a reputation for being a ball-buster of epic proportions. Her triangle mop of dishwater light brown hair and ill-fitting pant suits paired with functional loafers were rarely seen in the flesh. Olga preferred to belittle her employees with angry e-mails written in her immaculate kitchen two hours north of San Francisco, or via Henry Wadsworth, the most seasoned architect in the office.

"Thanks Henry. Any idea when we will move into our new office space?"

"Ummm, you should probably already know this," Henry paused and pursed his lips. "I pronounce my name *Henri* actually. Henry sounds so hetero, don't you think?"

"Hetero?" I asked as a heat of confusion crept up my legs. *Did this Henry/Henri character just tell me that he changed the pronunciation of his name so it would sound gayer?* Why would someone do that?

"Yes, darling, heterosexuality. You are familiar with this concept, no? Please make my day and tell me that Olga hired a lipstick lesbian cowgirl."

I shook my head and cleared my throat while I tried to make my brain stop acting like a pinball machine. "No, sir, I'm not a—what did you call it? Lipstick lesbian cowgirl?" I stammered as I set my tote on my new desk.

"Well, that should make your bumpkin cohort over there happy," Henry/Henri said, motioning toward our sole audience. "Meet Cameron."

"Hi, I'm Cameron. Let's go grab a coffee and then we can get started," he said, giving me a shoulder shrug that suggested that yes, Henry/Henri was in fact a bit nuts. Cameron was good-looking in a way that was just north of nerdy. He was tall, dressed like page 67 of a JCREW catalog with thick dark hair, and perfectly groomed without appearing to have "hair product," the guy's version of invisible makeup.

"Are you from Texas too?" I asked as he held the door open for me as we got into the elevator.

"Nah, I moved here from Philadelphia last year, but I'm a military brat, so I've lived all over the place. My folks are from Little Rock, and we moved back when I was in high school."

"So what brought you to San Francisco?" I said trying not to let him notice as I checked my hair in the reflection of the elevator's closed doors.

"Change of pace, I guess. I worked with Henry a few years back when I was first out of school."

"In Little Rock?" Good lord, I couldn't imagine Henry—excuse me, Henri—residing in Arkansas.

"Ha-ha, nah, we worked together in Philadelphia."

I followed him through the marble-tiled lobby and into the fog-filled madness that is Market Street at 9:00 a.m. Cameron gave me the thirty-second sound bite of his career for the past ten years: MBA from Northwestern, worked for one of the top commercial real estate developers in Philadelphia, moved to San Francisco to help Henry/Henri run the office.

"C'mon. Let's go to Peet's. They have this pumpkin spice blend you are gonna love."

Back at the office, Cameron sat down next to me, close enough for me to smell his cologne. Cameron seemed to take up even more space than necessary as he spread himself out as he explained to me the nuances of working for Henry/Henri. It was as if he was marking his territory with his masculine body language, allowing his long limbs to invade my personal space enough for it to feel flirtatious. After thirty minutes or so, Cameron went back to his desk and rarely spoke to me for the rest of the day while he jumped on and off conference calls. I tried to get myself situated and not catch the Southern gentleman sitting across the room from me staring at him. Sure, he was good-looking, but it was his bashfulness that made him endearing.

Henry Wadsworth was what I would describe as a sexual mullet—ya know, heterosexual in the front, homosexual in the back. Not in a literal kind of way, get your mind out of the gutter—in a fluid persona sort of way. When the occasion necessitated, Henry could pass as a beer-drinkin', golf playin', and pleated khaki-wearing guy's guy sort of dude. However, Henry was basically your typical Castro gay guy, but not in a blatantly flamboyant sort of way.

No one was more familiar with Henry's mullet homosexuality than his ex-wife Felicia. They were quintessential college sweethearts who met in ballet class sophomore year in college. Henry was the top male dancer, thanks to his twelve years of experience. But don't get fussy and fault Felicia for not noticing his suppressed sexuality. Henry overcompensated by being a lady's man among the ballerinas and sorority sisters of Kappa Kappa Gamma. By spring break of their junior year, it was assumed they would marry sometime in the near future, so that's what they did, because that is what everyone did back then.

A gold metal band around his ring finger and a wife in law school racking up countless hours studying left Henry home alone most nights and weekends, so he took up tennis, which is where he met his first on-the-down-low lover, Ricky, an exhilarating individual who looked magnificent in his tiny tennis shorts. Henry decided heterosexuality was not his happily ever after much to the dismay of his loving wife of seventeen years. This initially erupted into a wildly bitter divorce over Felicia's portion of his family's estate, until Henry did the unthinkable.

"Teddy, you're forty-three years old and haven't been married yet. Are you gay?" Henry asked his best friend since college.

"Look, just because I'm still single doesn't make me gay."

"You didn't answer my question."

"No, I'm not gay," Teddy responded.

"Well, I am, and you should see about dating Felicia." This was how Henry's former wife met the love of her life, Teddy. Henry was the best man at the wedding, just as Teddy was the best man at his.

Funny how life happens sometimes. The weekend cabin Felicia and Henry spent months negotiating the divide of during their divorce was the location of last Thanksgiving's ski trip. Henry brought his significant other, George, an interior decorator who recently completely refurnished the Lake Tahoe lodge shortly before the holiday trip.

It is absurd to divide people into good and bad.
People are either charming or tedious.

—Oscar Wilde

HEATHER JOY HAMPTON

Henry/Henri and I met up at an art gallery and happy hour spot in North Beach after work that day. It was like the cantina scene in Star Wars as I maneuvered through the maze of Mission Hipsters waxing on about the exhibit showcasing nude canvases. Henry was perched on a bench that resembled an amputated tree trunk, sipping a blended scotch on the rocks. I came to the conclusion that Henry looked like a middle-aged toad. He was five feet and seven inches on a good day, with a squatty build he attempted to camouflage with trendy yet mildly preppy clothing. If the proverbial gay best friend in every romantic comedy had a threesome with the Brooks Brothers, their offspring would be his wardrobe.

"Yoo-hoo!" Henry yelled in my direction over the pumping operatic music.

"Hi there," I shouted, sitting down next to him as a middle-aged man wearing a sign of random words meandered by.

"Oh goodie, the little Southern belle is here and ready to discover some actual culture. I didn't know what you like to drink, so I ordered you a light beer. You like light beer, don't you?" he said, smiling in my direction. Why would I like light beer?

"Thanks, appreciate it," I said, taking the longneck brown bottle from his hand.

"Isn't that all people drink down there?"

"Down where, Texas?" I took a deep swig out of the bottle. "Ummm, Texas is a pretty big place so I can't speak for everyone." I tried to dodge his question. Why do I feel the need to defend myself? Who cares if Henry/Henri convinced himself that I was some country bumpkin without getting to know me?

"Well, what's your drink of choice?"

"I like Crown Royal and 7-Up, or dirty martinis," I said, "but it really depends on the situation I'm in."

"Let's get you a big girl drink then. Those up there on the wall are called art," Henry/Henri said, assessing me with his eyes magnified purposely by the wire-rimmed spectacles that made his eyes look fishy. His philosophy about integrating a typical Texas girl into San Francisco was similar to throwing a toddler into the deep end of a swimming pool.

"The nudity doesn't bother you, does it?" he asked in a faux concerned tone. It did. "No, I can handle it," I said confidently as a tidal wave of panic came over me like a Gulf of Mexico hurricane.

Henry/Henri downshifted to a less-invasive conversation subject: himself, which I was quickly learning was his favorite topic to discuss.

Henry/Henri grew up in San Francisco, in the Marina neighborhood. "Ya know, it is the part of town cookie-cutter girls like you feel at home," he smarted.

"Total yuppie swamp, but the view of the Golden Gate Bridge from my grandmother's house along Marina Boulevard must be worth $10 million now."

The Marina girl is a San Francisco stereotype of a certain type of young woman that lives in the tiny neighborhood known as Marina/Cow Hollow. You need to know a bit about the history of the Marina to understand how and why the Marina girl developed into the albatross of San Francisco.

The Marina girl didn't exist in San Francisco's lexicon for most of the city's history. After the 1906 earthquake, the city of San Francisco pushed all the ashes and rubble north down the steep hills of Pacific Heights, creating a landfill adjacent to a former cow pasture that later became the Cow Hollow neighborhood.

Afterward, hundreds of Mediterranean-style homes were constructed in the 1920s on land that jiggled better than Bill Cosby's Jell-O when the 6.9 magnitude of the 1989 earthquake hit. Most of the longtime residents packed up and fled, leaving yuppie youngsters, perhaps less aware of their own mortality, to take over the neighborhood. Twenty years later, the Marina is the playground for the Republican rebels in the liberal mecca of America, the middle class of "fly-over" states, and San Francisco's worst nightmare, otherwise known as the Marina girl.

Three hours and five double scotches later, Henry/Henri had meandered into a monologue about convincing his life partner, George about the merits of a ruby engagement ring. "The mayor is simply one hot piece of ass. He loves the gays, you know. Gay marriage was legal in San Francisco for a minute, thanks to his tight rump."

I said my good-byes shortly after George arrived on the scene with an assortment of white leather fabric swatches and an attitude problem. Deciphering eggshell versus off-white was my last call moment with those two. Not because I was tired, but because I was coming to the quick realization that Henry/Henri was an asshole. From that evening forward, Henry/Henri became Bragasaurus in my head.

CHAPTER THREE

THE COPIES THAT BROUGHT ON THE CATFIGHT

Under certain circumstances, profanity provides a relief denied even to prayer.
—Mark Twain

"SO GEORGE AND I have an 'ugh-pointment' with the wedding planner at six o'clock, and I don't want to deal with another one of his drama productions if I'm late. Whatever, I need you to stop by the copy place on California and have two copies made of these site plans for my appointment with Paul Rogers in the a.m. Thanks, love, you're a dear." He ducked out of the "pit" with a hip jiggle and wrist flip.

I balanced my purse, laptop bag, and two heavy rolls of paper under my arms as I walked to the copy place on my way home from work. "Hi, can I order two copies of each?"

"You want it on this size paper?"

"The renderings are pretty detailed, so yeah, I think so, two identical copies of each roll."

"Hold on, let me see if we have this size paper in stock." He walked to the back room and I drummed my fingers on the counter, ogled the selection of stationary next to the register. Why don't people send letters anymore? A person's handwritten thoughts were poetic in a way e-mail could never demonstrate.

"Yep, looks like we should have enough paper this size. When do you need it by?"

"Tomorrow morning?" I crinkled my nose, fairly certain I was about to commit some sort of copy place travesty.

"Uh yeah, we can *do it* by then, but it will be a rush job. That costs a little extra." I leaned back on my left high heel and tried to remember Henry's specific instructions.

Meeting with Paul Rogers in the a.m.

"The copies are for a meeting tomorrow morning, so please do whatever you can."

The bells on the front door of the copy place jingled as I walked in bright and early the next morning.

"I have an order to pick up."

"Name, please?"

"Olivia Michaels."

"You brought in the big job yesterday?"

"Uh yeah, I dropped off two rolls of site plans yesterday after work." It didn't register that I dropped off a "big job" last night.

"Here we go, that will be $531.67," he said flatly.

"Um, okay." My fingers trembled as I fished out my emergency credit card from the back of my wallet. That was a lot more than I anticipated, but everything was a lot more than I anticipated in San Francisco. I balanced three rolls of site plans under each arm and kicked the door open with my butt as I finagled my way out of the copy place, as a mist of rain began to sprinkle.

"Here are the copies you wanted," I said as I lined all six tubes of rolled paper against the wall next to Henry's desk.

"Thanks, love." Bragasaurus said without looking up.

"My pleasure, the copy place is on my way home. Those babies sure were expensive, goodness." I wiped a bead of sweat off my forehead with the back of my hand.

"How much?" he said, still without looking up.

"Hold on, I have the receipt in my pocket, $531.67."

"What the hell is the matter with you? That is ridiculous." Henry sat back in his chair and crossed his arms across his chest. *Well I guess five hundys will get his attention.*

"I don't understand. I went to the place you told me to go to. I had them make copies exactly like you wanted. Honestly, everything seems expensive here." I shrugged my shoulders and nervously chewed on the inside of my mouth.

"The company is not going to pay for your lack of sophistication or common sense. Seriously, Olivia, you should have known better."

"What are you saying?"

"I'll tell you what I'm saying. The company is not being held responsible for that soggy receipt in your hand."

With moving and travel expenses still not reimbursed, I was situationally broke. The price tags in San Francisco were off the charts, so I had no understanding of the economy, just the $237 left in my checking account. My chin started to tremble so I clenched my teeth together and curled my fingers into fists. They were trembling too.

"You can take it up with Olga, I suppose, when she gets back from Germany."

I was speechless walking back to my desk in the "pit". *What a prick!* Not much work was done the rest of the day. I waited until he went home for the day before calling Olga's boss. I rationalized circumventing the chain of command was necessary as I tried to balance my checkbook in my head.

"This is Patrick."

"Hi Patrick, this is Olivia Michaels."

"Well hey there. How do you like San Francisco?"

"It's great." I lied. It wasn't great. It was exhausting. "I was wondering if you would be able to approve an expense report since Olga is out of the country."

"Sure, no problem. Just have Henry submit an office expense report."

"He, um, he actually wouldn't approve the expense."

"What was the expense for?"

"I had site plans copied last night. The bill was over 500 bucks."

"And he wouldn't approve *that*?"

"That's what he said."

"I swear, that guy, never mind. Just scan the receipt and send it to me. I'll take care of this."

The next morning, I boarded the cramped elevator and stabbed the twentieth-floor button as a chubby hand wearing a ruby pinkie ring peeked between the doors as they began to close shut, and when they slid open, Bragasaurus swaggers into the mirrored box. He directed a smug grin in my direction, and it was clear to me, he was enjoying watching me squirm. *Kiss my ass,* I said in my head as I stared at the floor buttons.

THE ROYAL EXCHANGE

"So me and a couple buddies I met when I hiked Half Dome are gonna grab some drinks at Royal Exchange after work, you in?" Cameron said without making eye contact as we both looked over a market analysis of office properties in Palo Alto that catered to venture capital firms.

"Sure," I said, smiling at the top of Cameron's head as his index finger traced under the property spec tenant improvement allowance for the swanky office space that would inevitably be occupied by people wearing attire only slightly more professional than pajamas.

"We'll need to get out of here before Henry comes back from his meeting," Cameron said, leaning back in his chair and rocking to a standing position.

I nodded my head and smiled. "Probably a good idea." Bragasaurus seemed to have at least a couple of long lunch meetings a week. Sometimes he returned to the office downright giddy or belligerent and surly. Either way, it wasn't pretty.

"So how do you like it here so far?"

"Umm, it's different . . .," I said, trailing off.

"You could say that, didn't answer my question though," Cameron said, smiling at me.

"I haven't really gotten used to it. Life is so different here."

"You're in the liberal mecca of America. The rules are different here. Life is harder in some ways, but it all balances out. Don't worry, you'll be fine, kiddo," Cameron said as he winked at me and walked out of the "pit". He started calling me kiddo a couple of weeks before. I wasn't really sure how I felt about his pet name seeing how my crush on Cameron and his perfect hair was growing by the day.

Promptly at four fifteen, I headed for the Royal Exchange with Cameron. The narrow pub three blocks from work was stocked full of financial types a little drunk from pints after market hours yelling at TV screens. It felt familiar, which felt particularly like silk. What I didn't particularly like was Bragasaurus. His misinterpretation of me was of a comical one-sided character, campy in a way that was out-of-date to the point of amusement.

Cameron high-fived and dude hugged a few guys. "What do you want from the bar?" He leaned in and put his hand on the small of my back, yelling in my ear over the roar of applause for a touchdown. I could smell his breath. It smelled like vanilla and toothpaste. I was tempted to "accidentally" turn while he spoke to me, just to see what would happen. Nah, his buddies were around. Maybe another time, scratch that, hopefully another time.

"Pyramid Hefeweizen." I leaned up and yelled into his ear as he leaned in and put his hand on the small of my back. I looked up at him, and he winked at me as he mouthed the word *nice* at my beer choice. Cameron's hand moved to squeeze my waist as he maneuvered around me to get to the bar. I watched him effortlessly flag the bartender and motion toward the Pyramid Hefeweizen beer tap and make a peace sign, ordering the same beer for himself. I shuffled through a pack of Brooks Brothers to grab my orange sliced beer pint from Cameron.

"I'm impressed, you know, about Pyramid. Cheers," Cameron said as we clinked our beer pints together.

"I hate shitty beer," I said, taking full advantage of the narrow, loud bar to get close to Cameron.

"Me too!" Cameron yelled. "My girlfriend loves Coors Light . . . so fucking annoying."

I almost spit back my $7 beer at this new tidbit of information. "You, ummm, you have a girlfriend?"

"Yeah yeah yeah, she's back in Philadelphia," Cameron said, his eyes focusing on the flat screen in front of us.

"That's cool," I said, beginning to nervously tear the edges of the cocktail napkin wrapped around my pint glass. "How long have y'all been dating?"

"Three years, maybe?" he said, leaning in, less so this time.

"Oh okay." I nodded up and down, focusing on an eight-inch-by-ten-inch framed black-and-white photo across the bar, hoping Cameron didn't notice that my blinking capabilities were temporarily not operating to the best of their capabilities. "Wait, I see that guy all the time!" I said, pointing to the guy wearing the sign.

"Oh, that guy. Yeah, he's everywhere. I don't know how he does it. I see him all the time. Anyways, she only drinks shitty beer, shitty wine, and diet caffeine free soda. Nice, right?" Cameron said, leaning closely into me again. I shrugged my shoulders as a non-response, trying to find the button to turn on my girl code odometer.

"What does she think of San Francisco?" I asked.

"She visited once when I first moved here. Hated it, hasn't been back since. I see her when I go to Philadelphia, or we'll meet up somewhere in between."

"That's cool," I said being as neutral as Sweden, or at least trying to fake my way to be.

"No, it's not, it's not cool," Cameron said, shaking his head and looking down at me. For a brief moment, the noise silenced, the world paused, and he stared for a long time into my eyes.

"I'm going to find the ladies' room. Can you hold my beer?" I asked, handing him my Hefeweizen pint.

"Down those stairs over there."

My T-strap heels clickety-clacked down the steep wooden stairs to the ladies' room as I fished my phone out of my purse. I pressed number 3 to dial my oldest friend back in Texas, Camille, whom I've known since the fifth grade.

"What's up?" she said in the low voice she only used at work. I cursed the two-hour time difference.

"Cameron has a *girlfriend!*" I hissed into the phone.

"No shit?"

"When did he tell you?"

"Just now . . . Cameron invited me to happy hour with his buddies. I order a beer, and he gets all flirty, and then tells me that his girlfriend back in Philadelphia only likes shitty beer," I replied as I assessed my hair in the ladies' room mirror.

"You're there with his buddies?"

"Yeah, some guys he went hiking with."

"Cameron hikes? Isn't that walking, but outside?" Camille said, laughing. I pictured Camille sitting in her corner cubicle with the Eiffel Tower poster I gave to her last year for her birthday tacked to the wall.

"What should I do?!" I dug through my makeup bag to fish out my lip gloss.

"Here's what you do: go back out there, keep being your super sweet self, but start flirting with boys, his friends if it's appropriate," she said matter-of-factly as I swept a fresh coast of peach lip gloss onto my lips.

"Got it. You're the best!"

"Go get 'em, girl. Call me when you get home. I want *details!*" Camille loudly whispered into the phone.

I flipped my head upside down to get some volume in my hair, undid two buttons of my blouse to reveal the rise in my cleavage, and checked all my cash 'n' prizes to make sure everything was working it like it was for sale and the rent was due. *Oh shit, let's not be obvious,* I thought as I buttoned back up one button before leaving the restroom.

Cameron was in a heated discussion, probably about fantasy football, with one of his buddies as I approached the group. I inched my way

HEATHER JOY HAMPTON

through his friends and made eye contact with a couple of them as I sashayed through the pile of stockbrokers back to Cameron to get my beer back.

"Hey, Jason, this is Olivia. She just moved here from Dallas," Cameron said, standing between me and his somewhat attractive friend.

"Nice to meet you," Jason probably said as I translated what I thought his lips mouthed. He stuck his hand out to shake mine, so I figured my lip reading was at least somewhat accurate.

"Where are you from?" I yelled into his ear. He was only five foot seven, so I didn't have to yell into the wilderness above when talking to Jason like I did with Cameron.

"Atlanta!" Jason yelled. "I moved here a couple years ago when I got out of grad school."

"That's awesome!" I yelled, hoping he could read lips too. "How do you know Cameron?" I said, pointing to Cameron in case his lip-reading abilities were unhampered by beer enough to need hand gestures.

"Ummm, he knows my buddy over there . . . Hey, listen, I need to get going, can I get your number? I would love to hang out sometime."

"Sure! Sure. Do you have a pen?"

"Nah, here's my card though. E-mail me," Jason said, handing me his business card.

"Nice to meet you, Miss Texas." He winked as he walked away.

Cameron must have been able to read lips, or body language, because as soon as Jason walked off, Cameron came from behind me and said, "Damn, girl, you move fast."

"What do you mean?" I yelled up to Cameron's wilderness.

"Already got a phone number?"

"He gave me his business card though."

"Yeah, so?"

"Why didn't he punch my number into his phone?"

"Ummm, I dunno. Maybe he's playing hard to get?" Cameron laughed.

"Shouldn't I be the one playing hard to get?"

"Not in this town. San Francisco isn't what you are used to, I guess."

"I guess so."

Sure, I second-guessed moving to San Francisco. Sure, I wondered if I had the balls to handle being this far out of my comfort zone. My building charged $500 bucks a month for parking, and work was only a few blocks away, so I didn't bring my beloved truck Boudreaux with me to San Francisco. Plus, driving up and down those steep-ass hills in a pickup truck scared me. Now, in the middle of Union Square, I found myself carless with a slippery bathroom floor.

"You should go to Bed, Bath & Beyond in SoMa, but not sommmme weekends, like the Folsom Street Festival, S&M my dear," George lisped into the phone. George pronounced his name *Whore-hey* and had eyeliner permanently tattooed to his eyelids. After meeting Bragasaurus a few years ago, Whore-hey began to go by the Spanish pronunciation, *Whore-hey*. Despite being 100 percent Chinese, Whore-hey was delusional enough to think everyone believed his faux Spanish accent and pompous enough to get away with it.

"Okay, I don't understand what that means. Can you help me? I really need a bath mat," I huffed into the phone.

"Oh gawds, Crate & Barrel, maybe?" Whore-hey yawned into the phone.

"Is that in Union Square?"

"Hold on, let me ask Henri."

"What are you confused about now?" Bragasaurus snarled into the phone.

"I'm trying to find a place that sells bath mats in Union Square."

"Jesus Christ, I'm not your tour guide." *Click.*

Nice, I thought to myself as I looked around trying to identify locals from tourists. I approached the only person I was certain who lived in San Francisco: the street performer spray-painted head-to-toe in silver shiny lacquer like C-3PO.

"Ummm, s'cuse me, can you tell me where Crate and Barrel is?"

The human C-3PO shrugged his shoulders and motioned to his mouth. Apparently, he was also a mute.

"At least can you tell me which direction?"

The human C-3PO rubbed his thumb with his fore and middle fingers in a gimme money motion. "Are you kidding me? Jackass," I huffed and walked toward Market Street, beginning the process of elimination, wandering Union Square.

Three hours later, I climbed into the Muni and leaned on the metal pole. My overpriced generic bath mat stuffed under my shoulder. I looked over to a hipster sitting in the corner angrily drawing into a moleskin journal, wearing an Eating Meat Is Murder T-shirt. I guess the hipster's aversion to animal murder didn't apply to his notebook. Hypocrite, thank God the grocery store sells hard liquor.

I kicked off my heels as I walked into my apartment, peeled off my clothes, threw on my college sweatshirt and pair of baggy cargo pants. *That's a beauty,* I thought as I checked out the new blister blossoming like a mushroom cap at the base of my ankle. I reached for the half-empty bottle of Crown Royal from the cupboard above the sink and poured myself a stiff one, topping it off with a splash of 7-Up. I took a sip and felt the burn in the back of my throat. It hurt so good. Then I plopped my tired ass onto the couch and clicked the TV on. A rerun of the *Cosby Show*: Mrs. Huxtable goes on a crash diet to fit into a formal dress. Her real-life sister, Debbie Allen, plays her overbearing trainer who whips Mrs. Huxtable into shape. Hours later, I woke up to an infomercial about some piece of exercise equipment that gave a money-back guarantee if it didn't peel off three inches from your gut. No wonder I was dreaming about Debbie Allen tying me to a hydro glide 3000. I met her once when I waited tables in college. She made me cry.

The ice in my half-finished Crown Royal on the rocks with a splash of 7-Up long since melted. I picked up the glass and downed the rest in one fatal swoop, wiping the perspiration from the glass off my coffee table with the arm of my sweatshirt.

The next morning, I woke up on the couch, the sun beaming into my apartment from the reflection of the office building across the park.. It was nice sometimes having one entire wall of my apartment comprised of two long windows with a sliding glass door. Just wish the apartment weren't only twenty-five feet long. Outside the sliding glass door was a large patio with a spectacular view of the Bay Bridge and a park where people went to smoke pot a lot. I peeled myself off the sofa and walked out onto the patio, getting my socks moist from the morning dew. I stretched, pulling my arms as high as possible, looking back at the clock on the wall. It was only 7:30 a.m. What the hell am I supposed to do with my Sunday?

I slipped off my wet socks and walked back into the apartment, peeling clothes off as I made my way to the bathroom. Maybe someone was in the office building across the park getting some work done on the weekends? Maybe they could see into my apartment? Frankly, I didn't give a shit. It felt a tad naughty that someone might see me naked. I was starting to feel androgynous lately. Men didn't look at me like they did in Texas. Men in Texas had no problem with approaching a woman and paying her a compliment. Whatever, let's not focus on Texas, let's focus on getting through the day without crying.

I forced myself to shake off the onset of Jessica Depressica and take a shower. Focus on the task at hand. Turn on the water. Check. Take a towel out of the wicker bin next to the sink and slide it onto the towel rack in the shower. Check. Step into the shower. Check. Get my hair wet. Check. I squeezed a quarter-sized dollop of shampoo into my hand, and my mind began to wander as I worked the bubbly volume-boosting lather into my hair. More shopping in Union Square? Nah, I had had enough of that yesterday. I could go to the Ferry Building and pick up cheese from Cowgirl Creamery, or some sourdough bread.

Sourdough bread kicked Texas Toast's ass. I swear I heard chanting from Justin Herman Plaza, probably another protest. The last Sunday I went to the Ferry Building during a protest, I ended up in the middle of pro-choice activists protesting a pro-life march. Pink-haired lesbians with black-and-white striped tights like deranged Strawberry Shortcakes screamed at Catholic school girls holding signs of aborted fetuses. I can always go to the Ferry Building on my lunch break. Besides, I wasn't in the mood for the National Guard this morning, at least not until I had my morning latte. Maybe I could jump on Muni and get off at a random stop? The better I got to know San Francisco, the more I might like it.

I scrubbed the sweat and whiskey off and then turned the shower to ice-cold while I rinsed my hair. *In Style* magazine told me last month that ice-cold water made hair shinier.

An hour later, I stuffed my wallet, phone, and city map into my purse before locking my apartment, letting my keys join the party in my casual weekend bag. It was small enough not to make my shoulder sore from carrying it all day and had plenty of compartments, always a plus. I walked two blocks to the Embarcadero MUNI/BART stop. A Rastafarian with braids as thick as my wrist and a matted beard played a steel guitar on the steps leading to the train platform. I turned down Tom Petty blaring from my ear buds to listen. He was playing a reggae version of Kenny Rogers's song "The Gambler," a marvelous melodic blend of home and now. My lethargic mood immediately perked up.

ACCIDENTAL ANOREXIA

The city of San Francisco was starving me to death. Sixty percent of food was inedible, for a myriad of reasons: Korean soup with the giant ball of hair, sweet-'n'-sour mystery meat, gummy tuna sandwiches, lumpy chicken noodle soup, even a toasted bagel turned into a culinary catastrophe when it was knocked out of my hand and landed cream cheese face down on the corner of Sansome and Market Street. The deranged transient flailing his arms and screaming about aliens attacking his chromosomes didn't notice. I guess he had bigger problems than my bagel.

The Financial District of San Francisco burst at the seams with delis, diners, sandwich shops, and coffee shops. I spent those first few weeks of January working late hours, often losing track of time in meetings that caused me to skip lunch since every eating establishment between 425 Market and my apartment closed by two o'clock.

Trekking up and down the city's forty-nine hills on the weekends, walking to and from work every day, I had dropped eight pounds in under a month. While you can never be too rich or too thin, the unfortunate bagging where my badonkadonk used to be in my jeans was becoming a serious problem. My diet was quickly becoming food that fell from a vending machine. One night, at around 6:30 p.m., I opened the plastic wrapping to a bag of microwavable popcorn and massaged the kernels to spread them out in the bag. I heard my cell phone ring to the tune of "All My Exes Live in Texas." Who else would have that ringtone? I quickly punched the universal Popcorn button on my microwave and jogged back to the pit. It was Jason from Royal Exchange, so I played it cool while I sauntered back to the kitchen area to get my evening treat.

"You should come to my buddy Kyle's cookout on Sunday. His wife, Kelly, is from Dallas. They live in the Marina. Cool people." Jason, with the semi-awkward flirtation tactics, was asking me on a date.

The break room was full of smoke. Somehow, two minutes in the microwave caused my $0.75 dinner to set off the smoke alarms . . . on the entire floor, causing panic for all the other workaholics on my floor, including Bragasaurus, who had regaled me as a campy idiot from the get-go. I ran back to my desk and scooped up all my personal belongings, meanwhile agreeing to accompany Jason to a BBQ the following weekend as the building's fire alarms went off.

Walking down twenty flights of stairs in four-inch heels is no small feat. I was breathless by the time I made it to the monstrous security desk in the lobby. There were two firemen in full gear talking to a security guard in an oversized polyester blazer.

"Hi," I said to no one in particular, just the group of hunkiness in general. "I work on the twentieth floor and burnt popcorn in the microwave so . . ." I saw Henri emerge from the stairwell blotting his forehead with a handkerchief, his bulbous pinkie ring reflecting the beads of sweat on his hands. "That's it. Thanks."

When you are only five foot two, you learn to walk quickly to keep up with longer-legged people in a big hurry. So that is exactly what I did, cutting in and out of the crowds of people mingling outside of our building. Both sides of Market Street were blocked off by four massive fire trucks. Trickles of sweat bled down my spine, the humiliation and panic sinking in.

I dug into my purse for my phone and punched the number of my former boss in Texas. He resembled Coronal Sanders, you know, Kentucky Fried Chicken, with a big pompadour of hair and a white goatee. He wore Wrangler jeans on casual Fridays and a big gold belt buckle. He thought I was ballsy and nuts for moving to San Francisco.

"You really wanna be around all them hippies?" he asked, with a thick slab of chewing tobacco lodged in his mouth, when I told him I was moving to San Francisco.

"Hey, Steve, it's the crazy girl that moved to San Francisco. Sorry if I sound out of breath, I just walked down twenty flights of stairs. Why? BECAUSE I CAUGHT THE BUILDING ON FIRE! No, not really. I burned popcorn. There were four fire trucks, and the whole building was evacuated. Oh shit, I think I stepped in pee-pee. Anyways, thought you would get a kick out of that. The fire, not the pee-pee. Okay then, bye."

Clothes make the man. Naked people have little or no influence on society.
—**Mark Twain**

MY DATE WITH WONDER WOMAN'S UNDERWEAR

What can I say? I'm from Texas and love a cookout, plus the potential to make new friends. Cookouts in Texas were always either because of football or when the weather was warm, so I drew a blank when it came to selecting an outfit for the chilly February function. I opted for a cable-knit sweater and my new Levi jeans with flap back pockets that I bought at the Levi flagship store in Union Square. It was rainy and chilly when Jason picked me up in his convertible BMW, top down of course.

"Do you mind putting the top up? It's a little cold," I asked Jason the stranger/date to cookout/new SF friend.

"Kinda, it would ruin the magic of Chinatown."

The dance party version of Fleetwood Mac's "Stand Back" blared from the convertible as we were propelled through northern San Francisco. I tried to admire the adorable Victorian walk-ups while I tried to forget that my hair was transforming into a wet cocker spaniel as the misty rain came down. The BBQ was stocked full of the frosty glares I was becoming all too familiar with. Friendly, casual conversations with strangers at a BBQ buffet line was the easiest social interaction I had known until this point. Even compliments were met with dull thuds when another partygoer complimented my jeans and I touched her shoulder to girl-bond chat about how I bought them for $30 bucks earlier that week.

Kyle, the BBQ host, burst into the small area where all the partygoers were crowded into with their longneck beers and Portobello mushroom burgers, wearing a gigantic sombrero, his wife's Wonder Woman underwear, cowboy boots, and nothin' else. Kyle grabbed my date's waist and proceeded to rub on him like a drunken douche bag lookin' to get his freak on at a dance club.

My white knuckles clamped down around my bottle neck beer, my breath like a hampered distress signal. "You have got to be kidding me," I said under my breath in a frosty whisper. I quickly excused myself into the nearest bathroom, barely locking the door as a single tear plopped onto my old cable-knit sweater. I fished through my purse looking for my makeup bag but found my wallet first. Two-bit Chelsea the cabdriver's business card shoved between two twenty-dollar bills was the magic concoction I needed to get out of this mess.

"This is Chelsea."

"Hey Chelsea. This is Olivia. You picked me up from the airport last month."

"Oh yeah, I remember you. Fresh meat, right? Well, the accent isn't getting any better."

"Hey, I'm at a party. Is there any way you can pick me up?"

"What neighborhood are you in?"

"I don't know exactly. I'm sorry; I should know that, right?"

"No worries. Just walk outside and go to the nearest street corner."

"Okay, I can do that." I said as I snuck out of the bathroom and down the main hallway. I softly closed the front door shut and jogged to the nearest street corner.

"I'm at Union and Gough."

"Sweet, I'm not too far from there. Hang tight fresh meat, I will be there in five minutes."

I decided then and there that the only man in my life would be George Foreman and his lean, mean, grilling machine.

CHAPTER FOUR

NOSE DONUTS

Most people are other people. Their thoughts are someone else's opinions,
their lives a mime-ery, their passions a quotation.

—Oscar Wilde

FOR MOST WOMEN, one of the most challenging aspects of moving to a new city is finding that special someone who will cherish their hair, bring out the best from their crowning glory, and artfully disguise all hair imperfections. I discovered Jackson shortly after moving to San Francisco on a recommendation from a girl I met at one of Whore-hey's parties whose hair looked like spun gold.

Jackson worked at an upscale hair salon nestled on the corner of Sacramento and Steiner in Pacific Heights. The interior of the salon was shabby chic meets contemporary stylishness, and they served complimentary wine, so of course, I loved this salon. Besides the bottomless glasses of vino and adorable interior, my favorite part of the salon was my hairstylist.

Jackson was a six-foot-three-inch Stunner from Seattle who had panache for chameleoning into his latest bennie every six weeks. There was Cock'r Spaniel the dog trainer, the unidentified older gentleman who was a cosmetic dermatologist specializing in Botox, the hoarder from San Diego, and Taco Paco. I spent the number 1 Muni bus ride over to his salon in Pacific Heights wondering what his latest bennie's issue/addiction/peccadillo would be.

"Jackson, I want to go blond . . ."

"No no no no no. I am not taking a head full of gorgeous red hair and turning it blond. You want to be some typical Marina girl?"

"What is a Marina girl?"

"Miss Texas, you are so fresh off the boat," he said in my ear, leaning onto the back of my shabby chic salon chair.

"It's my hair. I'm tired of being a redhead. I'm sick of people asking me if I have a temper or telling me I look like Lucille Ball." I crossed my arms across my chest defiantly.

"What about . . . working in some blond highlights around the face? That would look gorgeous on you!" Jackson said.

"C'mon, highlights would just be highlighted red hair. Why won't you just dye it?"

"Fine, whatever, you want it blond as mine or blonder than mine? I can always grab the Clorox from the janitor's closet . . ."

"Thank you." I hiccupped as a tear started to percolate. I had no idea why I was so emotional.

"I hope you don't have anything to do the rest of the afternoon. This is going to take a while, but that's just fine with me because I . . . have . . . so . . . much . . . to tell you about Benihana!"

"Like the hibachi place?"

"Sounds like that. Benihana isn't his name anyways. His name is, hang on a second . . . Thau Thau, maybe? I can't remember, doesn't matter, he's a Gaysian Freegan."

"Freegan?"

"Oh my gawd, girl . . . Freegans," he said, throwing his hands in the air.

One can always be kind to people about whom one cares nothing.
—Oscar Wilde

MARINA GIRLS

My first encounter with a Marina girl occurred three months into living in San Francisco. Erin, a friend I met at Royal Exchange the night I met Sombrero BBQ Jason, invited me to a Saturday jaunt to Napa with her friends. Two Marina girls were one of the half-dozen of us that piled into a stretch limo one rainy spring morning headed to Cakebread winery in Napa.

They were gorgeous in a homecoming queen meets Abercrombie sort of way with perfectly torn True Religion jeans tucked into Ugg boots. Hung over from their recent vacay to Fort Lauderdale, they inquired with a yawn about painkillers. My new friend's boyfriend, who resembled Fred Savage from the *Wonder Years*, pulled out an Altoid mint box from his back pocket and tossed it to one of the Marina girls.

"Mimosa?"

"Def, hold the OJ though."

After much drinking at a members-only wine event at Cakebread, a Marina guy in the group walked next to me back to the limo. "So are you going to the after-party, Miss Texas?" he slurred.

"Yeah, I think so . . ."

"Should be legit, lots of nose donuts." He coughed.

"Oh goodness, no donuts for me, I drank too much wine today. A donut would really upset my stomach."

"Hey, Wonder Years, can you toss me the Altoids?" said Marina Girl Number 2.

"This one is the E, right?" Number 2 said to Number 1.

"Duh, don't be such a lame ass."

Back at the after-party, Number 1, 2, and Marina Guy quickly retreated to the back bedroom for some "nose donuts."

"Who did you vote for anyways?" Wonder Years slurred from too much Cakebread merlot.

"I don't really like to talk politics, I think it's rude. Are they going to come out of that room soon? I think I am going to head home. Long day . . ."

"You're a fucking Republican, aren't you?"

"What?" I looked out the window at the twinkling lights.

"You heard me, you dumb bitch. You voted it for 'Dummbbbya,' didn't you?"

I spent the next day nursing my hangover, flipping through the TV channels in my old college sweatshirt. A rerun of the *Wonder Years* was on. That Fred Savage was a lot more personable than that piece of shit I encountered the day before. Who the hell runs around calling people dumb bitches for no good reason? Oh yeah, cokeheads, that is who. Drunken cokeheads run around belligerently calling people drunk bitches. Drunken cokeheads that keep ecstasy in Altoid boxes. What did Erin see in that guy anyways? Maybe he had a magical . . . oh, never mind.

"How was your first trip to Napa?" Cameron asked after we wrapped up our first conference call Monday morning.

"It was so beautiful!"

"It is even prettier in the summer before the vines are harvested. I took my parents to Napa last June."

"Did you have a good time with Erin and her friends?"

"They are, how do I say this, hard partiers?" I raised my eyebrow.

"Yeah, I heard that about them. They don't get that out of hand very often. Most of the time, they are good people, typical Marina girls. Did her boyfriend hassle you about Bush?"

"Yeah, you could say that. What is a Marina girl?"

"Well, there are girls that live in the Marina and the Marina girl stereotype. Girls that live in the Marina are probably more like you than anywhere else in the city. Ya know, a little on the preppy side, not as liberal as everyone else, has a good job, good girls. Then there are the Marina girls that usually come from some family money, party too hard, and generally are totally obnoxious. So some people in San Francisco assume that every girl in the Marina is like that. You should think about moving to the Marina."

"I don't want to live near those girls."

"Don't get me wrong. Those girls do live in the Marina, but most girls in the Marina are a lot like you."

NAKED DARTH VADER

"Honey, why don't you have dinner with friends?"

"Mom, I haven't really made any friends I would want to spend my birthday with, so I booked a few nights at a place in Napa for the week," I said, biting my thumbnail, firmly confirming I was a big fat loser.

"I know, sweetie. Save that vacation for when you meet a nice guy," she said with a deadpan yet optimistic inflection in her voice.

For my first birthday in San Francisco, I was all alone with no real friends to celebrate with. Going on a vacation solo made me feel lonely, yet I was thankful I had a job that allowed me to soothe my loneliness with fine wine and massages in the wine country. The daily grind of isolation became a normal part of life.

I rented a convertible and headed to Napa for the week. On the way back into the city, I went to China Beach. I sat down on a slightly weathered turquoise beach towel with my $3 striped IKEA cheapie beach tote at my side and pulled out my journal.

> *The Golden Gate Bridge is staring back at me in its magnificent, taunting, and deceiving glory. I always imagined that the bridge led to some sort of paradise or land of milk and honey. It does sort of, but it is the long route to the Wine Country.*

I snapped the leather-bound journal shut and took a walk on the beach toward the bridge. There were only a handful of people out that afternoon: a weekend dad making sand castles with two toddlers, a woman water coloring with an easel firmly planted in the sand and everything. I thought she took the cake for the oddest person on the beach, but then, there he was, in all his glory, *a man sunbathing naked wearing a Darth Vader mask.* I shit you not.

Was I living in San Francisco or on Mars?

CHAPTER FIVE

KAPPA KAPPA KRAIGSLIST

Friendship is born at that moment when one person says to another,
"What! You too? I thought I was the only one."
—CS Lewis

AN INCOMPETENT GENERAL contractor and overzealous housewife with too many interior decorating magazines were the cupids who inadvertently introduced Henry and Whore-hey as a result of a bloated budget and behind-schedule seven-bedroom Sea Cliff home construction project. If it wasn't for the home's intricate design, Henry never would have felt the need to grace the site with his presence for an inspection with the general contractor and lender. Whore-hey, the lead interior decorator for one of the top design firms in the city, was also requested to attend the meeting to go over the interior finishes as supporting evidence of the budget. An increasingly tense meeting led to drinks and conversation at Clift House afterward. Perhaps it was the breathtaking landscape near Ocean Beach, but a spark erupted that night between Henry and Whore-hey. Their first date was to an art gallery south of Market where the paintings were well worth the hefty price tags. They were inseparable ever since. Whore-hey had a jovial demeanor that brought out the warm papa bear quality often hidden in Henry's personality. I quickly came to adore Whore-hey and loved spending time with him enough to put up with Henry's consistent bragging after normal working hours.

"So, honey, what's been going on with you lately?" Whore-hey cooed when Bragasaurus left the table to go to the "little boy's room" as Whore-hey called it.

"Umm, just trying to figure out what my next move is when my lease is up at the end of the year."

"Oh! Really? I didn't realize it had been that long since you moved to San Francisco." I could tell by his tone that Bragasaurus enlisted Whore-hey to pick my brain if I was leaving when my relocation contract expired. This game would have been flawlessly played by Whore-hey except for one problem: Whore-hey sucked at being manipulative. I felt like I was on a date with an overly rambunctious guy a frenemy made me go out with.

"Yep, it has been almost a year believe it or not," I responded as I took a deep gulp of my vodka tonic.

"So what are you trying to figure out, doll face?" *And here come the pet names.* Whore-hey always reverted to pet names when he was fishing for information, or trying to get his way with Bragasaurus, in certain situations what Bragasaurus regaled to me was a bit on the TMI side though.

"Where I'm going to live when my lease is up."

"You aren't thinking about moving back to Sticksville, are you?" Game, set, match—it is on like Donkey Kong 'til the break o' dawn. If I play this right, I might get a promotion or at least a raise.

"C'mon, Whore-hey, you know I haven't exactly had the best year of my life. I feel like I don't fit in here, ya know?"

"Here's what you need to understand about San Francisco," Whore-hey said sternly. "There's no specific 'lifestyle.' Fitting in is just a matter of finding your niche, a small group of friends. Sure, there are all kinds of lifestyles running around this town. This isn't Dallas, honey, where everyone is marching to the beat of the same drum. Get your MRS degree, get married by twenty-five, have kids by thirty. You can live your life however you want, do what you want. Learn Mandarin, go paragliding, join a book club, carve out your little pocket of familiarity."

"Yeah, that's true." San Francisco was beautiful, extraordinary, and provided a buffet of every delicacy, activity, lifestyle choice, and human malfunction possible.

"Honey, why don't you move into an apartment with roommates somewhere in Russian Hill, or hell, even the Marina?" Whore-hey shooed as Bragasaurus came back to the table.

"What are we talking about?" Bragasaurus said as he folded his napkin back in his lap.

"I was telling our little friend here how she should move to Russian Hill or the Marina."

"Oh really, so you are thinking about staying in San Francisco?" Shit. I was hoping to ride the vague wave long enough to get my way.

"I'm really enjoying the job and like the projects I'm assigned. Management in SoCal said I might lead a design project soon if I keep working hard."

"Well, I haven't discussed your promotion with Olga or with them for that matter."

"You told me you would."

"You've only been in your current position a year. Normally, it takes someone two to three years to be promoted. You know that."

"I do, either three years or thirty-six projects, whichever comes first. I'm wrapping up my thirty-fourth project right now with the other two in the pipeline."

"We've been so busy, I haven't really kept count."

"Of course you haven't."

While their fact-finding expedition was annoying as all get out, Whore-hey did offer up a good suggestion. Maybe I needed to find a roommate. I checked out some roommate postings online and decided I would have a better living situation with a roommate.

FAUX FRENCHIE

San Francisco is a transient city full of people coming and going so more often than not. One month you have five close friends, and then poof, they disappear to graduate school or take a job in Denver. Occasionally, they may even get married and move to a suburb of the city where the cost of living is cheaper. Nonetheless, even the locals are constantly making new friends. I was having trouble making any at all. So I sucked it up and threw myself to the wolves. I went to at least one event each week in search of friends, more often than not coming home either frustrated or in tears.

The Wednesday night dinner club was a kaleidoscope of peculiar city dwellers. I called them the bourgeois bohemians in my head. Each week they met up at a new upscale restaurant for fine cuisine, conversation, and of course, wine.

I hung on to the cable car railing as it scooted through Nob Hill, hopping off at Hyde Street and Jackson and walking to Hyde Street Bistro. It made me nauseous to dine in such a romantic, cozy place with this hodgepodge of catastrophes. Bean the thirty-six-year-old perpetual Olive Oil, Mustafa the greasy Egyptian (although I believed him to be Libyan), popped-collared guy who introduced himself as Kool-Aid, a DOB from Hayes Valley, and Faux Frenchie.

"Eez so nice to meet you."

"Likewise."

"Vere do yew leave?"

"In the Financial District, at Jackson and Davis."

"Jew leave in za Goal dean Gate Towahs?"

"Exactly!"

"Zat eez so gooed fah jew!"

"Thanks, it is a nice building. What about you? Where do you live?"

"Eye leave in za mee shun."

"Oh okay. Where are you from originally?"

"Eye comb foam zee Burlingomm."

"The Burlingomm? Where is that?"

"Eez in za Zouth Bay."

"Oh! Burlingame! Sorry, I assumed you were from somewhere in Europe, like France."

"No, eye comb foam zee Burlingomm,"

Burlingame, a higher-end suburb, is located in San Mateo County directly south of San Francisco. *Does she have some sort of speech impediment? Why the hell is she talking like that?* I didn't want to get all in her business, so I smiled and pretended this was all normal, having dinner with a bunch of strangers: the bean, popped-collar Kool-Aid, the greasy Egyptian, the semi-creepy older dude, Faux Frenchie, and me. I rounded out the group as the random chick from Texas, so I guess that made all of us a hodgepodge of catastrophes.

The next evening, I went to a "roommate interview" at an apartment on North Point Street, half a block away from the infamous Marina grocery store nicknamed Dateway for its reputation as the unofficial best place for the heterosexual white wonder bread crowd to cruise for dates. The more granola SoMa crowd perused the cage-free eggs at Whole Foods on Fourth and Harrison while trying to pick up chicks. Of course, Castro has the Gayway on Market Street. The Marina Dateway is not a place to grab a gallon of milk in your pajamas. It is also not a place to gossip about Marina dudes for there is a 22 percent chance your cart will bump into them mid breath. Nor is it a place to purchase supersized tampons (or any size tampons for that matter), laxatives, or hemorrhoid cream (even if it is for under-eye circles). You better cross the Golden Gate Bridge to plug the vagessa or cure a code brown.

Vacating roommate, a nondescript girl in yoga pants and an oversized T-shirt, couldn't have been less interested as I oohed and aahed over the only apartment I had seen in San Francisco with real charm. The terra-cotta-colored walls, Mexican-tiled bathrooms, open floor plan, and original kitchen fixtures gave it a whimsical flair that reminded me of a single girl's apartment in romantic comedies.

The apartment's proximity to Dateway and the 30Sexpress's bus line made certain I was ready to sign on the dotted line—until the roommate remaining, Salsa Suzie, came home. She was a Latin ballroom instructor in her spare time from what big T-shirt and yoga pants told me. Her Blond Ambition Tour—inspired ponytail and dismissive, arched, ballroom makeup eyebrow gave me the sinking feeling that we would not become besties in the future. Damn shame, I really love Mexican-tiled bathrooms.

I had the pleasure of making the acquaintance of the Webster Girls the following week. The Webster Girls, which is how they signed the three e-mails we exchanged, lived in a steep walk-up at the top of Pacific Heights on Webster and Broadway. The apartment was a potpourri of IKEA furniture and Urban Outfitters decor. The Webster Girls had also invited twenty other girls, creating an after-Christmas sale environment, with twenty-three-year-olds gushing over the flaking robin's egg-colored paint in the living room. The room for rent was not actually a bedroom but a sitting area converted into a bedroom by a decorative room divider.

"Is there a closet?" I asked, doing the math in my head of exactly how many shoes I owned. You can never have a big enough closet, ever. In my wildest fantasies, I have a lavender velvet chaise lounge I luxuriate in while contemplating what to wear.

"Oh that. Well, you see, you will just need to get one of those rack thingies and maybe an over-the-door hanger for your shoes," Webster Girl Number 1 said with a concerned excitement. My dorm room in college was bigger than this bedroom.

"O.M.G., this is so retro," the statuesque Marina girl who I would have guesstimated to be twenty-one or so, exclaimed.

I broke the heel of my favorite pair of tall boots navigating down the steep Webster Street hill to Union Street where cabs frequented, picking up patrons of the restaurants and bars near Webster Street. After a solid ten minutes of trying to hail a cab, I sat down on a bench outside of Blue Light Bar and pulled out flip-flops from my purse. This was the fourth heel broken by one of San Francisco's forty-nine hills. After the second broken heel, I learned my lesson to carry an emergency pair of Old Navy $3 flip-flops at all times. It was a long, long walk back to the Financial District that evening but a pretty one, and the crisp fresh air was invigorating.

I am a mid-20s professional female who needs a room in SF with awesome female roommates (sorry, no boys). I'm moving back to the Bay Area after living in NYC for the past five years.

I'm a very social, bubbly person that loves to laugh and go out on the weekends to new bars and restaurants, but I'm definitely over the "woo-hoo partay" stage in my life. :) I don't bring any drama home (I hope you are the same). If you think we'd make a good match, perhaps we could meet up and look for places together. Feel free to shoot me an e-mail and tell me about yourself.

Great minds think alike I thought as I fluffed my newly platinum curls in the store-front window along Fillmore Street a week later. Her ad on craigslist mirrored the ad I mentally wrote as I walked home from the Webster house. We exchanged a few e-mails then agreed to meet for coffee. The brunette with the sunny smile staring back at me from my computer monitor looked approachable and sweet.

I walked into Jovino and ordered a cheese plate and glass of merlot before taking a seat at one of the outdoor patio tables. Although Zoe was a very pretty girl, she stood out among the ocean of blond ponytails enjoying $8 glasses of orange juice as she sat down in front of me. Zoe was petite like me with curly shoulder-length brown hair and a wide, toothy smile. She seemed friendly and a big bundle of energy.

Over red wine and a cheese plate, I learned Zoe was an enlightened Jewish American princess, the version that Northern California produces in small quantities. When I asked her about Judaism, just general questions, Zoe confessed she didn't really know about Judaism and had never stepped foot in a synagogue in her life. Huh? She explained she was ethnically Jewish but didn't practice the religion. Zoe was raised a vegetarian but ate any animal in the ocean. Sort of Jewish, sort of vegetarian, Zoe was a Jew-tarian. Zoe was opening a denim store on Union Street, Jean Genius, in January. Her passion for fashion combined with start-up money recently inherited from *an uncle who passed away the summer before would put her mark on the Union Street* fashion scene. We became fast friends and confirmed roommates despite not finding a place to live yet.

A few days later, Zoe and I went on our first apartment scouting trip. We toured an apartment off California Street in Nob Hill that reeked of Chinese food rotting in the fridge and another first-floor apartment off

Sutter and Hyde Street with metal bars on the windows. Afterward, we bonded over margaritas at La Barca on Lombard Street and decided to open up our search parameters to three bedrooms, just in case she could talk the landlord down to our price range. I thought she was optimistically aggressive, and I loved it.

There wasn't a legal parking space within five blocks of the three-story walk-up on Francisco Street, off Franklin, around the corner from Fort Mason, right in the middle of one of the most charming blocks in the Marina. A woman resembling Miss America and her husband emerged from the building as we were buzzed in. Miss America was nearly six feet tall with a halo of blond hair topping a blank canvas of Nordic features. She reminded me of one of those untouchable girls two grades above you in high school that everyone stared at as she crossed the cafeteria to hold court at the cool kids' lunch table. Her husband, wearing double-pleated Dockers and loafers sans socks, looked overstuffed into his business casual pants.

"Fat butt skinny legs," Zoe murmured, shaking her head. "Pleated khakis need to be outlawed."

Our heeled boots clapped against the hardwood floors as Zoe and I walked down the main hallway, admiring the apartment. It even had a backyard! The mossy bricks of the patio immediately felt like home.

Jeremiah, the landlord, was handsome in a blue collar sort of way, not the typical Marina guy with floppy blond hair, popped collar, $200 jeans, and flip-flops. He was also not the typical professor-type guy who wore trendy sneakers Zoe told me she preferred over drinks at Twenty-First Amendment a few days prior. I found Jeremiah's overgrown curly brown hair endearing, in a disheveled kind of way.

Jeremiah spent the past three months renovating the apartment from Animal House booting out "Franco Pizza Face" and "Couch Glue," he told us.

"We're *very* interested in the apartment. Is there any way you can knock a few hundred off the rent?"

"Ahh, the rent is pretty fixed really. I put a lot of work into this place."

"C'mon, Jeremiah, you know you want us to live here," Zoe cajoled, winking at him playfully. Damn, she was a good negotiator.

> *The total history of almost anyone would shock almost everyone.*
> **—Mignon McLaughlin**

"You guys can hang out here and meet with people if you want," our handsome landlord offered after five minutes of haggling with Zoe, who sweet-talked him down to a final rent price provided we found a third roommate.

With Jeremiah loafing in a lazy boy recliner, which was the only piece of furniture in the spacious living room, we met with the first potential roommate from our craigslist posting.

"Hello! Pleased to meet you, I'm Zoe and this is Olivia."

"I am Akiko," said the robotic voice coming from the exquisitely beautiful six-foot-tall Japanese android. Her body language, even the tick-tick-tick way she blinked her eyes, was automated. I contemplated if she was battery operated.

"So tell us about your current situation."

"I live with person," Akiko/R2-D2 said in her computerized voice.

Next up was Julie, a big-five accounting auditor who told us that having a communal stash of condoms was paramount for her nympho sex life, made Jeremiah start coughing uncontrollably from his lazy boy. "I'm sorry, that shit was funny. I had to leave the room."

Then Hurricane Carrie, an anorexic attorney from an exclusive suburb in the south bay, blew through, getting into an argument with Zoe over the shared parking situation. Watching Zoe and this broad was better than a fast-paced tennis match.

"I need a beer after that one. Want anything?" I asked my new partner in crime as we scouted the Grove for an available table. Two Pyramid Hefeweizens should get us through this next round.

"Whatever you are having if you're buying," Zoe said, sitting down at a four top near the window, taking off her trench coat.

Scheduled in increments of twenty minutes, we had three more potential roommates to meet that night, and Mama needed a big beer to get her through the stiff smiles and small talk.

Tonia or Tanya, the investment banker fresh off Wall Street who tried to lowball us to drop her potential portion of the rent, had a snooty attitude and Prada shoes.

Shannon, the interior designer with the adorable haircut, babbled about the improvement of her booty after a month taking Bar Method classes.

And then there was Katie. All smiles and shiny straight hair, Katie was bubbly, frank, and funny. She was a second-grade schoolteacher for a small private girl's school in Pacific Heights. Katie was a breath of fresh air and as sweet as a cupcake.

"That's Hefeweizen, right? I can tell by the lemon. I'm a beer girl too." She giggled.

Later on that night, clippety-clopping down Fillmore Street, Zoe and I mentally scotch-taped our happily ever after, deciding Katie was the ideal third roommate. This was going to be legendary: Zoe the Jew-tarian, Olivia the Texan, and Cupcake.

BOUDREAUX

"Dad and I thought we would drive your truck out to San Francisco for Thanksgiving," said my mom as she tossed a load of towels into the washing machine. I could hear the familiar tick of the cycle setting through the phone, and she felt so much closer than 1,800 miles away.

Ten days later, Mom, Dad, and my beloved old Ford pickup truck arrived at the doorstep of my new home in the Marina. A cardboard sign hung from the passenger side door that read "Frisco or Bust" in big child-like letters. The pickup truck was named Boudreaux Tibeadeaux but was rarely called by its full name since the usage of middle names is reserved for misbehavior, and Boudreaux had been a most dependable mode of transportation for years before I moved to San Francisco. I saw

Boudreaux's gun metal gray reflection out of the corner of my eye, nearly dropping the Breakfast at Tiffany framed photo I was nailing to the living room wall.

"Let me give you the grand tour." I waved my arm like one of Barker's beauties on the *Price Is Right* television show. We walked down the long hallway to the empty bedrooms, which provided my dad ample opportunity to examine each door hinge, bathroom fixture, windowpane, sliding closet door, bathroom tile, shower nozzle, you get the drift. Twenty minutes later, the tour and Dad's house autopsy were complete except for the kitchen. I knew that would keep him occupied for at least half an hour.

"So tell me all about your roommates," she said, pushing an unruly lock of hair behind my ear.

"Well, Zoe is a real sweetheart. She's like a big mug of hot chocolate, really warm and just a sweet person. Ummm, she's Jewish and she's a vegetarian but she eats fish."

"And what is the other roommate's name?"

"Katie. I think she went to school in Santa Monica, or Santa Barbara, I forget, one of those Christmas cities. Anyways, she's a second-grade teacher and really nice. Weird to be moving in with girls I barely know."

"Pumpkin, you could practically fit in this sink!"

"Mike, what is that beeping noise?"

"Livvy, there's pull-out drawers in the icebox. You could fit four gallons of milk down there!"

"The fridge makes a beeping noise if you leave the door open longer than thirty seconds."

"Mike, close the icebox. Her food is gonna go bad! You do have food in there, don't you?"

"Pumpkin, do you have a sheet of paper I can write on? I wanna make some notes for the kitchen remodel."

"When are your roommates moving in?"

"Zoe is moving in on Friday. I'm not sure about Katie. She's moving in sometime next week."

"Are Zoe's mom and dad helping her move?"

"Ya know, I asked her that and she said, 'We're Jews. We hire people for that sort of thing.' I'm not really sure what that means."

"Livvy, you gotta come see this. The cabinets have shock absorbers!"

"Goodness gracious, my knees are stiff," my mom muttered, getting up from the stone bench seat in front of the fireplace. Mom and I walked into my new twelve-by-sixteen-foot dream kitchen to find every cabinet door open as my dad scribbled notes onto the back of a take-out menu from Gatip Thai down on Lombard.

"Livvy, what do you think of this stone flooring?"

After my detail-oriented dad was finished taking enough notes to recreate my new kitchen for their DIY home remodel next spring, we hopped in Boudreaux and headed across the Golden Gate Bridge and into the Wine Country.

TRIP No. 1

DMV: Where is the title to the vehicle?

ME: Right here, ma'am.

DMV: We need an actual title, not a copy.

ME: Okay, this is what my bank provided for me since they technically have the title.

DMV: Guess you will have to get it from your bank then.

ME: Is all of the other information I've provided sufficient to get my registration once I get the title?

DMV: Yes.

TRIP No. 2

ME: So I have a certified letter from the bank saying that this copy serves as MY copy of the title.

DMV: That will do.

ME: Great!

DMV: Now we need to verify the vehicle.

ME: Okay, how long will that take?

DMV: You will have to come back another time. The verification person is on vacation this week.

TRIP No. 3

DMV: Your registration from outside of California isn't valid.

ME: What do you mean?

DMV: It needs to have a state seal.

ME: Motherfaq!

TRIP No. 4

DMV: Where is your smog test?

ME: What is a smog test?

TRIP No. 5
SMOG PLACE: DMV sucks, huh?
ME: You have no idea . . .
SMOG PLACE: It will be an hour wait to be tested.
ME: Motherfaq!

TRIP No. 6
Much like the entire process of getting my truck registered in California, I figured that I would have to wait a *really* long time to be smog tested and would inevitably fail with flying colors while being treated like an imbecile by some squishy dude with an attitude problem and slight body odor issue.

What? There is free Internet and *good* magazines in the waiting room? *Sweet!* This will make the, oh I don't know, one hour plus wait much better than I thought it would. What? I get a discount for mentioning yelp? *Jackpot!* Huh? S'cuse me? My car is *done*? I just got settled into this tasty complimentary donut and a Brooke Shields article on having perfect hair.

TRIP No. 7
DMV: Where is your weight certificate?
ME: Where do I go to get weighed?
DMV: We don't know. You're the A-hole trying to register a pickup from Texas.
ME: I guess so.

TRIP No. 8
ME: So here is my weight certificate I got from the city dump, title, registration, firstborn child, packet of Chiclets, AIDS test, and complete loss of self-esteem.
DMV: Well, that should be enough to get your car registered!
ME: Gee, thanks.

CHAPTER SIX

30SEXPRESS

If you can't get rid of the skeleton in your closet, you'd best teach it to dance.
—George Bernard Shaw

ONCE UPON A time, a few boyfriends far away, I pretended to watch the movie *Field of Dreams* while snuggling on the couch with my post-college sweetie pie using a technique I carefully crafted to disguise sleeping. I can't remember the characters' names, or the plot for that matter, but what stuck with me was the concept "If you build it, he will come." I certainly had no use for a baseball diamond in my back yard or even a backyard at the time; but yeah, at some point, having a diamond would be pretty sweet if the right fella crossed my path. I wanted a diamond for my finger, not my backyard, of course.

Fast-forward a few years, and the biggest bonus I've ever banked, I decided it was time to build my own field of dreams. Twenty minutes after delivery and assembly by the furniture company on Van Ness Street, I proclaimed, "This, my new friends, is the field of dreams!" In unison, Zoe and Cupcake cocked their heads to the side at their kooky new roommate with curious eyes.

"Olivia, that bed is gigantic!" Cupcake exclaimed at the monstrosity planted in the middle of my new bedroom.

"I know, it was the biggest bed I could find. I even got the high-profile pillow top mattress," I said as I struggled to pull the fitted sheet over a corner of the belt.

"How do you plan on getting into that thing every night?" Zoe asked as her eyes surveyed the bed's heavy mahogany frame, which came up to my waist.

"I'll get a stool or something," I said flippantly, straightening the velvet brown duvet. "What? I'm from Texas. We like everything bigger."

We spent the rest of our first afternoon unpacking. I rummaged through my Texas to San Francisco relocation paperwork and located my clothing inventory sheet required for relocation catastrophes. Every pair of jeans, heels, boots, coats, party tops, etc., were listed by category. It was a map for my new walk-in. Now that I had a closet bigger than a pack of cigarettes, my wardrobe could be organized properly. I began to stock my closet and check off items as they were hung with military precision. Once every item on the list had a new home in my new home, I stood back from the closet and smiled to myself, impressed at all the extra space I had to play with.

Wait a second, I thought to myself as I turned and looked at the piles of light sweaters, jackets, scarves, and wool blend blazers waiting to be organized. San Francisco and its eternally sixty-degree weather sure had made some changes to my wardrobe. By the time sunset came, I was so exhausted from trying to coerce and cram all my clothes into a jam-packed closet, all I wanted to do was take a bath and wash the remnants from wire hangers off my hands.

Later on that night, while Cupcake was buying three glasses of champagnes with a splash of Chambord, I settled onto the microfiber sofa at Notte and convinced myself for the hundredth time to stop comparing things to Texas. Our first roommate bonding night after unpacking at the new apartment was reason to celebrate, not be nostalgic about home. Notte did have a Miss Pac Man Machine and a sexy Argentinean bartender after all. We walked back home, and Zoe opened a bottle of Two-Buck-Chuck, and we giggled, gossiped, and sipped until past midnight.

Relishing in the joy of having my pickup truck Boudreaux with me again, or any vehicle for that matter, I raced up the steep Pacific Heights hill the next afternoon through the curvy, narrow tree-lined streets, driving through Hayes Valley with its quaint shops and city hall in its domed glory.

Approaching Market Street, I slowed a bit, careful not to run over any of the homeless people known to cross the street into oncoming traffic. I was in a big, gigantic hurry against time to make up to the top of Twin Peaks before the sun started to go down. Twin Peaks is one of those magical places in San Francisco that took my breath away. The city looked so quiet yet so full of life. The year prior, I cried because I knew I was utterly alone; this year, I cried for the opposite reason. After a solid year of bitter loneliness, I found my niche, and it felt amazing.

HOT WINGS

"So I was telling Cameron all about your store opening, and he asked if you and I would help him shop for some new clothes. Whaddya think?"

"Cameron's not the asshole with the decorator boyfriend, right?"

"No, that's Henri and Whore-hey. Cameron's the good-looking one with the Philadelphia girlfriend."

"Why can't his girlfriend help him shop?"

"No idea, I guess Cameron wants a professional."

"Hmmm, sounds suspect. I would be pissed if my boyfriend had some other chick help him shop."

"I get the feeling his girlfriend doesn't get pissed."

"Huh?" Cupcake said, joining the conversation.

"All Cameron told me about her is that she likes shitty beer and eats hot wings."

"What is a hot wing?" Cupcake asked.

"It is the wing of a tiny baby chicken. Like eating veal but the chicken version," Zoe said matter-of-factly.

"Are you serious?" I laughed out loud. "Zoe, you don't even eat meat."

"Well, that is what I assumed they were. Anyways, yeah, I want to meet Cameron."

My maiden voyage on the famed 30Sexpress required careful outfit consideration. Zoe and I spent the Sunday prior shopping and getting acquainted with all the high-end boutiques in Hayes Valley. I picked up a fantastic pair of jade earrings that would look fantastic with my favorite sweater.

"Getting ready for work?" Zoe asked, standing in the doorway of my bedroom with her cup of Sanka flowing with steam out of the Dallas mug I bought at Starbucks the last time I went home to Texas.

"Yeah . . . can't figure out what to wear for the bus," I said as I dragged my Coach tote bought on sale at the Petaluma Coach Outlet from a moving box and groaned softly as I sank onto my bed.

"Wear something fabooolous!" I couldn't figure out if this quasi-stranger I now lived with was being enthusiastic or patronizing. The typical Marina girl uniform was my decided outfit—consisting of a taupe Ann Taylor suit, white button-down blouse, new jade earrings, and sixteen-inch pearl necklace.

With my loaded up tote filled with the always necessary January umbrella, ear buds, makeup bag, cell phone, and laptop, I bundled a puffy scarf around my neck and put on my T-strap heels before heading to the Francisco Street 30Sexpress bus stop. I strolled down Franklin as Billy Joel sang about an uptown girl in my ear buds. The 30Sexpress bus doors opened and closed a few blocks down on Chestnut and Laguna Street, obviously jam-packed full of stockbrokers, attorneys, and Gap girls crammed in like sardines. When the doors opened at my stop, the bus looked too full, but a guy in a suit wearing a Timbuktu backpack forced his way inside. I realized that the only way I was going to spend the day with Bragasaurus was to learn the art of *cheerleader aggressive*, 30Sexpress style.

The next bus lumbered up to my stop three minutes later, and I finagled my way through the front of the bus, flashing my pass to the driver and saying hello. The middle-aged Asian man driving the bus nodded and smiled at me. *Okay, I'm inside, now what the hell do I do now?* I thought to myself. The bus lurched forward, and I would have fallen, but there wasn't anywhere to fall. Besides bus seating, there were floor-to-ceiling vertical metal bars and front-to-rear horizontal metal bars where everyone hung on for dear life. I grabbed the closest vertical bar near me since I was too short to reach the horizontal bars.

At the next and last stop in the Marina, four more people hopped on, one of which proceeded to grab the same vertical bar I was holding on to as the bus turned onto Van Ness. Our bodies pressed together as if we were sporadically spooning/dry-humping as we bumped into one another each time the bus hit a pothole or stopped abruptly in traffic along Van Ness Avenue. This is how I learned the appreciation of my neighborhood's hygiene. It felt nice. Many months without any attention to my cash 'n' prizes will cause a girl to appreciate some male attention any way she can, and there had not been a showcase showdown in my pants for a long time.

The bus careened onto Broadway as we entered Chinatown. Delivery vans and white trucks, most of which were graffiti covered, lined each side of the street. One of the white trucks was haphazardly unloading skinned animal carcasses hanging inside the truck. The pinky beige flesh looked rubbery and exposed to the animal's hooves bound and attached to hooks on the ceiling of the truck. I looked around the bus wide-eyed to see if anyone else was flabbergasted by the . . . I didn't even know what animal that was. Goats? Malnourished cows? Most of the twenty-something women on the bus wore either aviator or bug-eyed sunglasses. The men were either scanning their crackberry phones and/or listening to music. No one appeared to notice the carcasses but me. My mother taught me never to eat any meat I couldn't identify. Plus, the stench smelled like body funk and sweet 'n' sour sauce. This is how I vetoed ever eating in Chinatown again.

The first stop was Columbus Avenue where the advertising girls exited. I knew that from all the time I spent wandering around near my old apartment. Adorable little advertising companies nestled between North Beach and the Financial District, some of which had all-glass storefronts so you could see just how much your office environment sucked. Brightly colored walls, white lacquer tables, modern furniture that looked too delicate to sit on made me salivate. Oh, what a magical life it must be to spend all day in office space that I had only ever seen in magazines.

With the New Year, I was promoted and moved from the dumpy cubicle to my very own office, an upgrade from the doppelganger of the IKEA markdown section to another office building south of Market Street. While it wasn't nearly as amazing as those offices, it was all my own.

By the time we got to my stop at Mission and Beale Street, it was only me and the Gap girls with their smug "natural" makeup, ponytails, and indiscriminant outfits. The last stop on the 30Sexpress line was at Howard Street and the Embarcadero near the Gap corporate offices, and not much else. I shouldn't say they were smug. Who the hell knows if they were smug? For all I know, they were perfectly nice women, maybe just not morning people given the variations of scowls on their faces. They probably assumed I was "slow" since I had not quite mastered the navigation of the 30Sexpress experience.

"So I talked to Zoe and we're all set to go shopping tomorrow!" I said to Cameron as I took off my scarf and sat down in front of my computer.

"Awesome, I could really use your help."

"Really, I mean, you always look nice," I said, trying not to blush. For really reals, he always looked impeccable.

"Err, thanks," Cameron said, stuffing his head into the *Wall Street Journal*.

> *Beware of all enterprises that require new clothes.*
> **—Henry David Thoreau**

Cameron buzzed our doorbell at ten o'clock the next morning. One of the pluses to our pad we discovered after moving in was the corner of the bay window in our dining room that gave us full snooping access to anyone at our front door.

"Wow, he is cute!" Cupcake squealed, utilizing the snooping spot.

"Let me see," Zoe said. "Yeah, he is! This is going to be fun!" Our tastes in men rarely overlapped, Cameron was an exception. An hour later, Cameron was being fitted for a navy pin-striped suit, and I was getting grilled by Zoe outside the tailoring room.

"Are you sure nothing has ever happened with you two?"

"For one, I don't get my meat where I make my bread, and two, he has a girlfriend."

"Oh, they are just expiration dating. Long distance never works out."

"You think?"

"I guess sometimes it works out when there is an end in sight, but c'mon, *that guy* is dating a girl that her only attributes you know of are hot wings and shitty beer? Suspect if you ask me, either he's out of her league or she's great and he's got a . . ."

"Wow! Cameron, that looks nice!" I thanked Cameron in my head for interrupting our conversation.

"Yeah, I've really needed another suit."

"Say, Clarence, is there any way we can get a discount?" Sometimes Zoe liked to haggle for sport.

"We normally don't give discounts, ma'am."

"Oh, come on, Clarence. You love us! Come on, can't you knock 10 or 15 percent off?" Zoe cajoled. Cameron gave me his "what is she doing?" look he perfected working for Bragasaurus. I shrugged my shoulders. Clarence conceded to knocking 10 percent off the price of the suit.

After two short weeks of domestic bliss, we rang in the New Year with a house party. A few of my acquaintances accumulated that year, a very brief appearance from Bragasaurus and Whore-hey, and two dozen or so friends invited by Zoe and Cupcake made for a wild welcome into our new life.

A week or so later, one of the guests posted a review on yelp:

Amazing multi-level house perfect for parties, cotillions, and charity balls. Proprietress is a charming Southerner with a natural knack for entertaining and drawing together large groups of eligible young bachelors. Expansive downstairs patio available for various vices including smoking, drinking, and other activities proper ladies do not mention in public. Hot (single) landlord available on request.

Henceforth, our lovely new home would be known as the Princess Palace.

CHAPTER SEVEN

THE PRINCESS PALACE

From wine what sudden friendship springs!
—John Gay

THE RESIDENTS OF the Princess Palace settled into a routine quickly. Every evening Two-Buck-Chuck was enjoyed as we watched bad TV next to a crackling fireplace. Our Pottery Barn-esque decorated home—with its crown molding, Breakfast at Tiffany wall décor above the couch, and floor to ceiling bay windows—was cozier than any bar in Striped Shirt Alley. No one in bars really talked to one another anyways. And we could all hang out in our confirmed house uniforms we put on every night after work: me in cargo pants and fuzzy slippers, Zoe in yoga pants and zip-up hoodie, and Cupcake in her big beige bathrobe.

Zoe spent most of her non-TV time on the phone with one of her many close friends: the off Broadway director she met in college, Leticia. Clarissa, who Zoe met while studying acting in NYC, made a living from commercial residuals. Then there was Janice whom Zoe had known since the age of two. Last but not the least was Zoe's friend Becky. Katie and I referred to Becky as Miss Perfect.

CIAO BELLA

"Okay, what happened?" I asked as the Ciao Bella spa pedicure chairs began to flow with warm sudsy water.

"You don't want to know," Katie exclaimed, flipping her glossy straight hair over her left shoulder.

"You went to the Lounge, right?"

"Yeah, so I was standing at the bar when I saw this guy I hooked up with sitting over by the window. I recognized him right away because we got to know each other in the biblical sense last year."

"Biblical sense?" I asked with one eyebrow raised. What the heck does that mean? Did they pray together? Go to church together?

"Hooked up, fucked, whatever." She rolled her eyes, slightly embarrassed.

"Thank you." Whoa, nelly, I was *way* off.

"So I walked over to where he was sitting. Totally gorgeous in a Potrero Hill kind of way," Cupcake said, her eyes glazing over. Okay, now what does that mean? Are men better looking in Potrero Hill? I wanted to ask but bit my tongue until she was finished with her story.

"Well, Veronica was dating his friend who was DJ'ing the night we met, and he was there with some chick wearing a tube top. Veronica called tube top a skanky bitch, then she called Veronica a Mexican tramp, and then I threw my apple martini at her."

Zoe and I leaned forward and exchanged glances in the Shabby Chic spa pedicure chairs as Cupcake played with the back massager remote from her pedicure chair between us. This was an unusual development for soft-spoken Cupcake.

"Let's go to the bookstore later. I need to pick up *Eat, Pray, Love* for my book club," Zoe said.

"What do you guys think of hair extensions?" Zoe asked as Nancy the pedicurist tended to her tootsies.

"Ummm, why do you ask?" Cupcake said as she turned a page of her magazine.

"Well, I was thinking about getting them. There is a salon in the south bay where you can get human hair extensions from Indian women."

"I didn't know they sold their hair on reservations these days. Casinos or turquoise jewelry maybe, but not hair," I said as I sat back in my massage chair and changed the settings.

"Dot not feather Indian. From Indeeeahhhh, like the country," Zoe said in a tone all too reminiscent of Bragasaurus.

"Indians do have really nice hair," I said as I pushed out the image of Henri's head on Zoe's body.

Zoe beamed and I instantly forgave her.

"Well, I have an appointment next week, but I would have to redo all my profile photos on jDate.com."

"So you want to get some Indian hair to attract some Jewish guys?"

"I guess so."

"Get your hairs did, girl! It would be fun and you would look adorable," I said, doing a little dance in my chair.

"Oops, sorry!" I said to the pedicurist as she rolled her eyes at me. Note to self: no chair dancing while Ming Le paints my toes.

"I believe you," Zoe said firmly.

THE BOOK STORE

"So how do you pick out books in here anyways?" Cupcake asked, looking around in confusion.

"Hmmm," I muttered, looking around for Zoe who had made a beeline for the magazine section.

"Like how do you find the book you are looking for? Ugh, this is dumb," Cupcake said.

"What do you mean?" The dialogue in my head went something more like *"How in the hell can you be a teacher and not know how a bookstore operates?"*

Genius may have its limitations, but stupidity is not thus handicapped.
—Elbert Hubbard

Dropping the groceries from Trader Joe's onto the kitchen floor—Gouda cheese, morning star tofu sausages, and Two-Buck-Chuck—Zoe shuffled through the newly created kitchen junk drawer for the fireplace lighter.

"So I bought stuff to make muffins, but I don't think I have a muffin pan. Do you?" I asked as I opened and closed kitchen cabinets.

"I don't really have much kitchen stuff." She said, lighting the fire place.

"I can see that." In fact, all I could see in the cabinets was my sparse collection of cheap pots, pans, and mismatched dinner sets. The living area was comprised mostly of my stuff except for the forty-two-inch plasma TV courtesy of Cupcake's mom and dad and an oversized chair from Zoe. How did two women survive their adulthood since college with anything besides clothes and shoes? Cupcake shot Zoe her naughty girl look and sank into the cherry overstuffed club chair near the fireplace. Zoe dove onto the espresso leather couch and blinked lovingly at the fire.

"Zoe, your new hair extensions look great by the way," I remarked as I unpacked my groceries.

"Thanks, I feel like a whole new person."

JEAN GENIUS

"C'mon in, c'mon in, let me give you the grand tour!" Zoe squealed as I walked in the front door of Jean Genius. "So I wanted the walls to be like butta, took the contractors four tries to get the color right."

"You didn't paint the walls yourself?" I asked. Zoe had a blank look on her face of incomprehension as if I asked her why she didn't ride her magical unicorn today.

"Honey, I'm Jewish. We don't DIY," she said, rolling her eyes.

"Oh, let me show you what I added to the dressing rooms!" Zoe pulled back the heavy velvet curtain of one of the four dressing rooms and pointed to three pairs of heels neatly stacked in front of a three-way mirror. "I thought it would be a nice touch so ladies could try on the jeans with different heel heights," Zoe said, picking up a pair of Christian Louboutin black pumps with the signature red bottoms.

"Do you have designer shoes in every dressing room?" I asked her, crossing my arms. "Louboutin heels were $500, maybe $700 a pair?"

"Of course, they're not all this fancy. Some of them are BCBG," Zoe said, shrugging her shoulders. Zoe had a lot of things, common sense not being one of them. I loved her for being so idealistic to think that $700 shoes wouldn't be stolen in the first week of business.

CUPCAKE AND MR. APPLE

Cupcake was smitten with the twenty-four-year-old I introduced her to at our housewarming party. The twenty-four-year-old, one of the Man Child's horny man children friends, was tall, quirky sexy, and incredibly charming in the way that only engineers can be: a self-confessed "nerd" but with a glamorous job working at Apple headquarters on the design team. He wore skinny jeans, Puma sneakers, and tight-fitting T-shirts from eighties rock concerts. Their second date in South Beach over dim sum went so well that Cupcake didn't balk when he suggested heading back to his place for a nightcap.

Cupcake was surprised at his expert decorating ability but had a hard time absorbing it all because Mr. Apple couldn't stop kissing her neck. They did the magic waltz of the first kiss toward a platform bed in his loft apartment. He lifted her onto the bed with the precision of an ice skater, and Cupcake caught up in the moment, allowed him to remove her scarf and lightweight sweater. Her layer of white tank top under a boat-neck long sleeve was the only clothing separating her from rounding second base. Cupcake mentally did the math of what would constitute being a "good girl" while he nibbled at her neck. Her inhibitions were melting away then . . . "Who is that?" Cupcake whispered, pointing with her index finger.

"Oh, just a friend from college," Mr. Make-Out lifted his head slightly and looked in the direction of the pretty brunette in the eight-by-ten frame.

"It's a head shot on your nightstand though."

"Yeah, she's some girl I knew in college," he muffled into her neck.

"Ummm, did you date her?" Cupcake said, losing her focus. This dude was seriously a good kisser.

"I guess so. She lives in LA or something. We're just friends."

"It's the only picture you have in your bedroom . . ."

"Damn, I said she is just a friend. What is with you?!?" Mr. Apple said, breaking away from Cupcake and rolling to the other side of the bed.

"C'mon, you gotta admit. It's a little strange to have a photo of a girl on your nightstand when you're kissing me."

"Why are you so fucking psycho?" Mr. Apple said, furrowing his brow as much as a twenty-four-year-old was capable of. The dichotomy with a twenty-seven-year-old woman dating a twenty-four-year-old Peter Pan could not have been greater.

"That . . . is . . . a perfectly reasonable question," Cupcake said, slipping her arms through her lightweight sweater.

"Look, I'm not your boyfriend, so why the fuck are you so obsessed with some picture?" It was as if they were from two different planets, and on the planet inhabited by grown-ass women, dating meant something; whereas on Planet Peter Pan, dating was considered hooking up. Dinner was only a segue into foreplay. Whatever parts of his hooked up with parts of yours was irreverent in the grand scheme of his life. Peter Pans are like twelve-year-olds with bank accounts and BMWs.

"Maybe it is time I head home," Cupcake said, wrapping her scarf neatly around her neck.

"Whatever, you can call a cab or something," Mr. Apple said, rolling onto his back.

"Yeah . . . I'll do that," Cupcake said, grabbing her purse and stomping out of his apartment.

"Awhhh sookie sookie now, she's calling me!" I said to Zoe as I looked at the caller ID on my phone. Zoe was sitting Indian style on the couch with her laptop, trolling for future free dinners on jDate.com or match.com.

"Hey . . . are you busy?" Cupcake muffled into the phone.

"No, why?" I said, biting into a Granny Smith apple.

"Look, I need you to come get me."

"Where are you?"

"At that ass clown's apartment down in SoMa!"

"Okay, okay. What's the cross street?"

"Ummm . . . It's on Brannan I think."

"Is there any way you can check and make sure?"

"I'm too scared," Cupcake said in her little-girl voice that was meant to enforce sympathy.

"Can you ask him?"

"No! I'm in the lobby of his building. I'm not going back upstairs to ask that jerk," she huffed into the phone.

"Okay, let me call around and see if anyone else knows where he lives. I'll call you right back."

"She's in the lobby of his building," I said, scrolling my phone looking for Man Child's phone number.

"Hey, listen. Do you know where your friend lives?"

"Which friend? I have a lot of friends."

"The friend that is out with my friend tonight, I guess it didn't go so well because now she wants me to pick her up at his place."

"Oh wow, that sucks. He lives in the Avalon Towers. It's on Beale and Harrison."

"What does the building look like?"

"It's ten, maybe fifteen stories."

"I think I know which one."

"This info will cost you, you know, hehe," he said salaciously into the phone.

"Huh?"

"Meet me for a drink later this week. I'll let you pick up the tab as a thank-you."

"Thanks for the tip," I said, hanging up on him before he had another opportunity to be a dick. Birds of a feather flock together I guess.

"He is so fucking childish. I'm gonna go rescue our damsel in distress," I yawned, standing up from the oversized club chair.

Twenty minutes later, Cupcake climbed into my truck with a frightened and frustrated look on her face.

"How are ya, sweetie?" I asked as I pulled away from Mr. Ass Clown's building.

"I don't know. I'm fine, I guess, annoyed," Cupcake said, twisting her long shiny hair into a messy knot she secured with a hair band.

"Wanna tell me what happened?" I asked.

"Well, we went to dinner at Americana, had a nice time. He's super smart. Then he wanted to walk down the Embarcadero. He started talking about his phat new apartment, so we went back to his place, whatever. One thing led to another, and we were kissing in his bedroom. *Just kissing*. I looked over and saw a picture of this girl on his nightstand!"

"Maybe it was his sister," I said, shrugging my shoulders.

"It was an eight-by-ten black-and-white glossy. He for real tapped that. Anyways, so I asked him about it, and he said that she was 'just' a friend," Cupcake said, making air quotes as she said the word *just*.

"Yeah, she wasn't a friend . . .," I said, trailing off.

"He said she was, and then he got like really mad at me for asking about it. I stormed out, do you think I overreacted?"

"Did you want to leave?"

"Yeah . . ."

"Well then, you didn't overreact."

"Should I go out with him if he calls me?"

I made a mental pros-and-cons list of giving an honest opinion as I waited at the Columbus Street and Broadway stoplight.

Pros
1. She said she had fun.
2. He seemed like a nice guy when I met him. Horny and overeager, but nice.
3. Yeah, couldn't think of a number 3. Let's move onto the cons.

Cons
1. Cupcake thrives on childlike idealism masquerading as optimism.
2. If I tell her he's a douche and he does call again, I'm the jealous/judgmental bitch.
3. Telling her he's a douche will probably result in her calling and confronting him and, possibly, telling him that I said he's a douche, which would undoubtedly cause him to say, "Oh, she's just jealous."

Yeah, this is a no-win situation. I had an imaginary light bulb brilliant idea as the light turned green.

"Ya know, I'm not really good with these sorts of things. Zoe is much better at it. Let's ask her when we get home." Oh yeah, deflect the burden! Plus, in all honesty, Zoe was much better with this sort of situation.

As we pulled into our driveway, Cupcake's friend Veronica called. She was too busy telling her the details of her date that I had maybe a minute to run and warn Zoe, maybe develop a game plan if we had time.

I made the motion of "I'm gonna go upstairs" with my hands. Cupcake nodded and smiled as she listened to her friend give her opinion about tonight's events as she stood on our doorstep.

I ran up the stairs, into the apartment, and down the long hallway. Zoe was now sitting on her bed Indian style with her laptop. Same position, different location, still trolling for free dinners on jDate.com or match.com.

"Hey! What happened?!"

"Home slice had some chick's photo on his nightstand. They got into it and she stormed out. That's all I know," I said slightly out of breath.

"What did you tell her?" Zoe asked.

"I thought it would be better if we talked about it together. Ya know, two heads are better than one?" I said, shrugging my shoulders.

"Oh yeah, yeah, that makes sense," Zoe said, lowering her voice as Cupcake shut the front door.

"Hey!" Cupcake said to Zoe as she stood behind me.

"Hey is for horses!" Zoe exclaimed, confirming that I hadn't said anything about her date.

"Hhhhoooowwwww was your date?" Zoe said, feigning excitement.

"Ummmm, it was good—okay, I guess, I had fun, but it got a little weird towards the end."

"How so?" Zoe said, taking a sip of water from the bottle on her nightstand and setting the laptop on her bed.

"We went to Americana. I had the tuna tartare. Afterward, he was talking about his sixty-inch plasma that he wanted to show me at his apartment. I was like, 'Okay, it's still a little early.' So we go to his place and start kissing. Anyways, totally not a big deal, but there was this picture in his room that I asked him about. Totally not my business, because I mean, we're not exclusive. This is our first date! I asked him about the picture, and he got totally upset. I mean, I was *really* in his business about it. I freaked out, probably had too much vino, and bolted. Do you think I should text him and apologize for leaving so abruptly?" Cupcake said, dipping more and more into her little-girl voice. It was as if she warped the story into some warped version of the actual events so she would get the reaction she wanted from Zoe.

Zoe looked at her, looked at me, looked at her, looked at me, looked at her, and then folded her hands in her lap. "What do you want to do?" Zoe said as she looked back at me and gave me the "this doesn't make sense" look while Cupcake rolled her eyes upward and thought about it.

"I mean, it was pretty rude of me to leave like I did, I should probably text him at least. That would be the right thing to do," Cupcake said as she turned around on her stiletto heel and went to her room. "Night, ladies," she said.

"Night!" Zoe and I chimed simultaneously.

"Shut the door," Zoe mouthed to me as soon as Cupcake was out of earshot.

"What the hell?!" Zoe whispered.

"I don't know. She called me, totally upset. Then when I got there, she wasn't really all that upset. She said she asked about some girl's picture on his nightstand, and he got mad at her for asking about it."

"Well, if he got mad about it, then there might be something to it."

"Maybe I should ask the Man Child? I had to call him to find out where that ass clown lived."

"She couldn't tell you?"

"No, she said she was too scared to step outside and look."

"Where was his apartment?" Zoe asked, confused.

"Right off of Beale Street in South Beach. I don't understand what she was so scared of. That's a safe building."

"I don't blame her. I heard that there's a restaurant nearby that employs actual ex-convicts!" Zoe said.

"Yeah, Delancey Street, I've eaten there. They have really good home fries. I figured you would be all about giving people a second chance." A very heated discussion occurred a few nights prior among Zoe, Veronica, Cupcake's Berkeley friend, some guy she met the week prior, and me. I was the only "conservative" person in the group, and they treated me like an elitist asshole.

"We just designed the building across the street. I've seen the crime records. It's a safe area, trust me."

"Well, anyways, I don't blame her," Zoe said. "I'm gonna go take my face off."

OLIVIA: *Thanks for the directions. I guess she got upset about some picture she saw in his bedroom.*

MAN CHILD: *LMAO, prob the pic of Julie.*

OLIVIA: *Who is Julie?*

MAN CHILD: *His GF.*

OLIVIA: *WTF, why were you trying to hook them up @ my party then?*

MAN CHILD: *I dunno. Your roomie is hot.*

OLIVIA: *Yeah, your friend is taken.*

MAN CHILD: *I'm not . . . how bouts me n u later?*

OLIVIA: *G'nite.*

"Well?" Zoe said, patting her face as she stood in the doorway of my bedroom.

"Here, read my phone," I said, tossing it to Zoe.

"I mean, are you kidding me?!? Ewwww!" she said, jumping onto my bed.

"Yeah, no shit. What are we gonna do?" I asked.

"We're gonna stay out of it is what we're gonna do. If she asks you, then tell her what that Man Child said. If she doesn't, then it is her situation," Zoe said, climbing off my bed.

"G'night," she whispered as she closed the door of my bedroom.

I was puzzled as I climbed into bed that night. The situation didn't make sense. Why would Cupcake tell me one version of the story and then tell Zoe a totally other version of the story? Granted, the facts were the same: date with guy, photo on nightstand, left his apartment. I fluffed the pillow underneath me and wiggled my legs a little bit to get some warmth underneath the comforter. Did the conversation with her friend sway her opinion about the date? I met that girl at the house party. She was the queen of bennies from Cupcake's stories, so I didn't understand why Cupcake blessed her opinion with a magic wand.

I turned onto my back and started my nightly routine of mentally drilling holes into the ceiling. Hours—sometimes only one or two, sometimes six—spent unable to sleep, countless questions and concerns were lassoing my brain. Did I remember to pay my phone bill? I miss my parents. How many calories did I eat today? I should probably do my laundry tomorrow. Oh wait, I'm supposed to fly to Orange County for the day. Did I remember to print my boarding pass? What was that guy's name that I'm supposed to meet with? Did I remember to pick up the dress I'm wearing tomorrow from the dry cleaners? I'm thirsty. If I get up to get a glass of water, I will probably wake up to go pee in a few hours. I do have a bladder the size of a lima bean. Why do I have to pee so much? Is there something wrong with my plumbing? Maybe it is a concentration thing holding the pee. How do I train my bladder to get bigger? That should be my New Year's resolution. What will I tell people though? The truth? *I'm vowing to hold my pee longer this year. Yep, that's what I will say next New Year's,* I thought to myself as I drifted off to sleep.

CHAPTER EIGHT

STANLEY SORRENSTEIN

Are we not like two volumes of one book?
—**Marceline Desbordes-Valmore**

ZOE, HOPEFUL THAT her Jewish *Fiddler on the Roof* fantasy would come to fruition, asked her childhood girlfriend, Miss Perfect, to fix her up with one of her fiancé's friends.

Becky, otherwise known as Miss Perfect, grew up in a perfect house with doting parents in a posh suburb of San Francisco. Zoe became fast friends with Miss Perfect one adolescent summer while they were camp counselors. Miss Perfect danced her way through undergrad and law school without spilling Pabst Blue Ribbon beer on her cashmere or ever having one of her pristine highlighted tresses out of place. In fact, Miss Perfect never even had her heart broken. By the ripe age of twenty-eight, Miss Perfect had a three-carat princess cut engagement ring and a townhouse in the tony Pacific Heights neighborhood. Zoe looked up to Miss Perfect with little sister adoration, always seeking her advice on fashion and dating despite her guidance resulting in future insecurities. So when Miss Perfect told Zoe her fiancé had a neighbor who would be an ideal match for her, Zoe jumped at the double-date invitation to dinner.

Zoe walked into Circa with a burst of first-date anticipation clad in a new sapphire silk wrap top, her favorite pair of jeans, and patent leather peep-toe heels. Miss Perfect and her fiancé were already seated in a booth deep in conversation.

"Well, hey there, lovebirds!"

"Hello. You remember my fiancé, Mr. Moneybags." That wasn't his name. In fact, I'm not sure Zoe ever told me his name. He was a wildly successful investment banker who resembled a frumpy tenth-grade science teacher, tweed jacket with the patch elbows and penny loafers.

"What's going on you two?"

"We ordered ahi tuna tartare for everyone."

"Great!" Zoe gave her wool blazer to the hostess and picked up a leather-bound menu.

"We also ordered wine for the table. Stanley should be here any second. He's walking over from the Grove."

"So what's the story with this neighbor of yours?" Zoe asked as she leaned in, practicing her cleavage thoughtful look.

"Yeah, he's a, ummm, what did he tell you he was, sweetie?" Miss Perfect said, picking a piece of lint off the velvet-covered booth.

"Well, he said he was an inventor."

"Inventor? Inventor of what? Pooooooooost-Iiiiiiits?" Zoe said playfully.

"Zoe, compose yourself, he's walking over," Miss Perfect said with exasperated undertones.

"What's up, guys?"

In a nanosecond, Miss Perfect transformed into a perky matchmaker.

"Stanley, I would like to introduce you to my very good friend Zoe. Zoe, allow me to introduce you to Stanley." Zoe locked her jaw and attempted a smile in her dinner companion's general vicinity. Miss Perfect's build up of how Dr. Moneybag's neighbor was a superb potential boyfriend candidate built up a certain level of expectations in Zoe's mind. Appearance wasn't at the top of her list when it came to guys, so she never bothered to inquire about what he looked like. The troll with the stained sweatshirt sliding into the booth next to her was certainly not what she had in mind.

"Wow. This is kismet. Look at you two, like two bookends!" Miss Perfect exclaimed before taking a sip of wine.

Zoe's nostrils flared a bit as she used all her theatrical training to crust a smile onto her face. The muppet sitting next to her pretended not to hear the comment, which relieved Zoe.

"Look at these prices! Hope we are going Dutch!" Stanley said, casting a scowl at the menu. Zoe froze and cast a steely gaze in Miss Perfect's direction.

MISS AMERICA

"She called us bookends!" Zoe snarled under her voice as she eased into the spa pedicure chair at Ciao Bella the next day.

"Awkward," I said, crinkling my nose at Zoe. Between pretending to ignore me when I waved at her on the 30Sexpress to convincing Zoe she should check off the "voluptuous" physical description on jDate.com, Miss Perfect wasn't my favorite.

"Well, hello neighbors!" Miss America gushed as she walked into Ciao Bella with a matching pair of blond tweens traveling behind her. Miss America was the epitome of chic casual weekend wear in her burgundy crushed leather jacket, Hermes "H" belt, and dark denim jeans.

"Hey, neighbor!"

"Ladies, this is my niece Chloe and my niece Clara. Say hello to the nice neighbor girls," Miss America instructed as she pointed in our direction.

"Hello," the tweens said in unison.

"My sister's daughters, in town for spring break," Miss America mouthed to us as if she was excusing herself for accidentally burping. "Tom, is there a—I don't know, kiddie pedicure you can do for these two?"

"Auve quorse, we ave a chai-ild pedoocure we can do fer yoo."

"Not me, silly, you know I always get the deluxe with paraffin."

"We can do chai-ild pedoocure fer them, no problem."

"Great, and can I get a glass of chard? Thanks, love."

"Wha cahlur you wan?" Ming Le asked as she rubbed lotion onto my feet.

"This one," I said, handing over my favorite shade of OPI nail color. It was creamy, natural, classy, and basically heaven in a teeny tiny bottle.

"Dat nace," Ming Le said as she took the nail color from me.

"You have boyfriend?" Ming Le asked as she worked on my feet.

"No, no boyfriend," I said as my cheeks began to flush.

"Oh, honey, why you no have? You so pretee and skeen so why."

"Yeah," I coughed. "My skin is really pale."

"Just haven't met the right guy maybe?" I shrugged, glaring at Zoe whose mouth was firmly pressed against her fist as she made her best attempt not to burst out laughing.

"Soooo, let me see the piggies!" Cupcake squealed as Zoe and I walked in the front door. Both of us, wearing flip-flops, thrust our left feet in Cupcake's direction in our best Dreamgirls' stance.

"OPI belle of the ball again?"

"You know it!" I squealed.

"Zoe, what color did you get?"

"It's called 'I'm not a waitress,' I think."

"Fierce," Cupcake confirmed. "What else is going on?"

"We saw Miss America and her nieces at Ciao Bella," Zoe said as she bit into an apple.

"She was totally awkward with them, and oh yeah, I should have a boyfriend because I'm so why."

"You're so what?"

"Why, as in no tan, pasty, Elmer's Glue, Snowflake, blah, blah, blah," I said, rolling my hand in the air.

"Wasn't Snowflake your nickname in high school?" Zoe chimed in, her mouth full of apple bits.

"I really need to stop drinking wine," I said, looking down at my feet.

"Hells no, your Texas stories are fun-knee!"

"We like how your accent slips after a couple of glasses," Cupcake said, winking at me.

"My accent slips?" I gave her a dirty look. I thought about that taxi driver my first day in San Francisco, infuriated she may have been right.

"Sure, when you're drunk," Cupcake said definitively as she flipped through the latest Pottery Barn catalog.

"Or on the phone with your parents," Zoe said, opening the pantry to get some peanut butter for her apple.

San Francisco used the Panama-Pacific Exposition of 1915 as inspiration to create the Palace of Fine Arts historical landmark on Lyon Street, which is also rumored to have been George Lucas's inspiration for some of the architecture in the Star Wars films. Fast-forward nearly a century later, the Palace of Fine Arts was the backdrop for countless engagement photos, capturing that definitive moment in time when two people are on the cusp of committing their lives to each other, and also the primary location where Zoe, Cupcake, and I did most of our sunbathing and gossiping.

"Fuck, gimme your magazine!" Zoe demanded as she nudged my shoulder.

HEATHER JOY HAMPTON

"No, I'm in the middle of a very important article about celebrities without makeup." I shook my head and pushed my sunglasses into my hair.

"That guy over there walking towards us, that's Stanley Sorrenstein."

"Who? That guy? Really?" I followed her disgusted gaze to the disheveled, angry dude stomping across the lawn.

"Yes!" Zoe hissed. "Now gimme your damn magazine!"

"Fine, don't turn the page though. I want to finish reading it when you are done," I said, handing the magazine to her as she proceeded to block her face with it. I lay back down on my beach towel and tossed my wide-brim straw hat over my face. It was seventy-two degrees outside, and I was wearing a long sleeve shirt, but it was just warm enough for the sun to tickle your skin.

"Okay, whew! He didn't see me," Zoe said, wiping her forehead and handing me back my tabloid magazine. I rolled onto my stomach, propping myself up on my elbows, and continued reading.

"I don't understand why you read that trash."

"What am I supposed to do? Sit out here and read Kafka? I use my brain at work. I'm entitled to give it a break and read trash."

"You could relax and enjoy the sunshine."

"Have we met?"

"Good point. Did you bring sunscreen?"

"Left pocket, by my knee."

"Thanks. You know, I think cargo pants look so adorable on some girls, but I look like butchy."

"Bushy?"

"Butchy, like a lesbian," Zoe said as she rubbed SPF30 onto her face.

"What's wrong with that?" I said half-listening, getting sucked back into the article about celebrities without makeup.

"Nothing, but I mean, what's the point in wearing them if I'm trying to look cute for guys?"

CHAPTER NINE

DR. PARTY GIRL AND THE WASABI YENTA

Friends do not live in harmony, as some say, but in melody.
—Henry David Thoreau

CUPCAKE WAS DEMURE 90 percent of the time. Her hair was always shiny and meticulously straight ironed. She often wore fuzzy twin sets, Abercrombie sweatshirts, and ballet slippers. Her day time attire could easily have been worn by one of her second grade students. Then at night, Slutty McShoweverything came out to play: silky tops that plunged to her midriff, mini-dresses too short to sit in, sky-high stilettos, black eyeliner, and gaudy accessories. Walking into a bar with Cupcake was like walking in with a high school marching band following behind us. The room would often pause and stare. When it came to Katie showing the Marina Peter Pans her goodies, yeah, she showed her cupcakes.

One martini into an evening and Cupcake would hug anyone within reach. Three martinis and she would make out with any "cute boy" without having more than a thirty-second conversation. At Mamacita one Saturday night, Cupcake approached a guy wearing a Pac-Man T-shirt and was kissing him before I came back from the bar with margaritas. Cupcake always dismissed them as being assholes when they never called her again.

ZOE'S REVOLVING DOOR OF DATES

On a rainy Tuesday evening, I answered the buzzer for date du jour. "Hey there, Zoe is almost ready. Let me go check."

"Hey, hot stuff, your meal ticket has arrived." Zoe couldn't decide between seven pairs of patent leather peep-toes.

Some people enjoy the theater or live music or an outdoor hobby. Zoe loved to be taken to dinner by men she met online. Night after night, Zoe would carefully put on makeup to enhance her chocolate brown eyes and olive skin. Her outfits were always structured, jewel-toned tops paired with "good jeans," and sassy peep-toe heels. She would clippety-clop her way down to Ottimista on Union Street, A16 on Chestnut Street, or Starbucks if the guy was cheap. A busy week was four or five dates, a slow week was two or three, but rarely a second date. What was most interesting was how little she cared. Men were simply yummy snacks, and her social bonding diet was fed by close friendships with us and Leticia and Clarissa and Janice and many others.

Zoe would often have a dating horror story or three to regale Cupcake and I with. At least these Peter Pan jokesters made us laugh, but sometimes the giggling with the girls reminded me of how sad I was. Finding these two wonderful friends and getting out of that cramped studio apartment in the Financial District boosted my spirits immensely. Unfortunately, I longed for male companionship, and my only romances since moving to San Francisco were with a guy that barely spoke English and a Man Child that carried a man purse. I sat there perched on the arm of Cupcake's oversized chair and tried to drum up encouraging, witty repertoire in response to Zoe's review of her date.

"Did you have a good time?"

"He was, meh." She shrugged her shoulders. "Dinner was so good though. I had the salmon in a tarragon sauce. Then he was so cute, he wanted to get donut holes at that bakery on Chestnut that stays open late. Oh! So then, we're sitting on the bench outside the bakery eating our donut holes and guess who walks by?"

Cupcake and I said in unison, "Stanley Sorrenstein."

"Of course, there he was, walking out of the Grove with his dirty laptop backpack. Seriously, is the Grove his personal office? I've seen him in or around the Grove three times!"

"I'm surprised he goes there so much. I thought you said he was cheap. That place ain't cheap."

"He probably orders the two-dollar tea and sips it all day."

THE WASABI YENTA

Before Zoe, all I knew about Jews was from the single Jewish person to cross my path in Texas: my beloved fourth-grade teacher. I had assumed that the Jewish stereotypes seen in movies or heard in off-color jokes were ignorant opinions from prejudice.

The dichotomy between this Shiksa Texan and the yenta Zoe initially reared its head at the annual Sushi and Martini Ball, a semiformal Jewish event she invited me to. I love sushi. I love martinis. I had an unworn black cocktail dress bought on sale, waiting for the right occasion. So the two of us hopped in a cab headed to a nondescript building south of Market Street where I met a brigade of walking Jewish stereotypes:

Jude, the Jewish American princess: In a prim black knee-length dress and round brushed tresses, she had firmly planted her existence into Zoe's life by the second martini. Her polite smiles never passed her carefully highlighted cheekbones.

Isaac: His chest hair burst from his sweaty button-down shirt clad over a stocky frame. With horn-rimmed glasses and a strategically placed goatee, we made small-talk about men's facial hair as Jude paraded her new gal pal Zoe around the party. After initially warning Isaac that I was not one of God's chosen people, he laughed and said that he was already taken. His girlfriend, Isabella, had the face of an angel and the appetite of a horse apparently, never venturing more than two feet from the sushi buffet line all night. Isaac eventually went back to Isabella for couple bonding, so I kept a fake plant in the corner company.

"Jude's friend Charlotte is a columnist. She writes, like articles about wine, and interviews celebrities."

"That's nice, sweetie," I said but could barely hear myself over the throbbing techno music blaring over the sound system.

"Why aren't you having fuuunnnnnn?" Zoe asked, doing a drunken version of some nineties dance I couldn't put my finger on at that moment. I was also a few sheets to the wind, and not in a good way.

"Zoe, I think I want to go home soon."

"Boooo, Jude said you might say that."

"S'cuse me?" I asked, pulling out lipstick from my clutch.

"Oh, I don't know. She said that you didn't really fit in with this crowd," Zoe said in a singsong voice fueled with apple martinis and euphoria.

"Because I'm bonding with the plant over here?" I muttered, rubbing my lips together.

"Nooooooo," Zoe said with a bobble head nod. "Because you're not Jewwwwishhhhh." And she tapped my nose with her forefinger unsteadily balancing in her heels. She was drunkety drunk. I was not too far behind her. And it was time for this non-Jewish American princess to go home to her Princess Palace.

The combination of martinis, my four-inch heels, and a snag in the entryway worn-down indoor-outdoor carpet caused all the caboodles in my clutch to spill out as I caught the stairway railing to catch myself from tumbling. Camera, lipstick, keys, and strawberry-banana-flavored gum. I sat down on the stairs and gained composure from the near-plunge.

Zoe was the first person I truly connected with in San Francisco, and I didn't want to feel the disappointment or growing fruition that our friendship wouldn't be a long-term bond. The following morning, with the martini cloudiness still brewing in my head, I was sick with disappointment. Zoe was raised in an affluent, pampered lifestyle of extreme liberalness. My upbringing was the polar opposite. With our two opposing schools of thought on everything but clothing and girl-bonding, I worried that the closest friend I had made in San Francisco would abandon me for her new Jew Crew.

For the next few months, I tried to rally, going with Zoe and bitchy Jude to second Saturdays at the Cellar, a monthly Jewish mixer with a $5 cover charge and open bar. Her new Jew Crew was a tight-knit bunch, comingling together so frequently that it required a timeline and flow chart to keep straight.

During my immersion into the Jew Crew, the Windy City blew in Zoe's friend from her five-year stint in NYC. Sharing a fishbowl of God-knows-what mixed drink at Betelnut, the three of us compared notes about dating in San Francisco, Chicago, NYC, and Dallas. Granted, Miss Windy City was gorgeous in an unassuming way, but her ability to rope in talent was impressive.

"Tell her how you met your last boyfriend," Zoe yelled over the techno music blaring from the restaurant's crimson walls.

"Oh, te-hee-hee, craigslist missed connections! I was on the subway and saw this guy and then . . . saw him *again* that same afternoon," Windy City said with momentum building. "Sooooo much eye contact! The next day, I checked craigslist missed connections that there he was . . . asking about a brunette wearing a tie-dye scarf. Anyways, he turned out to have a tiny penis and his *cunnilingus* was less than fabulous. Hey, that rhymed!" She was vulgar in an adorable sort of way.

Miss Windy City's tale of finding love from craigslist missed connections inspired me, or at least entertained me while Cupcake and Zoe watched *Dancing with the Stars* in the living room, searching for a description of an outfit I wore on the day specified. This was over-analysis and desperation personified.

32 DEGREES

The boxing class in SoMa Cupcake coerced me into trying looked more like a day spa than a boxing gym. Instead of *Apollo Creed* sort of men sparring in a dusty boxing ring with sweat flinging in the air after each jab, I was handed a pair of ladies' lavender boxing gloves and a small bottle of antibacterial lotion from an upscale store nearby.

Cupcake unwrapped herself from her many layers of overly bundledness. Two scarves, North Face pullover, hoodie, tunic, and then finally, a tank top underneath. A bit much for September, but this was San Francisco after all, and Cupcake loved her layers when it was chilly and windy.

"It was totally snowing while I was walking over here!" Cupcake squealed.

"Snowing, like artificial snow?" San Francisco could always be counted on for some random theatrics, like when the sidewalk in front of the Ferry Building is covered in down feathers after the annual Valentine's Day pillow fight. What it couldn't be counted on for was snow in early fall.

"No, real snow!"

"Babe, it can't be less than fifty-five degrees outside . . ." As a Marina girl, trivialities such as this factoid were meaningless in her world. In fact, her entire existence was a quintessential cliché: grew up in Pasadena where she was a cheerleader, dated her high school's version of 90210 Dylan, wearing her $300 sunglasses indoors, and then the good times rolled on in college. She was in a sorority I couldn't remember the name of, and she frequently went to showers celebrating a sorority sister's wedding or upcoming baby Saturday afternoons. Cupcake always seemed bewildered by what to buy or bring even though she attended more of them than anyone else I knew.

"So what does that have to do with it?" she asked as she stretched on the mat.

"It has to be thirty-two degrees outside to snow . . . Could it have been hail maybe? I heard it might hail on the news this morning."

"What is *hail*?" I often wondered if Cupcake could be an idiot savant. I knew the girl was bright, I promise, but wowza, she caught me off guard sometimes. Forty-five minutes and a few hundred punches with her magenta boxing gloves, Cupcake became Mike Tyson in her mind.

"I should totally start boxing!"

"Yeah, you're like a mini muscle man . . ."

ZOE AND THE LATE NIGHT OUTDOORSMAN

Dearest Roomie,

To a lady whom I enjoy, count on, LOVE, and adore . . .

Happy birthday! You have done so much and I'm proud to have you as a friend. You are beautiful, loyal, caring, funny, a great listener, and fabulous.

XOXO,

Zoe

Wearing toy-store tiaras, we giggled the entire cab ride to the Mission neighborhood. Velvet Cantina, my favorite kitschy restaurant in San Francisco, was a tiny place with only three waiters who served a margarita that was mucho plenty strong and amazing chicken enchiladas. Situated at the Velvet Cantina was a hodgepodge of my entire posse in San Francisco.

I was determined to meet someone, anyone, I could relate to my first year in San Francisco. So I sought out groups where I thought there would be similarly minded people.

At the suggestion of Bragasaurus, I went to a young Republicans gathering where mildly socially awkward intellectuals wearing double pleated khaki pants and loafers without socks protested the liberal abominations of San Francisco lifestyle. I wasn't Republican in Texas, and while I may have been considered conservative in San Francisco, I found the young Republicans to be dull knockoffs of what they saw on television about conservative people.

The women in the group dressed in extremes:

- There was the girl with hair that looked like she stuck her finger in the electrical socket and wore fluorescent-colored clothing, which gave her the facade of having a slight case of jaundice. Her appearance gave the impression of "Notice me!" yet she was incredibly shy and walked away from me midsentence while making polite conversation.

- The speech writer who slept with everyone—and I mean everyone—yet dressed like my grandmother going to church on Sundays.
- The exotically beautiful woman in the group who laughed like a hyena filled with helium.

I labored through half a dozen or so young Republican happy hours before meeting Missy, a former debutante and co-chair of a non-profit organization that taught E.S.L. to children from refugee families. Missy loved wine, men fifteen years her senior, and liked to buy *very* expensive dresses. I found this fascinating and entertaining from a spectator sport view.

Then there were my buddies I met while crashing a University of Texas alumni even though I didn't go to University of Texas. Yes, I made friends by crashing events I wasn't invited to since I graduated from a private university in Texas that was too small to have an alumni group across the country, so I sought out people similar to me from the college football team I cheered for the most. That was where I met my two San Francisco guy friends—Ford and Rahim—my two miscellaneous ethnic snapshots into the mind of the San Francisco man. Miscellaneous ethnic is one of my favorite kinds of physical beauty, as if the best of natural selection had a party at the time of their conception.

Ford was good-lookin' in a tall, dark, handsome, charismatic, charming, yet approachable and unassuming. He was fairly certain his ability to sleep with every girl in town was his personality, which was probably true, but his looks gave him the confidence to approach any woman he desired. Ford also viewed women like a decadent dessert. As much as Ford loved the ladies, a commitment with anyone made about as much sense as eating funnel cake three times a day.

Rahim was a whimsical, well-dressed bundle of energy, always the life of the party, always the person that remembered everyone's name, and usually the first to arrive and the last to leave at every party. The first night I met Rahim, we drank until 2:00 a.m. Then Rahim asked me if I want to go on a picnic at Ocean Beach, at 3:00 a.m., in the rain, so I did.

Rounding out the group was a handful of Zoe's Jew Crew friends I had somewhat casual-befriended: Jude, Charlotte, Isaac, and his beautiful girlfriend Isabella. Cupcake invited her friend Felix, who worked for the mayor's campaign and not so secretly harbored a crush on her.

For such a diverse group, everyone had a great time. Religion, political views, football rivalries, all of it was put aside for the night. Many pitchers of margaritas were poured, and I was beaming with glee. The meal was topped off by a surprise s'more-nacho dessert with candles. It was my best night in San Francisco yet.

Afterward, we danced until one o' clock in the morning at Beauty Bar and posed for silly pictures in the vintage hair-dryer chairs. Across the dance floor, I saw Zoe and Rahim, the 3:00 a.m. picnicker, locked in a drunken smooch. Good for her! I never pictured the two of them together, but hey, I ain't a matchmaker. That night, still drunk, I peeled my clothes off and climbed into bed still wearing my toy-store tiara: the princess for the night sleeping in my field of dreams.

A week later, Zoe and I had spent nearly a dozen hours giggling about the 3:00 a.m. picnicker and her upcoming date. At least half of the time, we discussed outfit options, depending on date locales if that makes us any less neurotic. It was a just-add-water mini "I like him but let's be real. He isn't my husband."

CHAPTER TEN

THE MAYOR WITH
THE MOUSSE

You go to heaven for the climate; hell for the company.
— **Mark Twain**

THE NEXT FEW months flew by in a fluid motion. Cupcake went on a two-week trip to Italy, coming back with a slightly thicker waistline and laissez-faire view about life.

I went with Zoe's family to their vacation home in Palm Springs for Thanksgiving, and then spent a week home back in Texas for Christmas. Zoe continued to date her ass off.

I just worked my ass off. Flying from location to location, scraping track marks across the USA continental map, placing a much-higher importance on my career above anything else. My paycheck was the only bimonthly blessing I could count on to arrive on time, although Bragasaurus was becoming increasingly irresponsible, irrational, and abrasive. All his behavior I accepted as normal. I simply filed it away in the folder marked Eccentricity in the box labeled San Francisco. That Bragasaurus, and some of his behavior, might have been more complicated (that he may be battling internal demons, for instance) was always glossed over whenever I broached the subject in an attempt to better understand his behavior.

"Cheer up. Don't let that jerk get you down!" Cupcake said in her cheerleader voice.

"Hey, I have a teacher-in-service day next week. Let's meet for lunch. We can check out the hot guys on their lunch breaks." Cupcake envisioned the Financial District as being a sausage factory full of hot men carousing in search of pretty girls. I envisioned her job as molding the minds of angelic children in pressed uniforms. Both of us were more than a little off in our assumptions about each other.

The next week, I strolled down Mission and Front Street, walking past my favorite street dweller, a man who arrived every morning in front of my building like clockwork to arrange an intricate display of dog bowls filled with toys. He bowed and prayed to the dog bowls as if micro machines and plastic monkeys were his Allah. The toys varied daily, and he never asked for money. Once, he replaced the Hot Wheels with a picture of Britney Spears. This was during her meltdown shortly after the head shaving incident, yet I found it peculiar what a pop star meltdown had in common with toys.

The tasty sandwiches and the friendly counter staff at Working Girls Café reminded me of home and were worth the overpriced subs Cupcake and I ordered. We walked down to the Embarcadero and sat down on a park bench near the Ferry Building.

"Cheer up, sweetie. This is gonna be the year it happens." Cupcake patted my leg with her delicately manicured fingers.

"I'm not sure if San Francisco is for me. It's been two solid years, and my closest relationship with a man is that dude infatuated with Fisher Price. Men here suck!" I exhaled, apprehensive to confess all my frustrations about San Francisco and how I continued to feel overwhelmed.

"Well. Now might not be a good time to mention it, but Felix scored us tickets to the mayor's re-election party next week at the De Young Museum."

Our "simply one hot piece of ass" mayor's re-election party invitation, scored by one of Cupcake's admirers, Felix, to the mayor's reelection party held at the De Young Museum was ambiguous about the dress code. I interpreted it to be upscale work attire and paired a gray lightweight wool dress I bought in Palm Springs last Thanksgiving with a bold turquoise necklace and black patent leather heels.

I was crouched over my work tote dumped onto the coffee table, sorting through what to shove into my deceitfully small clutch for the evening, when Cupcake sauntered into the living room wearing some sort of Fredericks of Hollywood-esque black slip dress with a plunging neckline and five-inch fuck-me stilettos. Her back, completely exposed down to the crack of her ass, threw me over the edge.

"Is this that kind of party?" I asked, feeling like Miss Matronly, clutching my work tote in a motherly embrace. "Oh, I was in the mood to dress up," Cupcake said, adjusting her straps, giving me one of those implied looks that I was required to comment on her outfit. It was as if two abrasively slutty dresses conceived, and Cupcake was wearing their offspring.

"That is some dress you have on," I said. That was the best response I could muster. Albeit Cupcake was known for her Slutty McShoweverything alter ego, this dress surpassed all her hoochie-coochie-look-at-my-booty costumes to date.

"You like it? My mom picked it out when we went shopping last week," Cupcake said, jutting out one bony hip bone.

"Mmmmm hmmm," I murmured, stuffing everything back into my work tote before making a beeline into Zoe's room to see if she was planning on showcasing her cash and prizes to the mayor that evening.

"Hey, can I come in?" I said underneath my breath as I lightly knocked on her bedroom door. Our home sweet home with crown molding and beautiful fixtures had one major flaw: paper-thin walls.

"What's up, buttercup?" Zoe said, opening her bedroom door a crack to reveal her warm brown eyes and a bed topped with outfits that were rejected for tonight's event.

I mouthed, pointing toward the living room, "Wearing . . . dress . . . that . . . miming boobs exposed, ass sticking out."

Zoe nodded her head and shrugged her shoulders. "Hell, if I know."

I spent the first hour at the party watching for Dr. Party Girl boobie slippage and munching on shrimp the size of my fist.

"Where did Zoe go?" I asked, interrupting Cupcake flirting with a dapper-looking fellow with slick backed hair nearly as stiff with mousse as the mayor's hair. I had to hand it to the Democrats in San Francisco. That side of the political spectrum sure had hotter guys.

"Oh, she's over in the dessert room with Miss America," Cupcake said without breaking eye contact with Mr. Mousse Part Deuce, leaning on a cocktail table with one elbow. I swear I almost saw a hint of areola.

The dessert room, catered by *Willa Wonka and the Chocolate Factory* apparently, had knocked Zoe into a sugar coma. She was sitting alone against the wall, finishing off a slice of cheesecake. Her eyes looked glazed over, and I looked back at Cupcake as she walked over to us. I questioned whether paramedics should be involved as I pried the plate from Zoe.

"Hey! There's Cameron over here," Cupcake loudly whispered, pointing. Dr. Party Girl was drunkety drunk. I looked in the direction of her red lacquered finger. *So that was Emily*, I thought to myself.

"Who is that with him?" Cupcake asked, taking a sip of an apple martini she grabbed from a waiter passing drinks.

"That's his girlfriend, Emily, she lives in Philadelphia." The girlfriend had mousy straight brown hair that hung a few inches past her shoulders, probably the same haircut since the fifth grade. She looked like the kind of girl whose favorite hobby was tennis, wore turtlenecks in neutral colors, and the highlight of girl's night out was dancing to "Living on a Prayer" with three friends she met freshmen year in college.

"She looks like she's from Philadelphia," Zoe commented.

"What do you mean?" I asked, taking a sip of my dirty martini, trying my best not to stare at Cameron's girlfriend.

"There are some gorgeous women in Philadelphia, don't get me wrong, but a lot of women look like that. I think it has something to do with the weather, too cold to bother with hair and makeup," Zoe explained.

"She's cute." Cameron and I made eye contact. *Shit.* "I'm going to go over and say hi." I swallowed the last sip of my martini and braced myself to cross the room and meet Emily.

As the main room erupted into a thunderous applause. "I guess the mayor is here. Let's go get our picture taken with him," Cupcake said, taking a last swig of her martini. Downed in less than a minute flat. Nice job, Dr. Party Girl.

"I should probably go over and say hi, doncha think?" I said nervously, fluffing my hair a bit in the back. "Why bother? They're expiration dating," Cupcake dismissed.

"You two go ahead. I need to sit down for a sec . . .," Zoe said with a crooked smile as she parked it at a cocktail table.

"You sure?" I asked Zoe as Cupcake walked toward the main room.

"Oh yeah, her dress needs to be supervised. The mayor can't see her cash 'n' prizes," Zoe laughed.

The mayor, with his spackled head of coiffed golden waves, was head and shoulders taller than the crowd pressed toward him with the same MO. Felix intercepted Cupcake and I via the biggest burly bear hug his 140-pound Korean frame could handle and thrust the two of us into a throbbing crowd of flashing cameras as we pushed into the mob of people. Camera flashes were coming from every angle around him. Gracious and patient with his party of disciples, the Mayor with the Mousse posed for pictures with a painted-on frosted smile. His fiancée, Jennifer something or another, was a sometimes actress who dated George Clooney a few years ago according to last month's article in the newspaper. Her Chanel suit, so very Jackie O, was the cherry on the JFK part deux political sundae.

CHAPTER ELEVEN

LOOKIN' FOR LOVE IN ONLINE PLACES

Leap and the net will appear.

—Zen saying

A T A QUARTER 'til eleven, I finally climbed into a cab and headed home, another fourteen-hour day down the drain. My back ached and hands were stained with blue ink. Occasionally, I wondered if I was tired from the long hours. Truth be told, I loved my job, loved everything about being an architect. However, I often felt like a fraud, a pretend grown-up, a con artist living the scam of a career girl.

I heard giggling from the living room as I jabbed my key in the front door. "What are y'all doing?" I asked as I unbuttoned my jacket and leaned over to peer into the living room. Not one but two bottles of wine were open.

"You will never believe what we did!" Cupcake said as she stood up slightly off balance, spilling a bit of wine onto the hardwood floor.

"We made a man chart!"

"You made a what?" I laughed out loud as I peeled six paper towel sheets off and wiped the spilled wine off the floor.

"Like a flowchart, so we can remember all of the dudes!" Cupcake exclaimed, throwing her hands in the air and plopping back down on the couch.

"Where did you get poster board?"

"I teach second grade silly!"

The Princess Palace devised a man chart for all the men in our lives. Each of our three names inside a circle with lines sprouting in various directions: straight lines, double straight lines, lines next to a dotted line, just a dotted line, so on and so forth. Each of the lines signified romantic encounters, flirtations, crushes, dates, mini-boyfriends, etc.

The noticeably few lines around my name only made it more obvious I was alone, so I tried my best to drink my feelings. After an hour reminiscing about all the Peter Pan shenanigans we experienced since meeting each other, I went into my bedroom, dropped my laptop bag, and picked up my internal baggage. I changed into my pajamas and washed my face, splashing cold water against my skin, hoping the icy sting would knock some happiness into me.

My frustrations felt radical and bizarre compared to what I was accustomed to. After two years, my spirit had begun to break, and a chip was beginning to grow on my shoulder. The selfishness of my surroundings, the hopelessness of finding someone special, forced me to make a concerted effort to jump into the cauldron of Peter Pans. So I did. I jumped into the deep end of the proverbial dating pool in San Francisco: online dating.

Zoe began teaching me the ropes. She was a pro at online dating. Her craft at roping in talent was a total reflection of her personality: warm, witty, stylish, and endearing. At Jean Genius late one night, as I helped her take inventory, Zoe taught me her five rules of online dating.

Rule Number 1: Sir Spam a Lot

A guy that can't be bothered to send a personalized e-mail about your profile wasn't worth an awkward first coffee date, like this treasure chest of faux sincere spammyness:

"Hey, check out this e-mail I just got!" I yelled to Zoe as she scooped egg whites onto a plate.

FROM: ISSOSSFL
TO: SAN_FRAN_TEXAN
SUBJECT: BEAUTIFUL EYES

Hello! Normally I would never e-mail a woman as beautiful as you, but I was beset with staring at your beautiful eyes.

I groaned in my deepest voice possible.

"*Shut the front door!* I got that same e-mail. Hold on, let me wash my hands real quick," Zoe said, abandoning her breakfast.

"Okay, start over and do one sentence at a time," she said with dramatic undertones as if she was directing an orchestra.

"Hello," I moaned.

"Normally I would never e-mail a woman as beautiful as you, but I was beset with staring at your beautiful eyes," Zoe said in her best deep "man voice."

"Besides being just a pretty face, your profile spoke of inner beauty as well," I said, articulating his oh-so-thought-out words.

"I would love to take you out somewhere expensive and treat you like a queen," she said.

"My name is Frank," I said with a deadpan voice, laughing.

"I am a forty-two-year-old IT guy from Silicon Valley, and I would love to get to know you better." Zoe laughed out.

"Well, at least he didn't say, 'I like your mouth,' or something like that," I said, shrugging my shoulders. "How weird, we're not even on the same website."

"Some of them are on *all* the websites," Zoe said flatly.

Rule Number 2: Under no circumstance should you ever go out with a guy who has a shirtless picture he took of himself in the bathroom, otherwise known as the douche bag picture.

Garrett's profile said he was a pediatrician, volunteered at a pet rescue on the weekends, and loved to cook pasta at home. He recognized my friend Ford in one of my pictures, so it felt as if he was a mutual friend. Especially when he tracked me down on Ford's Facebook profile and friended me a couple of hours before our date. I cruised through some of his Facebook pictures after I finished getting ready for the date.

"Jean Genius, this is Zoe."

"He has one of those douchy MySpace pictures on Facebook."

"Stalk much?" Zoe said, laughing. "That picture wasn't on his match profile, was it?"

"No! There are like four of them in front of the bathroom mirror, and in one of them, he's making the duck face."

"The stick-your-lips-out duck face?"

"Yes, he's pouting for goodness sake!"

"Gotta go, someone just walked in." *Click.* Shit. I had to walk into this one blind. Could I cancel? What would be my reason? Would it make it back to Ford? Let's think about this. Those pictures were taken a couple of years ago. Maybe he's matured since then. He's a pediatrician. Are pediatricians even allowed to be a douche bag?

GARRETT: Can't wait to meet you, sexy.

Ewww! Only a douche bag would call someone they had not ever met sexy. I switched gears and tried to get reexcited about the date. I repeated the word *pediatrician* over and over in my head, like one of those yoga meditation mantras.

> Pee-dee-ah-trish-an,
> Pee-dee-ah-trish-an,
> Pee-dee-ah-trish-an.

Plus, he was taking me to Houston's, totally not a douche bag move. If he was a douche bag, he would have wanted to meet up at City Tavern or somewhere else in the Bermuda Triangle.

Dinner was nice with Garrett, except he insisted on sitting in the booth next to me. Forward. Plus, we were cutting up steak. Hello, elbow room? He smelled good though. After dinner, he suggested we grab an after-dinner drink in Nob Hill.

Garrett hailed a cab and said, "I've got a secret for you," after we were in the cab.

He was sort of leering at me. "Check these out," he said, giving me a sly look, pulling his jeans down to show me a pair of mesh see-through boxers.

Just the sound of his zipper made my stomach churn.

"Put your damn pants back on!" I screamed.

"Not a bad package though, huh?" he said, winking at me. When did he decide his pecan and walnuts were a secret he needed to show me?

"Sir, can you pull over right here, please?" I asked the cab driver politely.

"Are you serious?" Garrett stammered, zipping up his jeans.

"Yeah, take care." I hopped out of the cab at the intersection of Columbus and Broadway, in North Beach, by all the strip clubs. I stood at the corner waiting for the cross signal to turn green and watched Garrett's cab make a U-turn and pull up to the Shimmy Shack. He hopped out and high-fived the burly bouncer. *Nice!*

I slammed the front door and wrestled my coat off when I walked into the living room. Zoe and Isaac were eating Pad Thai at the kitchen table.

"Uh-oh, bad date?" Isaac said with a mouthful of food.

"You've got a tiny piece of tofu on your chin. So yeah, you could say it was a bad date. Do we have any wine?"

"Yeah, there's a bottle already open," Zoe replied, pointing to the bottle of merlot on the counter.

"All right, I gotta hear this one." Isaac wiped his hands with a paper napkin and locked his fingers together behind his head.

"So home slice sat next to me on the same side of the booth."

"That's odd," Zoe said, cocking her head with a scowl.

"Oh no, that's only the beginning." I shook my finger.

"We get into a cab to get an after-dinner drink. Then he pulls down his pants to show me his see-through boxers!"

"What color were they?" Isaac laughed out loud, one of those belly laughs too. "I gotta know, what color were they?"

"Red. Red mesh see-through boxers . . .," I said, taking a big gulp of wine.

"I can't . . . I can't . . .," Zoe said, laughing so hard she was crying and waving her napkin like one of those Spanish bull fighters. "What did you do? Did you freak?"

"I hopped out of the cab at the next stoplight."

"Where were you at?"

"In North Beach at Columbus and Broadway."

"That's not a safe area." Mama Zoe tsk-tsked.

"It gets better. So I hop out. Then I watch the cab make a U-turn, and he gets out and goes into one of those strip clubs."

"Which one?" Isaac asked, gaining composure.

"The Shimmy Shack."

"That's not even one of the good clubs," Isaac said matter-of-factly.

Rule number 3: Don't be down with DOB.

"Zoe, what's your cut off age?" I asked as we watched TV one Tuesday night, drinking Two-Buck-Chuck and shopping for dates. It was extra chilly outside, and my laptop was like a heating pad against my thighs.

"Thirty-five."

"What about if he has a phat job?"

"Thirty-five."

"What about if he has a six-pack?"

"Thirty-five, no wait, please don't tell me he has one of those douche bag photos."

"Hell no, he's on vacation. See, look. He's the guy on the left."

"Wow, he's cute," Zoe confirmed, checking out one of his profile pictures. "How old is he?"

"He's thirty-eight."

"That's a little old for you."

"The older the berry, the sweeter the juice."

"I thought it was the blacker the berry."

"Yeah, but berries get juicier the older they get, like when they ripen."

"And then they go bad, wom, wom, wommm," Zoe said in her game show voice.

The DOB was a venture capitalist who lived in San Mateo. I didn't realize until I walked into Bin 38 and saw the balding DOB that he had a hat on of some sort in all his profile pictures. He looked youthful and in shape wearing a baseball cap with his buddies in Mexico, ironic wearing a sombrero with a mariachi band in another vacation picture. His somewhat high-waisted jeans and tucked in black turtleneck masked whatever muscles were underneath. Things were quickly stacking up against his favor. I crossed my fingers that his personality would make up for his packaging.

First glass of wine conversation consisted of his opinion about Tahoe and how Squaw Creek was his favorite place to snowboard, which was about as interesting to me as watching paint dry, so when the waitress came back around, I nodded my head yes in a bobble head sort of way. DOB got a little frisky with wineglass number 2, suggesting we move locations out to the patio and then putting his hand on my knee.

"You know, changing locations is almost like a whole other date," he purred in my ear. I could smell his breath and the slight hint of Newport menthols.

"We're at the same place, just outside," I said lazily, taking a big gulp of wine. My knee had not been rubbed in months. I'm not proud of it, but I ordered a third glass thinking I could drink until he became sexy. I was officially buzzed when the waitress handed me glass number 3.

I fluffed my hair while DOB was in the restroom, hoping that the third glass would bring sexy back. I asked him when he came back, "So where did you hear this theory about changing locations?"

"There's this book I've been reading called *The Game*, and that's one of the theories," he explained.

"Theories for what?" I asked in my third glass of wine haze.

"Well, umm, you see. The guy that wrote it used to strike out with girls all the time. Then he learned a few tricks and wrote a book about it."

"Wait, oh you mean *The Game*! You're reading *The Game*?" Oh snap. DOB had to be drunk too, or an idiot. It is one thing to read the book, another to tell a girl about it. Sort of like no girl will admit to reading *The Rules*.

"How did your date go last night with the thirty-eight-year-old?"

"Well, he had on bad jeans . . ." Zoe and I had many a discussion about the merits of "good jeans" versus "bad jeans." Her philosophy was that if a man was oblivious enough to know he had on "bad jeans," then he was too oblivious to be dateable. "And a tucked in mock turtleneck." I winced.

"Did he look thirty-eight?"

"Hell yeah in that outfit! He was balding too which only made it worse!"

"Really? I figured you had a good time. I heard you come in at like eleven."

"Yeah, I tried to drink 'til he was sexy."

"How did that work out for you?"

"He told me he used one of the techniques in that douche bag book *The Game* on me."

"Which technique?"

"Changing locations or something—doesn't matter. He had no game."

"I'm not going to say I told you so but . . ."

Rule Number 4: Face Don't Know

I had also been exchanging e-mails with a lawyer who came across as smart, witty, and cute from what I could see in his pictures. All of them were from a distance: in front of the Grand Canyon, skiing, catching a fish on a boat. So on and so forth. His height was listed at six feet and three inches, and he described his build as athletic, so I took a leap of faith that he was at least somewhat cute. *What would I be walking into?* I wondered as I waited for him at Hime. He was late, I mean really late. Face don't know walked in and introduced himself to me. Err, sure. He was nice enough, no spark.

Rule Number 5: Let the Men Be Hunters

"Zoe, check out COASTGUARD81's profile. Cute, huh?"

"He's holding a gun in one of his photos."

"I think that might be a machine gun, or a rifle, I'm not sure of the difference." I was more concerned with his biceps at the time.

"I don't know why that military thing does it for you. I think it's a little barbaric."

"C'mon, you seriously think a guy in uniform isn't sexy? Look at his third photo, holy crap!" I bit my bottom lip and cocked my head to the side while I stared at one of his pictures. "What about the whole 'protecting our country' thing?"

"Military guys seem so working class. Besides, I thought you only liked guys that were educated."

"Wait, let me get this straight . . . You think that everyone in the military is barbaric and uneducated?"

"Well, not when you put it like that. Okay, what's the story with this guy?" Zoe asked rhetorically as she read through his profile. "Oh wow, he did go to college!"

I couldn't help but roll my eyes at Zoe. For someone that claimed to be super open-minded, she certainly didn't have an open mind when it came to anything different than what she was used to.

"He comes across like a good guy on his profile."

"What did he say in his e-mail?" Zoe asked. I could tell she wasn't listening to me, figures.

"The usual, he liked that I've been skydiving."

"Did he ask you out?"

"No, but he gave me his phone number."

"E-mail him back an equally long response and give him your number. Do the 'feel free' sentence." Zoe would say "feel free" for just about anything. She said it was casual and breezy. Instead of "give me a call," say "feel free to give me a call." I didn't really understand the difference, but it worked like a charm.

Later that night, Jason McAllister, a.k.a. COASTGUARD81, called and asked me out on a date Friday night. I wore one of my favorite outfits: fitted white button-down shirt, my magic jeans, and the sassiest red patent leather pumps ever.

"Wow, you're even prettier than your pictures," were Jason's first words as he greeted me.

"Goodness, thank you, you too!" I said as I clanked the rickety gate of the Princess Palace.

"A girl like you needs flowers on a first date." He pulled three peony flowers out from his coat.

"Peony flowers are my absolute favorite."

"I'm really racking out the points, huh?" Jason grinned. "I was thinking we could walk over to this cute Italian place not too far from here."

It was the best date I had been on in years, at least since moving to San Francisco. He wasn't like the Marina Peter Pans. He didn't use *party* as a verb or wear a popped collar.

The following Thursday, Jason came over and cooked dinner for me and the roommates.

"He is so hot!" Cupcake mouthed as she walked in after work.

"I'm whipping up some tacos. I've got plenty of fixins if you want a couple." Jason smiled at Cupcake.

"I thought she was the only one that used the word *fixins*," Cupcake said as she opened her mail.

Jason tried so hard to make the girls laugh that night, and I was smitten because of it.

"All right, well I'm going to go watch *Dancing with the Stars*. It was really nice to meet you," Cupcake said.

"You too, hope to see you real soon," Jason said.

We hung out and watched a little TV in the living room, doing the "Let's see how we fit together" first cuddle. It was niiiiccceeee. Around nine or so, Jason went in for the first kiss. *All right, let's see if this one has sea legs,* I thought as we started to kiss. An hour later, I came up for air, agreeing to take a spin on his boat that Saturday in the bay.

Jason McAllister lived in Alameda, on the other side of the bay past Oakland, in a boutique community near the Coast Guard base. I rapped on the knocker of his front door and looked down at my outfit, second-guessing its appropriateness for boat attire since it was seventy degrees outside: a long-sleeve T-shirt over a bikini top with jeans and flip-flops.

"Hey, pretty girl, c'mon in! I'm getting everything ready. Want the grand tour before we head out?"

"Sure."

Jason showed me the living room area and kitchen downstairs, then walked me upstairs to the bedrooms. "This is Mike's room, Matt's room, and this is my room."

"I recognize this photo." I pointed to a picture on his match.com profile of Jason and his family, which was one of my favorite photos on his profile. Jason was so tall and tan and happy standing with his parents and brother. Then I noticed another photo next to it, nearly identical except for the addition of an attractive brunette in the group.

"Are you ready to get going?" Jason asked.

"Yeah, I'm excited." I followed Jason back downstairs and counted four more photos of Jason with the same brunette, in addition to three other photos of Jason in various couple of embraces with other girls, all of them petite and wholesome-looking like me.

The water was peaceful that afternoon, and I tried my best to let the spark with Jason relight as we toured the bay on his boat. I didn't do a very good job of it though. The photos left an acidic taste in my mouth that even the cream soda and turkey sandwiches we ate out on his back patio afterward couldn't wash down.

"Nice flowers," I said, pointing toward a plastic pitcher filled with wilted daisies.

"Ummm, thanks. They were for my mom when she was in town last week."

"Awhh, that's sweet, you bought flowers for your mom." I smiled at him.

"I didn't buy them. Annie did."

"Annie?"

"Yeah, she's a girl I used to date a while back. We're just friends now though."

Under what circumstances would a girl buy an ex-boyfriend's mother flowers? I pondered as I drove over the Bay Bridge back into the city. I didn't know. What I did know was that I had this immeasurable silo of affection, sitting there in my heart, waiting for someone special to come into my life to give love to. Walking around with that much of an appendage strapped to my chest made life paralyzing sometimes.

CHAPTER TWELVE

THE PACIFIC HEIGHTS GENTLEMAN

I can believe anything, provided that it is quite incredible.
—Oscar Wilde

IT WAS A typical Monday morning, well almost typical. Let me rephrase that statement: it was a typical Monday morning only for San Francisco standards. A small group of angry people, maybe a dozen or so were protesting on the sidewalk in front of the building across the street.

All it really takes to organize a protest are the following ingredients:

1. Gotta have a bullhorn to yell and chant.
2. A big drum helps keep the stomping protesters in rhythm.
3. Signs, normally that say nothing that makes sense to anyone else but your buddies, marching to the beat with you.

Don't get me wrong, freedom of speech is great. Organizing large groups to express your convictions can be effective and inspiring to the masses. Many great changes have occurred in American history—thanks to peaceful protests. However, banging on pots and pans because you're pissed you didn't get a designated parking spot in the building's underground parking—well, that's just silly. The last time I acted that way, my mom took away my favorite doll for two days.

"We want parking!"
"We want parking!"
"What do we want?"
"We want parking!"

I plopped into my chair and plugged my laptop into the docking station. I went to my drawing table and leaned on the design I had been working on for the past week or two: a three-story condo development south of Market I was sort of falling in love with. After I logged in and reread the e-mail messages I checked from my BlackBerry over the weekend, I logged in to match.com to see if I had any new prospects.

FROM: PeteyMagee23
TO: San_Fran_Texan
SUBJECT: Hello

I really enjoyed reading your profile. It is remarkable to encounter a woman as unique and attractive as yourself. Would it be possible to meet for coffee or a glass of wine the next evening you are free?

Take care,
Peter Paxter

His online profile picture looking back at me was a fellow with dark curly hair and a sheepish smile, perhaps resembling Abraham Lincoln in a Jonas Brothers sort of way. He was handsome, but not *too* handsome.

I clicked on his picture and went to his profile:

Wine, a great dinner, intellectual conversation, and a guy to hold the door for you, that's me in a nutshell.

When I get the chance to relax, I like to break out my guitar. I've been playing everything from classical to rock since I was a kid. Music is a big thing in my life, and I've got a wide range of tastes from the Killers to the SF symphony. Keeping my body as healthy as my mind is also important to me. I like to hit the gym or go for a jog around the city every day. It's just great to be outside. I try to camp and hike whenever I get the chance. SF has so many places that are fun. You can always find my friends and me at the local coffee bar. We're even learning more about wine and are hoping to bottle our own Syrah. All in all, you'll find that I'm a loyal guy who always puts family and friends first.

I'm throwing the bar scene out the window. I'm hoping to find a girl who wants to share life's journeys with me. She's a woman who is comfortable with who she is. Let's meet and have some fun and see where it leads.

Pacific Heights boasts some of the most scenic views of the Golden Gate Bridge, but even more coveted than the views are the gentlemen who call the neighborhood home. The Pacific Heights Gentleman is yet another stereotype in the San Francisco social scene that exists for a very good reason: there are a lot of these characters running around. Typically late thirties or older, the Pacific Heights Gentleman woos with fine wines, dinners at A16, and holding the door open.

Two years into my San Francisco social experiment, I came to meet my own Pacific Heights Gentleman. In typical San Francisco fashion, my Pacific Heights Gentleman had overworked and cajoled his way past partying Peter Pans, to the top of his law firm where he ran the research department. He was successful by anyone's definition: a law degree from Stanford hung above the mantle in his posh condo in Pacific Heights. He was often the public face of his firm, speaking to large audiences, and had even taught pre-law classes at Berkeley the semester prior.

Having had little to no experience in the subtle art of Marina-style flirtation—identifying Marina girls drunk enough that they were willing to let down their social walls, yet sober enough to recall the conversation with the nondescript guy at the bar when he called the next day. Preferring hiking in Marin or Santa Cruz versus wading through the waters of Bar None, his friends had long since given up on him finding a Marina girl of his own. Then I came into the picture after an intellectually charged first date at Coffee Bar in SoMa where I told him I thought he was adorable when he walked me to my truck and held both my hands.

Getting dressed for our second date put me in a fashion tizzy. I stood in front of my closet wearing only a Victoria Secret Angel push-up, matching panties, and patent leather espadrilles that I had spent a solid five minutes lacing perfectly around my ankles. I decided on a periwinkle wrap top and loose-fitting black city shorts that hugged my hips.

Our Saturday afternoon date required a pre-date touch up at MAC on Union Street. With a new shimmery blush that brought out my cheek bones, I stopped by Zoe's store for a predate evaluation. Zoe was with a customer, but she gave me two thumbs-up approval through the windows of Jean Genius, and I flashed her two-handed "cross my fingers," then made my walk down to Polk Street.

Peter was standing at the corner of Polk Street and Broadway waiting for me. He smiled at first from ear to ear, and then I watched as the corners of his mouth started to fade out of grin mode.

"Wow! You look great." He looked down, shuffled his feet, and then looked at me again, grinning at me with the biggest smile in the world.

"Thanks," I said in my best faux humble voice. Truth be told, I worked my ass off to look this pretty, so the compliment was more of a relief than a feel-good moment.

"I was thinking we could either grab a bite at Pesce or maybe the Thai place across the street," he said.

"I've never been to either place, so whichever one is your favorite," I said, squeezing the handle of my Burberry handbag tightly. I was pleasantly nervous, and it felt exhilarating.

"Let's try Pesce," he said, shrugging his shoulders.

"I hear their tapas are amazing," I said.

Over a bottle of white wine and scallops, Peter told me how he conquered his fear of public speaking.

"I thought about what sort of man I wanted to become, and being comfortable talking to a group of people was a fear I needed to get over to become that man," he said, dipping a piece of bread into the olive tapenade dip.

"The definition of courage is having the ability to face fear without being derailed from a chosen course of action. Without those moments in time where you are forced to be courageous, courage can never become a part of you. Public speaking is nothing compared to what my brother experiences in the military," he said, smiling at me.

I sat back in my chair and took a sip of wine. "I think you are wonderful," I said, letting a smile creep over my face.

After lunch, we grabbed coffee at Royal Ground where he told me I was beautiful for the first time. We took the long way back to my house, slowly walking and sharing our stories with each other. After our four-hour date, in front of the Princess Palace, Peter hugged me for the first. He smelled like soap, aftershave, and fresh laundry. It was intoxicating and took at least thirty seconds to break away.

"Mmmmm," I purred, curled up on the couch with my feet tucked under me and a lazy smile on my face.

"I'm going to live vicariously through you," Zoe said, unbuckling her sandals after a cookout at one of the Jew Crew condos.

"Don't count your blessings, no first kiss!" I tsk-tsked, inspecting my cuticles and looking out our big bay window onto our empty street.

"I know, right!" Zoe said, slamming the refrigerator shut with her foot.

The mood had been all wrong: blazing afternoon sun, cars driving by jammed with drunken Marina guys, even the infamous Sign Guy stood in front of Pesce staring at us for a good five minutes.

"You should totally call him. He told you he wasn't doing anything tonight, right?" Zoe said, opening a bottle of merlot.

"Should I?" I said, sitting up questioning myself.

"Totally! Why wouldn't you?" Zoe said as she opened a container of hummus.

"Doesn't that go against one of your rules?"

"Nah, this one really likes you."

"Okay, don't make me laugh," I mouthed as I took my phone from the coffee table, dialing his number as I walked into my bedroom, creating a distance that would make not giggling possible.

"Hey there, this may sound weird. I'm not doing anything right now, and if you aren't doing anything right now, I thought it would be fun if we hung out. Hope you are having a great night. Take care. Bye," I said all in one breath, then collapsed onto my bed. What did I do? I sat up, shook my hair out, and then threw the phone on my bed as if it had cooties. I did a quick victory dance as I walked back into the living room and jumped on the couch opposite Zoe.

"I did it!" I said victoriously.

"So he didn't pick up?" Zoe said, spreading hummus onto a piece of bread and popping it into her mouth.

"Nah, I left a voice mail," I said as my phone started to ring from my bedroom.

"Shit! Maybe it's Peter."

"Well, go get your phone!" Zoe said with her mouth full.

I jogged back to my room and saw his name on the screen. I fluffed my hair and then answered. Somehow, an extra centimeter of hair volume would add courage.

"Hello." I crossed my eyes at myself in the mirror for no particular reason, nerves I guess.

"Hey, sorry I missed your call. I just got back from running the Lyon Street Steps."

"Oh, I run those sometimes."

"No, you don't. If you did, I would have noticed you," he said.

"Sure, maybe different times," I said absentmindedly, flipping through tops in my closet.

"Anyways, what are you up to?"

"Ummmm, nothing," I said as I walked back into the kitchen.

"If you want to, I would love it if you came over, or I could come over there. Whatever," he said.

"Ummm, maybe I can come over there?" I said, making eye contact with Zoe who was now doing her "happy dance" in celebration. As much as I loved that girl, Peter and I needed some p-r-i-v-a-c-y.

I sprayed on a bit of perfume and changed my outfit into sexy yet super casual: scoop neck tank, flattering jeans, wraparound sweater, and flip-flops for the walk up the hill to Pacific Heights. He lived four blocks away in an art deco building with a menacing front porch overhang. The walk up the Gough Street steep hill took nearly fifteen minutes. Peter had a smile as wide as the Golden Gate Bridge as he walked through the polished marble foyer of his building to open the door for me. We embraced for the second time that day. The crevice between his pectoral muscles was the perfect hiding place for my endlessly worried forehead. It felt like home.

Walking into Peter's apartment was like walking into a bachelor library. Everything from the taupe wraparound sofa, mahogany bookcases, expansive windows, and sixty-inch plasma television were impressive. I dropped my bag next to an oversized leather club chair and walked toward the wall-to-wall windows in his living room.

"Do you want a glass of wine maybe?" he asked with his hands stuffed into baggy cargo shorts.

"Yeah sure, that would be awesome," I said, picking up a Joseph Campbell book off one of his shelves.

"You have a lot of Joseph Campbell books," I said, running my forefinger along the book bindings.

"I really like his work, sort of changed my life." He smiled.

"Let me give you the grand tour," he said, cocking his head in a "follow me" nod.

"So here's the kitchen. I don't really hang out in here too much. But here's the coolest thing in here: the Wine Rabbit," he said, producing a large contraption for opening wine bottles. "I'm really glad you called. I was thinking about you on my run earlier." He grabbed a wine bottle and two glasses from the pantry.

"What were you thinking about?" I smiled at the beautifully honest man fumbling with his wine bottle opener.

"How I should have kissed you," he said triumphantly, opening a bottle of Syrah.

I scrunched up my nose. "The mood wasn't right though," I said as he handed a glass to me.

He blushed and raised his wine glass. "That's what I thought. Here's to great minds thinking alike." Our glasses clinked and our eyes locked. I felt light-headed. His hand touched between my shoulder blades and slowly grazed down my back as we walked through the dining room into his living room. I could feel the warmth of his hand.

"This is sort of the reason that I got this place." He pointed to the window with a stunning view of the Golden Gate Bridge. We stood there for a moment with our bodies within inches of each other and his hand on the small of my back. I could sense his warmth and felt goose bumps crawl up my arms. I had to get away. This place, this man, was too much.

"Huh, I wonder if you could see my house from here." I walked to his floor-to-ceiling windows to gaze out onto the night sky. The Princess Palace twinkled off into the distance at the bottom of the hill. I turned to look at him; his brown eyes were sparkling. He walked over bashful and nervous to the window.

"Ya know, I can almost see some striped shirt Peter Pans from here," I said, pointing at the Bermuda Triangle.

"Striped shirt Peter Pans, huh?" His left arm went around my shoulder, and we gazed down at the twinkling lights of the Marina in the distance.

"Yup, ya know, those guys that *just want to be a boy for-ev-er!*" I laughed, shaking my fists.

"I like your freckles right here." He traced his forefinger along the top of my shoulder, the steam of his breath tickling my neck.

"Really?" I wrinkled my nose at him.

"I do," he quietly said out of breath. We locked eyes, both filled with fear and anticipation, and then he softly kissed me. My world collapsed. In that moment, my whole life changed. My mind raced as kisses in front of the window turned into kisses sharing the club chair turned into kisses on the couch. Hours and hours passed. We were both breathless and giddy.

"Ummm, this might make me seem like an ass, but I would love it if you would stay over," he said, taking a lock of hair out of my eyes and running it behind my ear.

"No funny business," I said as seriously as I could.

"You are funny business," he said, kissing me again, propping his head on his hand, tracing the outline of my collarbone with the other hand. Damn near took my breath away.

"C'mon, let's go lie down," he said. It was early morning by that point, and we both collapsed onto his bed, facing the same direction, my back against the soft cotton of his T-shirt. He wrapped his arm around my waist and kissed the back of my neck. I barely slept, and so did he. We asked all those questions you want to know about someone when you begin to fall in love.

Early that next morning, after the sun came up, I turned around and faced him. He was beaming. So was I, and so was my bladder. "Where is your bathroom?"

"The door on the right." He motioned to the door less than ten feet away.

"'M 'kay, I'll be right back."

I dropped trou and did a double take at his toothbrush holder while I used the facilities. "You've got a Batman toothbrush," I said, scratching my bed head, doing a mental recalculation of our conversations while I climbed back into bed.

Did I blank out while staring at his perfect ringlets of Armenian hair? How could I have missed the need-to-know fact "has kids" on his match. com profile? It certainly would have been weird if he did seeing as how no one had children in San Francisco, let alone a Pacific Heights Gentleman.

"I do have a Batman toothbrush, he guards the bathroom," he said in a deadpan tone. I turned to face him, and he was grinning ear to ear. He had finally encountered a weirdo too.

Fingers entwined, we walked to Rex Café on Polk Street in a cloud of initial romance. It was nearly empty that Sunday morning as we munched on apple wood-smoked bacon and strong coffee. Afterward, Peter walked me home, pulling me close in an embrace filled with a newfound passion that was temporarily paused as Miss America careened into the driveway in her newly purchased Mercedes SUV.

"Hey, neighbor, this is Peter. Did y'all get a new car?"

"Oh yeah, we are going to need a bigger car soon," Miss America said, glowing like an angel. Sometimes I wondered if she secretly walked around with her own personal lighting crew.

"Are you and the girls going to be home tonight? We wanted to stop by and chat for a bit. We, well, we have some big news."

"I'm not sure, but probably."

"Great! I'm sorry. Hey, I'm the neighbor from upstairs," Miss America said as she thrust her hand to Peter.

"Pleasure to meet you."

"Nice to meet you too, Peter."

Peter cocked his head and smiled at me, developing our own facial expression inside joke. Miss America mouthed, "He's so cute," behind Peter's back as she walked through the front gate.

"Well, well, well," Cupcake tsk-tsked as I walked in the front door.

"I need a marker," I said as I dropped my purse down onto the kitchen counter.

"For what," Cupcake giggled. She knew damn good and well what I needed a marker for.

"The man chart." I twisted my mouth nervously and folded my arms.

"Are we ready to add your Pacific Heights Gentleman to the chart?"

"Oh yeah." I looked down at my feet and smiled.

"I think I've got one in my purse." Cupcake scooted down the hallway to her bedroom and returned with two permanent markers and a highlighter.

"I didn't know which colors you wanted to use," she said, waving them in my direction.

"All of them, Katie, I need to use all of them," I said as I took the Breakfast at Tiffany's iconic movie poster down from above the couch, where we hid the man chart behind it. I drew a fat baby cupid holding an arrow-shooting chubby red hearts connected by a thick black line from my name to a corner of the poster board. Then I wrote Peter Paxter in big black letters.

"Wow," Cupcake sighed as she sunk into the opposite side of the couch.

"Yeah, wow is right." I sighed back. "I feel like I need to go pry one of Cupid's arrows from between my boobies." Which was true; it also felt like I hit the jackpot in dating, my own Pacific Heights Gentleman: the blue ribbon winner in the competitive Marina dating world.

CHAPTER THIRTEEN

THE AFRICAN DOG

The heart has its reasons which reason knows nothing of.
—Blaise Pascal

A T A QUARTER past five, Miss America and Mr. Khakis knocked on our door. Cupcake, clad in her big beige bathrobe house uniform, let them in for their big announcement. "We decided to get a . . . Rhodesian ridgeback. It's a lion-hunting dog from Africa we are having shipped in."

I had questions of the logistical nature.

How do you ship a dog from *Africa*?

Miss America explained as if she was answering before a panel of beauty pageant judges, her baby blues gleaming from our fireplace, and a basket of "bribe the neighbor" goodies under her cashmere-clad arm.

"So here's a box of chocolates from that adorable chocolate store on Fillmore, a bottle of Syrah from California Wine Merchant, and a gift certificate to Dragon Well."

"We love gifts!" exclaimed Zoe in her typical enthusiastic nature.

That night I went for a long run as the sun started to set. The strip of compact sand nestled between the Marina Green and the water felt the *tap-tap-tap* of my Nikes as I thought about last night. I had run this path dozens of times before without noticing an old wooden bench next to the choppy blue waters. It reminded me of a bench the couple who finally find love would sit on at the ending of a romantic comedy as the credits start to roll. The neurotic actress with invisible makeup would lean her perfectly styled head on the shoulder of her leading man, who was more patient than ever occurs in real-life romances, as the music swells and the screen fades to black. I walked over to the wooden bench and sat down as I pulled my ear buds out to listen to the water. I closed my eyes, and I wished that the butterflies in my stomach about Peter would last as long as possible.

"Okay, honey bear, what are we doing today?" Jackson said as we walked to his stylist chair.

"Umm, just a trim and a few highlights."

"So how are the girls?"

"They're good."

"Any new prospects?" Jackson asked as he brushed my hair.

"I met someone," I said with a hint of determination in my voice.

"Awhhh shit! Spill!"

"He's a Pacific Heights Gentleman."

"Damn girl, gimme five!"

"So have y'all fucked yet?" Jackson whispered, lowering his voice.

"Not yet, but I think soon maybe."

"Well, whatever you do, be safe. Girly pills, condoms, spermicide, lubricide, cervix hats, whatever."

"I'm on birth control. It's a ring I put in my lady parts for three weeks, so I won't have to worry about taking a pill."

"Vagina jewelry, huh? Well, all right then . . ."

At Bin 38, over expensive glasses of wine, we started to tell each other all our stories. I was falling in love by the minute. Afterward, we puttered around the bookstore. Then we smoked cigars on his rooftop patio and watched the sunset. He gave me his thick wool sweater to fight off the San Francisco wind. I wore it home that morning and inhaled his scent from the collar. It smelled like his soap.

The next week, we jumped into the deep end of the proverbial dating pool: the sleepover where the clothes come off. My bedroom had been carefully groomed for my Pacific Heights Gentleman's arrival. The sheets were washed and scented with lavender; miscellaneous toiletries that usually stayed on the bathroom counter were tucked away in the bottom of my lingerie drawer. My fingers trembled noticeably as I twisted a lock of my hair around the curling iron. I sat the curling iron down on the counter and massaged my temples with both hands. Peter made me weak in the knees, terrified my heart, and entangled my mind. He was everything I had ever wanted in a man. How is it possible to get everything you ever want? I wanted to cling to the dust ruffle of my bed, but even more, I wanted to cling to the idea that I might get what I deserved in life.

Peter peeled off his Henley gray T-shirt revealing the body of a comic book hero, all eight stomach muscles so protruded that they looked downright angry. Covering the unbelievable muscle situation was skin the color of honey and the most perfectly masculine chest I had ever seen. A successful chest of hair depends on many factors: color and placement of the hair, curliness, physique, I could go on and on. His chest was nothing short of spectacular.

"Goodness gracious."

He emptied out his pockets absentmindedly without looking up: cell phone, leather wallet, keys. He looked up at me bashfully. "What?" he said embarrassed.

"Sorry, I wasn't expecting that."

"That? That what?" He chuckled. It took five or ten seconds to answer him. I didn't know how to say what I was feeling. How do you tell someone that they are the most beautiful thing you have ever seen and convince them to believe you?

Instead, I stuttered, "Ummmm, God did good," as I smiled, embarrassed, while I circled my arms around his shoulders.

"You are a goofball," he said as he pulled me close, his hands around my waist, and kissed me.

I bit my lip. What if my body wasn't everything he wanted it to be? I climbed onto my bed, my feet dangling over the edge, hands sitting on top of my thighs. I glared at my cuticles, only one of the many things about my appearance I wanted to change.

"We can do or not do whatever you are comfortable with tonight, okay?" Peter encircled his fingers in mine. "I just want to hold you all night." He touched his forehead to mine and looked into my eyes; then he kissed me. Peter made me feel at ease in an intangible, magnificent way I had not experienced before.

He kissed my neck down to my collarbone, finding freckles scattered along the top of my shoulders as he slipped my cardigan off my shoulders. He ran his thumbs up and down the back of my neck, then took my face in his hands. He stroked my cheek with the back side of his fingers that trailed down to the top of my camisole. His fingers were feathers against my skin. I ran my fingers through his hair as his hand slid down to the small of my back. He lifted me off the edge of the bed and lay down next to me with one hand propping his head and the other holding my cheek as we kissed. Eventually, his hand trailed down my side, against my breast, and down my stomach. I giggled a little when he reached a ticklish spot. He smiled back at me and ran his fingers through my hair. "You are so beautiful," he whispered.

CAMERON'S QUANDRY

"Knock, knock," Cameron said, tapping the opened door of my office. He looked tired with the hint of a five o'clock shadow.

"How are you? How was your weekend?" I said, straightening a stack of papers on my desk. I assumed he went to Philadelphia since he left after lunch on Friday. My friendly banter with Cameron had been strained ever since he put his hand on my knee in the backseat of a cab we shared after a wine-infused dinner with Bragasaurus and the Real Businessmen of Orange County a month after I moved in with Zoe and Cupcake.

Every time the two real estate developers from Irvine came into town, they took Cameron, Bragasaurus, and I out to dinner. Cameron and I always drank too much at these dinners. We needed the liquid courage to stop fidgeting with our forks while Bragasaurus pretended to be heterosexual. The Real Businessmen of Orange County were the type of men who dressed like they just played golf, drove hummers with Bush bumper stickers, and had overly botoxed wives. I guess it made sense why Henri reverted to Henry.

This particular evening at Morton's Steakhouse, one of the Real Businessmen of Orange County said he read an article about estrogen in the San Francisco water system. Needless to say, Cameron and I drank more than usual and left before dessert. "I call Henri Bragasaurus in my head, you know," I confessed to Cameron in the cab. He let out a big hearty laugh, then put his hand on my knee, and told me I was hysterical. Cameron squeezed my knee cap and let his hand linger there. I was too drunk and stunned to push it away. Stunned because he did it but more stunned because I let it happen. He had a girlfriend, but the warmth of his palm felt too good to push away. We never discussed it, and our friendship wasn't the same afterward.

"It was good. Went to Philadelphia to see Emily." Cameron stuffed both of his hands in his unpressed pockets.

"How is Emily doing?"

"We, uh, she's engaged, I guess," the words stumbled out of his mouth.

"You guess she's engaged?" I laughed a bit. Sure, I nursed a crush on Cameron for over a year, but I was dating Peter now, which made Cameron's engagement irrelevant to me. I guess not to Cameron as I judged by his awkward demeanor.

"No—I mean, yes, I proposed."

"Congratulations!"

"Yeah, I guess it was time."

"Don't get too excited about it," I said, trying to make the conversation light hearted.

"I'm a dude, we don't get that excited about getting engaged."

"Yeah . . . I guess you are right," I lied, taking a sip of water. That was a big bag of bullshit. I knew it. Cameron knew it. Even Bragasaurus knew it.

I stopped by Jean Genius after work to get Zoe's opinion on Cameron's engagement.

"What do you think about these?" Zoe asked, holding up a pair of dark wash True Religion jeans with white stitching on the back flap button pockets.

"Holy shit," I whistled as she handed them to me.

"I know, gorgeous, right?" Zoe cocked one hip to the side and looked lovingly at the denim craftsmanship. "You gotta try them on, I know you are going to love them, I promise!"

"Guess what Cameron did over the weekend?"

"Oh, I don't know. Eat hot wings and drink shitty beer with Emily?"

"Yep, and he popped the question too," I said as I undressed in the fitting room.

"It's probably time for him to get married."

"I assumed they were long-distance expiration dating," I said as I jumped up then down and pulled the jeans up my thighs. Swear to God, my ass had never looked this good.

"That's what I thought too," Zoe said from the other side of the dressing room curtain. "What do you think?"

"I'm happy for him. Sure, I just don't understand men. They can date a girl and be totally in love, then drop her for no reason," I said, posing in front of the three-way mirror, then pulling back the dressing room curtain.

"I meant 'what do you think about the jeans,' but damn, girl! Those look amazing!" Zoe said, motioning with her forefinger to twirl around.

"It is all about timing for men," Zoe advised. "The girl they happen to meet once they decide they are settled enough in their careers is the girl they end up with." She was the Dalai Lama of dating sometimes.

"Are you bothered that Cameron proposed or that a relationship like Cameron's ended up engaged?"

"Both, neither, I don't know. I shouldn't really care I guess. I'm dating Peter now," I said as I pulled the dressing room curtain closed and changed back into my work clothes.

"So what do you and your Pacific Heights Gentleman have on the agenda for the evening?"

"Just dinner, maybe drinks afterwards."

"Well, you know what I think you should wear."

"These jeans." I folded them over my arm and mentally came to terms that I was about to purchase a pair of jeans that were as expensive as my first apartment's rent.

The horror of dating a man with an impeccable physique left my stomach turning like an early nineteenth-century butter churner, with each phone call from Peter rendering a roundabout of my ego that made eating a full meal impossible. *The new boyfriend diet was definitely taking its toll,* I thought to myself as I slipped on a navy top from American Apparel and into my new jeans.

With a scarf tied as a belt and bright yellow ballet flats, I was ready for a casual supper with Peter. He was waiting on my doorstep when I skipped down the stairs after hearing the buzzer, wearing a blue checkered Brooks Brothers button-down shirt from work that day and a pair of worn-in jeans. Fuck, I was attracted to him I thought to myself as I opened up the gate outside my building.

"What do you think about having some sushi?" he asked and smiled, knowing it was my favorite. His mother told me months later, once we met and became close, how much Peter despised sushi.

We walked over to Marina Sushi on Lombard Street, halfway between his place and mine, for a light dinner. We ordered a Japanese beer and sake as we looked over the menus.

"Are you ready to order?" the Harakuju waitress asked us as she poured water into our glasses.

"We were sort of wondering how big the hand rolls are," Peter said, scrolling down the sushi order sheet.

"Size of ice cream cone."

"Oh okay, we're going to order two spicy tuna ice cream cones, a spicy tuna roll, and the yellow tail sashimi."

The atmosphere at Marina Sushi was sleek, trendy, and dimly lit. The conversation at the table next to us trumped all of it.

Marina Dude No. 1: "Dude, I got so wasted Saturday night . . . I had, like, four vodka red bulls at City Tavern."

Marina Dude No. 2: "Sweet, me and JC were at Balboa, you should have come over, tons of drunken honeys."

Marina Dude No. 1: "Yeah, I was a little fucked up by then. I had three sake bombs at Ace Wasabi."

Marina Dude No. 2: "No worries, I was pretty fucked up, gotta drink wine at Balboa to get in with the cougars, then fuckin' Kristy showed up with her skank patrol and put me on lockdown. Total waste of my striped shirt, dude."

Peter leaned in and whispered, "Marina dudes only like to talk about two topics: where they went and how much they drank. Oh yeah, and chasing tail." Peter took a big bite of his spicy tuna roll ice cream cone and winked at me.

BRAGASAURUS

"I need your final site plans no later than the end of the week," Bragasaurus said, tapping the eraser stem of a pencil on my desk. The *tap-tap-tap* rhythmic sound reminded me of a six-year-old girl tapping her patent leather Mary Jane shoes out of impatience five minutes before a full-on temper tantrum erupted.

"Of course, I will have to work all weekend revising your work, so try your best not to have any errors this time." He smirked. The stench of too much cologne remained well after he left my office with about forty additional hours of work.

Negotiating time lines and due dates was only more fodder for him to use as ammunition. "Oh, you know how she is, I told her it had to be done, and all she wanted to do was complain about it. Prissy little redneck," he would say to clients once I left his office. The less said the better.

"I'll have it to you by the end of the day on Friday," I said, doing a mental calculation of everything I would need to cancel in the next couple of days: dinner plans with Zoe and Ford, Pilates, and a hair appointment with Jackson I had already rescheduled three other times. Cancelled doctor appointments at the last minute for a conference call were on my expense reports as miscellaneous expenditures at the request of Bragasaurus. Deadlines created late night working, leaving crumbs of my time for any ambition of a social life, but I always made time for Zoe. Jean Genius closed at eight o'clock, and I would often take a cab straight from work over to the store since the 30Sexpress made its last stop shortly after six o'clock.

I was at work hours after my window went dark and night fell on San Francisco, dozing off in a cab on the way home. The white noise of the street traffic was a lullaby. All the lights were turned off in the Princess Palace when I walked in.

The following day, I was the special kind of stupid that forgets to eat. By three o'clock, I looked up from my desk thinking it was midmorning. Shit! All the delis were closed by then, and it wasn't like I had time to grocery shop once I got off work. Oh well, I kicked off my heels and walked in stocking feet to the soda machine down the hall, taking the long way to avoid Bragasaurus and his big bag of bullshit.

I took the first bus leaving the Marina Friday morning. My bloodshot eyes matched some of the other passengers', mostly stockbroker types that worked market hours. If I made it into work by seven o'clock, that would give me ten straight hours to wrap everything up before the long weekend.

At least I have a great weekend to look forward to, I thought to myself. Peter and I were going to Napa on Saturday.

I stopped by Bragasaurus's office around noon to get some last-minute feedback from him. "Oh there you are. I was about to come see you. Listen, Whore-hey and I are heading up to Tahoe this afternoon around two o'clock, so I will need to have your site plan proposal by then so I can take it with me."

All the color disappeared from my face, and I had to remind myself of the necessity of blinking. "I'll try my best to get it to you by then."

I scooted out of his office and ran back to mine. Finishing this type of project was like preparing Thanksgiving dinner. Everything was sort of all over the place until the meal is served.

At 1:58 p.m., I ran back to his desk and handed him the report.

"Thanks, love. Have a great weekend, ciao!" Bragasaurus flashed a triumphant smile and waddled off wearing ski pants that made him look like a marshmallow.

"No problem," I sighed with relief.

A few hours later, I decided to call it a day. This had been a seventy-hour work week, so I had no qualms about heading out a few hours early. I stopped in my tracks in front of Bragasaurus's desk. There it was. My report. Sitting on his desk. That motherfucker.

I would have been angrier had this not been a pattern with him. I stomped the four miles back to the Marina fuming. What a jackass! Why does he pull those power trips on me? After living together this long, Zoe knew all my faces.

"Uh-oh, what did he do now?" Zoe asked as I walked into Jean Genius.

"It is like he purposely does this shit." I slammed my laptop bag onto the counter.

"I mean, why not take the damn proposal with you? Why leave it there knowing I'm going to see it," I said, taking my jacket off.

"Did you walk home again?" Zoe taunted with one raised eyebrow, turning into the overbearing mother I never had. Zoe thought walking home wasn't safe. She thought a lot of things weren't safe. My philosophy was more "you can't go through life worrying about that sort of stuff," which created a seesaw balance to our friendship. I gave her the push to step outside of her comfort zone, and she gave me enough guilt to think twice before cutting through the Tenderloin. The extra four blocks to walk through North Beach took another fifteen minutes, but Zoe's lectures took longer.

"Yeah, I like your top." The color was somewhere between rhubarb and raspberry, and the flow of the silk fabric whittled her waist into the size of a toothpick.

NAKED ROLLERSKATING

Except for outlying neighborhoods like the West Portal or Ocean Beach, finding parking in San Francisco was always a challenge. Metered street parking in Union Square or the Financial District was unfeasible, so venturing to those areas with Zoe revealed a level of neurosis I had only seen in Woody Allen films. You see, Zoe was terrified of underground parking garages.

To add insult to injury, she was also certain we would be mugged, raped, or attacked if left alone on the street, so shopping together in downtown required a minimum of three people so one person could park and the other act as Zoe's bodyguard. Cupcake and I weren't in any way, shape, or form the bodyguard type of person, so I'm not sure what sort of protection we could offer, but we humored her nonetheless.

It was one of those crystal clear days where the weather was warm but not hot. Cupcake dropped Zoe and I off at the entrance to the parking garage on Post Street. She tried to look comfortable, but I knew she wasn't. Zoe looked like a germaphobe cleaning out the toilet of a gas station bathroom.

"Hey, what a second! That guy is nekkid!" Zoe pointed to a man roller-skating toward us. It was a spectacle to behold—a middle-aged man wearing a junior varsity lettermen jacket circa 1983, tennis headband, rainbow tube socks, and nothing else. No pants. No underwear, no thong, nothing. Totally nude and not the good kind of nude; he was the nekkid kind of nude. To make it worse, he wasn't just roller-skating, he was bebopping to whatever was blaring in his cassette walkman. That's right, folks. Circa now, cassette walkman, and pantless.

"Is that what Ford's friend's package looked like?" Zoe giggled.

"Well, his ding-a-ling wasn't swinging around like that . . . Goodness he is one hot shitty mess," I tsk-tsked, shaking my head.

JEWISH GUILT

Zoe decided to keep the Mexican fiesta birthday theme going and had her shin-dig at La Barca on Lombard Street where we had bonded while apartment hunting. We planned on having dinner there then pumping out some karaoke at Silver Cloud. Zoe's interpretation of busta move was legendary. Cupcake and I were surprising Zoe with a Swedish princess cake from Schubert's Bakery on Clement Street. At least that was the plan until I walked into work that morning.

The Real Businessmen of Orange County were a duo of high-rolling commercial real estate developers. They were charismatic, fast on their feet, and knew the business inside and out. The only thing the Real Businessmen of Orange County loved more than golf was dropping atomic F-bombs. Granted, usage of fuck can be extremely useful when delivered in a tenacious manner, but these two flung fuck around like a woman with DD breasts wearing a plunging neckline, saying fuck or showing cleavage will catch someone's attention but too much boobie or too much fuck loses its value.

"Hey, guys. I didn't know y'all were in town today," I said to the Real Businessmen of Orange County.

"Got in late last night. We're headed up to Seattle to meet with the John Brightwell about the new condo development he's working on in the South Lake Union area."

"The one on the trolley line?"

"Yeah, you know what that fucking thing is called? The SLUT! Get it?! South Lake Union Trolley! Whatta bunch of idiots."

Saying no to them simply was not an option, only what was your degree of yes. Watching them work from the sidelines was impressive; however, being a part of their storm could cause you whiplash.

Five minutes later in my office, I was personally steamrolled. "You see, going to Seattle today isn't negotiable. You've worked your ass off to get to this point and had to deal with fuckin' Henry to boot. You don't wanna lose out on this opportunity," Orange County Number 1 said to me.

"He prefers Henri, ya know," I said, staring off into the window, looking out onto the San Francisco Bay in the distance. Thank goodness the window was directly behind them, so it appeared I was decisive instead of perplexed.

"Yeah, we know," they said in unison.

"So here's the deal, you're gonna be at San Francisco International in ninety minutes. End of story," Orange County Number 2 said, standing up out of his cheaply upholstered chair and looking toward his counterpart.

"Let's bounce, our car is downstairs," Number 2 said as he turned to Number 1.

"See ya at the airport," Number 1 said to me, shaking my hand.

CHAPTER FOURTEEN

DATEWAY

When the Gods wish to punish us, they answer our prayers.
—Oscar Wilde

I WAS TOTALLY SCREWED, possibly dead, and the cause of death would be asphyxiation from Jewish guilt. "Please don't be home! Please don't be home!" I prayed as I jiggled my key in the front door of the Princess Palace.

"Hey, pretty girl! What are you doing home?" Zoe said, lacing her boot.

This was an ideal moment to scream the word *fuck* in my head. "Ummm, that's a good question. I have to go to Seattle today, well like in seventy-five minutes."

"You'll be back by tonight, won't you?"

"I'm sorry, honey. I don't really have a choice."

"But what about my party?"

"All your other friends will be there. You'll have a good time. I'll take you out when I get back, so now you're getting two birthday parties. That's exciting, right?" Zoe gave me her best *Scarlett O'Hara* glare before she walked out the front door. I would have sat there and sulked at my shittyness at being a friend, but I had exactly no minutes to pack and get my butt to the airport. Hell, the cab downstairs had the meter running.

After my meeting with John Brightwell the next afternoon, I called Zoe to find out how the birthday party went. "It sucked. That's how it went. It was completely awkward." This was my first taste of Jewish guilt. It didn't taste very good, like an antacid covered in baby powder, totally capable of asphyxiating me.

"Jude drank three apple martinis then kissed Felix."

"She didn't."

"Jude and Felix? Fuck, I can't make this stuff up."

You can't cross a sea by merely staring into the water.
—Oscar Wilde

Cupcake stood in the driveway smiling and waving as I pulled rear end first into the driveway of an empty house in Pacific Heights. One of her students, the heir to some dot com fortune his father stumbled upon, moved to Seattle, leaving several pieces of furniture behind and for the use of anyone who cared to take (what they considered to be) junk off their hands.

"It's only a small loveseat, but it has a pull-out sleeper, so I thought it would be a nice addition to the living room. Whaddya think?" Cupcake asked as she swept a lock of hair behind her ear.

"I think it's probably a bitch to carry up a flight of stairs." I guesstimating how much that sumabitch weighted.

Cupcake threw me her "poor me" eyes she used only when absolutely necessary, always wielding her prey helpless. "Err, I could see if Peter can help us?"

"Hey babe, sup?"

"Well, what's up is a loveseat sitting in an empty living room a few blocks away from you, what's down is hopefully this nice addition to my living room. Can you help us carry it upstairs?"

"Oh yeah, sure, no problem."

"Thank you, thank you, thank you! I'll text you the address."

Peter met us and our loveseat at six o' clock on the dot with his adorable mop of brunette curls going hay wire into angelic ringlets around his sweaty forehead, his muscles bulging from his workout.

"Sorry, I'm sweaty." He said after he helped us lug the love seat out of the Pacific Heights mansion and into our Princess Palace.

"Don't be sorry, babe. You look sexy all sweaty like that."

"So do you," he said, blushing.

"I'm not sweaty," I said, flirting a bit with my boobies in my low cut V-neck T-shirt.

"We'll see about that." He winked at me. The decrepit elevator of his building inched up to the top floor, and Peter nuzzled my neck, rubbing his sweaty nose all over it. I had to admit. He smelled amazing, even all sweaty. What can I say? I love his stink.

I thumbed through one of his thousand-plus books stacked in his living room while he showered. He emerged from his bedroom wearing only a pair of cargo shorts and looked like an Adonis.

"Want to watch the new Star Wars Revenge of the Sith cartoon? I DVR'ed it." Adonis he may have looked, but Peter was a nerd through and through, and I loved the combination.

BAY TO BREAKERS

Cupcake's Dr. Party Girl alter ego was a lot of things, but a night owl was not one of them. You see, Dr. Party Girl loved to "day-drink." The months of May through July in San Francisco were packed with some sort of excuse to be drunkety, drunk, drunk by early afternoon nearly every weekend. The arrival of day-drunk season begins with a bang: Bay to Breakers.

Bay to Breakers is an annual 12K race through the heart of San Francisco, and the longest consecutively run footrace in the world, according to urban legend. The participants dress for debauchery, San Francisco style, in strange costumes, elaborate contraptions, or plain old butt-naked. That's right, running a 12K with your junk bouncing around for all the spectators to see.

"I'm afraid you'll have to count me out," I said, pouring a cup of coffee.

"Relax, Republican, we already have enough girls to carry the beer stroller. You could maybe hang out along the way and people watch. C'mon, it would be fun. Oh yeah, and most people drink before, during, and after the race. It starts before eight a.m. by the way."

"No way, José, I'll never wanna see that much butt-nakedness."

"Give it time. You'll see. Next year, I guarantee you'll be in," Zoe added with a smirk.

"Fat chance," I said as I blew into my cup of coffee.

Cupcake encountered a tribe of dudes wearing ballerina tutus at Bay to Breakers somewhere near the entrance to Golden Gate Park. Later on that afternoon, with Cupcake's sunglasses cocked slightly crooked from one too many red plastic cups filled with various libations, she wrote her phone number down on one of the Mr. Tutu's lower thigh with a Sharpie . . . using her mouth, as his friends and strangers alike cheered on. Cupcake read us her IM exchanges from her laptop later that week as the three of us watched *Project Runway*. Hopefully, Mr. Tutu wouldn't mimic Heidi Klum's "auf Wiedersehen."

Zoe and I dropped Cupcake off at Mr. Tutu's condo on Van Ness Avenue the following Saturday night for a casual date. Mr. Tutu, Jason

Barnes, otherwise known as Aqua Man was a marine biologist with two passions in life: S.C.U.B.A. and being a douche bag. He was a former army deep sea diver, where he developed a love for the ocean and preserving aquatic creatures in their natural habitat. Aqua Man was also a sociopath with a heart of gold, creating a combustible blend of charm and erratic behavior in a solid six-pack abs of a container with the label firmly stamped "Douche Bag". Unfortunately for Cupcake, she only read labels for fat and calorie content, and didn't realize Aqua Man's primary ingredient was douche baggery.

Their first date was a casual lunch on a sunny Saturday afternoon. After taking Cupcake for a ride on his motorcycle along Highway 1, she was hooked. Aqua Man was gorgeous in regular clothes (minus the tutu), exciting, funny, and spontaneous: the total package in her eyes. That's the thing about getting hooked. You begin to overlook signs that will inevitably lead to getting your heart broken. His obsessive compulsive cleaning habits, immature jokes, and pretentious posing were interpreted as being tidy, hysterical, and a love for the finer things in life.

"I'm heading to Washington for three weeks tomorrow. Why don't you come with me? We can check out Vancouver for a couple days." Aqua Man said as he drove Cupcake home after an afternoon up in Napa. His spontaneous invitation was flattering, but spending an indefinite amount of time with someone you've been on five dates with was a little over the top.

"That sounds like fun, but I'm really trying to save money right now."

"Don't worry about your ticket. I'll pay for it."

"Really?" She was off for the summer and bored, so she said yes . . . and immediately questioned her decision.

"So, Jason invited me to hang out in Washington for a while." Cupcake said as she sat on my bathroom countertop while I sprayed perfume in front of me and stepped into the scent, shimmying my shoulders back and forth.

"Why don't you spray perfume on your wrists like normal people?"

"Have we met?"

"Yeah, guess you're right."

"Okay, so, Aqua Man invited you to hang out in Washington, and?" I confirmed as I twisted open a tube of mascara.

"Well, he said he would buy my ticket to fly up there on Friday and hang out." She said as she leaned into the mirror to stare at her complexion. As always, it was flawless.

"So, he's buying your ticket?" I pumped the mascara wand before pulling it out of the tube.

"Yep." Cupcake contorted her face in the mirror, checking for invisible lines.

"Where are you staying?" I asked as I raked the mascara wand through my eyelashes.

"He's staying in corporate housing. I would have my own room and all that . . . I don't know O, what should I do?"

"Katie," I said as I twisted the mascara tube closed. "It's okay to take chances every now and then. You're wonderful and everyone loves being around you. He will too."

"So you think I should go?" Cupcake said as she slid off the counter and twirled her hair into a pineapple shaped mound on top of her head.

"I do. I think you should go."

"I don't know. I can't decide." She said, securing her hair with two chopsticks.

Before I had a chance to rebuttal, our door bell buzzed. "Shit, that's Peter." I yanked a jacket off the hanger and fluffed my hair.

"Do you mind asking Peter about it? I could use a guy's perspective."

The next morning Peter and I went in search of omelets and the newspaper. "Have you ever eaten there?" I asked, pointing to a diner joint attached to one of those drive-up motels in the Lombard/Van Ness corridor.

"Nope, let's check it out." Peter twirled me around and we walked over to the diner. The decor could not have been more kitschy: Marilyn Monroe commemorative plate in the display case near the front door, Mr. Potato Head on the shelf near the coffee maker, one of those scenic pictures of a beach that looks like it is moving, plastic tables that are "faux wood" color. Over chicken habanera omelets, I told Peter about Cupcake's Aqua Man quandary.

"Where did she meet him?"

"Bay to Breakers."

"Were either of them naked at the time?"

"No, but he was wearing a pink tutu."

Peter raised his eyebrow and took a big bite of his toast.

"All of his friends were in pink tutus."

Peter raised his other eyebrow and looked the other direction.

"I know, I know." I said, squeezing his wrist and laughing.

"Well, there are only two explanations: he's either fallen for her or a big ol' douche bag. Inviting a girl out of town after five dates, he's probably a douche," Peter decided, grabbing a home-style hash brown from my plate.

"I wouldn't tell her that though. What the hell do I know, anyways? You know I don't have any game."

"No, babe, you don't have any game." I said, mimicking his response by raising my eyebrow and looking the other direction.

AQUA MAN

Cupcake took a chance and went on her Aqua Man adventure. She flew into Seattle then took a regional puddle jumper to some town I had never heard of near the coast in Washington. The plane made two stops at local airports smaller than her parent's house, before arriving at the last airport before Canada where Aqua Man was there to pick her up. Despite the non-glamorous locale, there was something exotic and exciting about traveling for hours, just for a date.

Aqua Man smelled like oysters, not in the good kind of way, when he hugged her before grabbing her suitcase and tossing it into the back seat of his muddy jeep. "So I was thinking that we could go white water rafting tomorrow a few hours south of here."

"White water rafting? That's sounds dangerous."

"Nah, it'll be fun. You're adventurous, right?" he said, patting her knee and shooting a beaming toothy grin her direction. *I thought just coming here was an adventure*, Cupcake thought as she half-smiled in his direction.

The next morning, two hours before the sun came up, Aqua Man banged on Cupcake's bedroom door, drill sergeant style. "Rise and shine, sleepyhead, the wilderness waits for no one, he, he," he said, leaning against the door frame. Cupcake did as she was told. She changed out of her pajamas, splashed some ice cold water onto her face, brushed her teeth, and slapped a baseball game onto her head before encountering one of the most horrific days of her life.

For starters, she had to change into a rented wet suit . . . in front of over a dozen people . . . and since she thought she would be spending the day in Vancouver, she didn't pack a swimsuit. Aqua Man bobbed his head up and down in approval, commenting "Nice!" several times as Cupcake wiggled, jiggled, and finagled into the wet suit. She struck rock bottom when Aqua Man noticed her lips turning blue when they boarded the raft.

"You cold?" he asked as he took his place in the back row of the raft.

"Little bit." She sat down in the raft in front of him and slightly to the left.

"Just pee in your suit then. That's what you're supposed to do to stay warm."

"What?"

"Pee in your suit!"

"I'm not peeing on myself or on everyone else!" she hissed turning around and glaring at him.

"Why not? I just did, he he." He sat back against the raft with his hands locked behind his head and a defiant smirk across his face. Disgusted, she turned back around and watched a trickle of urine flow down the middle of the raft toward the raft instructor's feet. A day can be nothing more than of epically bad proportions when it begins with watching your date' piss in public. Who knows? Maybe everyone urinated in their wetsuits. All Cupcake knew was that every time the raft slammed into a wall of water, she was disappointed that the water didn't wash away the boy's locker room smell.

"That was off the hook!" Aqua Man yelled as he high fived two guys at the dock then stuck his palm in Cupcake's direction. She looked around for something to throw at him, didn't see any blunt objects within reach, so she gave him a dirty look instead.

The next morning, another rapid fire knock on her bedroom door woke her up. She cursed herself for not locking it. "Hey, ah, so I just got a call from the airline and your plane is leaving this morning instead of Tuesday."

"What? What do you mean?"

"They didn't really tell me. Just that your flight was re-scheduled for this morning. You should probably pack up and everything."

"No, that can't be possible." She said as she rolled over and patted her hand against the nightstand for her glasses.

"I don't know what to tell you. We should probably go check it out."

"Seriously?"

"Seriously."

"All right, I'm up. Just give me a minute."

"You should pack your stuff just in case."

"Really?"

"Well, yeah. These small airports are funny. This stuff happens all the time."

"Err, okay, just give me a second to get my things together." Cupcake pulled her dress and two blouses off their hangers, dumped her makeup and hair products into her toiletry bag, and put on her college sweatshirt over her pajamas.

"Why don't you go inside and see what's going on? I'll stay out here with your suitcase." Jason said as he flipped on the hazard lights in front of the airport entrance.

"What am I supposed to ask them anyways?"

"Just go in and figure out what's up with your flight, make sure it isn't leaving this morning. I'll stay out here with your suitcase."

Cupcake padded into the airport in her fuzzy slippers and over to the ticket counter. She pushed her coke-bottle thick glasses back up onto the bridge of her nose and cursed herself for not putting in contacts. "Hi, I'm not supposed to fly out until Tuesday, but I guess flights were cancelled?"

"No ma'am. They weren't."

"That's weird. My, um, my friend out there said he got a call this morning about my flight for Tuesday being cancelled."

"Nope, that flight wasn't cancelled."

"Whew! Thank you so much." Katie unzipped her sweatshirt and breathed a sigh of relief before she turned away from the ticket counter and looked out the window of the tiny airport. Jason and his muddy jeep were gone. *Motherfucker!* Cupcake ran outside and saw her suitcase sitting next to the curb.

"That your bag, miss?" an older gentleman sitting on a cement bench smoking a cigarette motioned in her suitcase's direction.

"It is."

"Some fella in a jeep left it there. Figured it belonged to you since it's just us and Marge here right now," he said as he stubbed his cigarette butt into the receptacle on top of the trash can. Cupcake turned and looked at Marge through the smudged glass door, recognizing her as the person who helped taxi her plane from the runway into the airport on Friday.

"Is she the only person that works here?"

"Nah, her sister Betty works part-time on the weekends."

"Gotcha," Cupcake sat down next to him on the cement bench. She wanted to punch Jason, throw a martini in his face or pop his tires. It didn't matter which. She just wanted revenge, but she was too sore from the day before, and too enraged, to come up with a good scheme.

"Are you Katie?" Marge asked as Cupcake wheeled her suitcase back over to the ticket counter.

"Yeah, I am." She looked down at her ridiculous outfit, realizing the last time she went out in public looking like this she was wearing the same sweatshirt and pajama bottoms. It was finals week her senior year in college and everyone dressed like shit so that make it at least somewhat excusable. Seven years later, not so much. "Ummm, so it looks like I'm stranded here. Can you check and see when the next flight is leaving?"

"Should be leaving in two hours or so, I can check you in right now if you want."

"Wait, so I am on the next flight?"

"Yeppers."

"Thank you."

Cupcake walked back outside and sat down next to her new buddy, the cement bench smoker. "So what happened with you and the fella?" he asked as he lit another smoky treat.

"He switched my flight, I guess."

"Must've cost him a pretty penny, these small airlines don't let you switch flights. You gotta book a whole new ticket."

"You think?"

"Well yeah, they don't like to make all those stops before Sea-Tac if they don't have to."

Cupcake frowned as she fished her phone out of her purse and called information for the airline's number.

"Hi, I was supposed to fly from Middle-of-No-Where, Washington to San Francisco on Tuesday but someone cancelled that flight and booked another flight for this morning." Cupcake bit her nails and paced as she waited for the customer service rep to look up her information.

"Yes, your ticket was changed yesterday morning."

"What *time* yesterday morning?" Now Cupcake was totally confused since she spent all morning with Aqua Man and the urine coated white water raft.

"Looks like the new ticket was purchased at 5:12 a.m."

"Oh, okay. Thank you. Just out of curiosity, how much was the flight?"

"Your original round trip ticket was $782.37 and the total for your flight today is $532.08."

"Wow! Great, thanks, you've been a big help."

"Katie, he's a douche bag," Zoe said in her hate-to-break-it-to-you tone that afternoon when Cupcake came home unexpectedly.

"Really?" she said, eating her feelings via a pint of Ben and Jerry's chunky monkey ice cream. She was relieved that his behavior was not a reflection on her specifically.

"Yeah, why don't you put the ice cream down? Let's go blow off some steam at Dateway."

"Oh okay, fine," Cupcake said, blowing her nose into a tissue. "Let me change clothes."

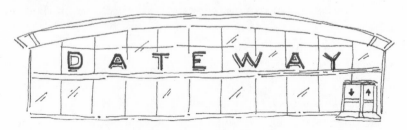

Cupcake was a slow-ass grocery shopper. She was a browser and I was a bumblebee. I usually tore through Dateway like a bat out of hell, grabbing the recipe items on my list without regard to their location in the store. If I would have worn a pedometer, I could have easily clocked half a mile each trip to Dateway. While Cupcake contemplated her mango purchase, I grabbed two cherries and held them at my chest with my fiercest pose in front of her cart.

"Stop it! You're embarrassing me!" Cupcake said in her second-grade teacher tone as she tried not to laugh. Orlando Bloom's doppelganger walked passed us and smiled at our silliness.

"Whoa . . . he's looking at bananas. You should go over there," I said to Cupcake, motioning toward Mr. Bloom's twin.

"I am not hitting on some dude!" Cupcake said, frowning at my suggestion. I raised my eyebrow. Oh yeah, she was sober, that only happened when she was drinking.

"You already had a moment, he totally smiled at you."

"Why don't you look it up on missed connections for me later then?" Cupcake rolled her eyes.

"You make yourself too available."

"By walking over to the bananas?"

"*You* are bananas."

I wouldn't go to Bay to Breaker, but I did however go with Dr. Party Girl to the Union Street Festival a month later. It was in Striped Shirt Alley, and I had nothing better to do that Saturday. By late afternoon, we were both trashed at Betelnut when Jeremiah the Landlord stumbled over. He was drunkety drunk and sweatier than usual, with his mop of curls drooping into ringlets around his neck.

It was more crowded in the bar area of Betelnut than the 7:30 a.m. 30Sexpress. Jeremiah leaned over me and tried to wink at me, but he was too drunk to properly execute lowering one eyelid. I awkwardly smiled and turned my head, scanning the room for Dr. Party Girl, and then I felt sweaty cargo shorts rubbing against my favorite skirt as the loud techno music blared over the speakers. *Shenanigans, shenanigans,* I thought to myself. I am getting dry-humped by my landlord.

"Ummm, please don't grope me, I pay you rent," I said robotically to him, searching for Cupcake in the crowds of people. She was lip-locked with a guy she met earlier that day. Jeremiah walked off, taking a hot mess express Marina girl into the unisex bathroom.

"Hey, is that guy over there Stanley Sorrenstein?" Cupcake squealed. "We should totally go over and tell him what a dick he was for dissing Zoe!"

"No, sweetie, I don't think we should. We don't know that man, okay?"

CHAPTER FIFTEEN

BUTTERFLIES ON BROADWAY

One's real life is often the life that one does not lead.
—**Oscar Wilde**

AS USUAL THE 30Sexpress was a zoo. I rushed to the 30Sexpress stop, noticing that the bus was already standing-room only. I smiled at Dolores the driver as I showed her my monthly MUNI pass and inched through the crowd of cologne to an empty standing spot near the back exit of the bus. While attempting to etch out my own friendlier version of San Francisco, I made it a point to learn the names of all the 30Sexpress bus drivers. I looked around on the bus and noticed a girl who often had her mustache waxed when I got my brows tinted at Benefit. Zoe's friend Miss Perfect was holding on to one of the vertical bars reading a *US Weekly* magazine, blinding all the other passengers with her engagement ring.

I wore my favorite three button blazer with my $330 jeans from Zoe's store and patent leather peep-toe pumps to work that day. Bragasaurus, and his big bag of bullshit, was a pain in the ass; but at least my paycheck provided certain amenities that made living in San Francisco more pleasing. It was in that moment I realized I had become one of those stylish and hurried Marina girls I admired my first few days in San Francisco. I thought about another moment when I came to a realization about myself.

There are moments in life that define who you are. Moments in time when a line is crossed, for better, for worse, and you cross over to the other side. When I was nineteen years old, I saved up $300, a fortune at the time, to buy my first suit. I chose it carefully. It had to be classic, make me look older, make me look taller, and last until whenever. Standing in front of the three-way mirror in the dressing room, the sales clerk fussed with the cuffs of my pants. After deciding how many inches would need to be hemmed, she smiled and left the room. I looked at myself in the mirror, and for the first time, I realized *I'm a woman.* No going back. This would be my life, in a suit. No more waiting tables, no more wondering and waiting for my future to start. I was no longer a child. My life was no longer a dress rehearsal that I would find myself sitting in the audience watching others learn their lines. Many years later on that 30Sexpress bus, I smiled inwardly and gave myself a high five for how far I had come.

I walked over to Divisadero and up to the Lyon Street Steps. It was cold outside and getting windy, but I didn't care. The view from the top at sunset made any of the pain running up the stairs more than worth it. Thirty minutes later, I took off my ear buds and pressed the call button at Peter's house. For such a swanky place, the buzzer sounded like it was on its last leg. The "burrrrrp" noise it made sounded more like a fifth beer burp than a buzz. I was wearing my favorite Lulumon running pants and my puffy jacket, with running shoes. My hair was piled on top of my head in a messy bun that he always loved. I thought I looked stupid.

"Hey, babe," he said, enveloping me in a hug.

"Hey, monkey," I said, taking a deep inhale of the mixture of his sweat and soap.

"You look like a lollipop in this getup," he said, laughing at me.

"What? What do you mean?" I was totally confused.

"Ya know, big puffy jacket on top and narrow bottom." He laughed, punching the elevator up button.

"You're crazy. My bottom isn't narrow!" I smacked him on the chest.

"Really? Let me see," he said as we got into the elevator. He pulled me close and playfully squeezed my butt. I took off my puffy jacket and pushed my body against his. If I stood on my tippy toes, we were almost eye to eye. I looked up into his brown eyes, and he leaned over and put his forehead against mine.

"Not quite narrow in all the right places," he whispered in my ear and then kissed my neck. His archaic elevator opened and we broke apart.

THE GAME

When Peter came to the Princess Palace, I almost always cooked an elaborate meal, and he always brought a book he would read after dinner out on my patio. Miss America's husband, who often took out the African dog while we were outside, would chat with Peter about the weather and sports and politics, like men do.

"You two remind me of how my wife and I were before we got married," Mr. Khakis said. After he went inside, Peter turned my chin up toward his and kissed me gently on the lips.

The future did come up from time to time, and he used *when* instead of *if* in our language, inflating something as simple as taking a few days to drive Highway 1 down to Santa Barbara. After months and months of dating, it felt natural to look out onto the sunny horizon of our future.

"When we have kids, I hope they have hair like yours," Peter said one night, gathering my hair into a ponytail with his forefinger and thumb after turning a page in his book, as if what he said was as inconsequential as "I could really go for some ice cream right now."

> *The course of true love never did run smooth.*
> —**William Shakespeare,** *A Midsummer Night's Dream*

For the first time in our relationship, Peter was running late . . . I knew he was working from home that Saturday to finish a project for work.

I was already at Union and Gough when I received the first message:

PETER: Hey, running late, see you in 20

So I walked up and down Union Street, basking in the bright sun. I walked down to Starbucks, sometimes known as Starfucks for its hookup atmosphere, for an espresso. I walked down Fillmore one block to the cute boutique near the Bermuda Quadrangle when I got the next text message.

PETER: Still working, meet me in 15

All right, for once, Mr. Perfect was running late. No problem, right? That's what I thought to myself as I waved at Zoe's newest store clerk perched neatly on the bench inside the store. I made a mental note to congratulate Zoe on finding the effortlessly chic sales clerk when he sent the next text message.

PETER: Meet me at my place in twenty minutes.

I now had ten minutes to spare altogether, so I ducked into Zoe's shop to meet the newest member of her denim family.

"How ya doing? I'm Zoe's roommate, so nice to meet you!"

"Hi, I'm Jessica," she said bashfully, hiding underneath her thick layer of bangs. "You are the roommate from Texas, right?"

"Yep, so what's going on today? Sell me some jeans that will make my butt look like two scoops of butter pecan ice cream."

I sat in a cab in front of his building for nearly five minutes, apologizing to the driver and redialing his number, each time immediately rolling to voice mail. He finally came out from the art deco entry with a weathered look on his face. I felt so far away from him that moment and didn't know why.

Our seats at the baseball stadium were directly behind home plate that sunny and unusually warm afternoon. I made a few attempts to cajole him out of his sullen mood then scrambled into the bottomless pit that was filling up with anxiousness in my heart. I was terrified and didn't know why.

After the game, we took a taxi back to my place first, and he gave me a quick peck on the lips before I exited. My keys had trouble fitting into the gate, and I dropped them as I turned around, Peter and the yellow cab already gone. He had always waited for me to get into my apartment before.

A few minutes later, I took out my after-game ensemble I planned on sleeping in at his house from my purse. *What a waste of a perfectly sexy nightgown*, I thought as I pulled the white cotton nightgown over my shoulders before climbing onto my bed and flipping on the TV. I heard Zoe come home and turned down the sound so she wouldn't know I was in my bedroom, too embarrassed to tell her that my baseball game date didn't go as planned, or that everything wasn't perfect with Peter.

PETER: Had a blast at the game today, want to grab dinner?
OLIVIA: SURE.
PETER: K, I'll be over in 10

Everything was right with the world once again.

Each time I had plans to see Peter, I repeated my hour-long morning routine of showering and primping all over again, even if we were just going to watch TV. I would pretend that I was always this effortless. I became insecure that I wouldn't be beautiful enough and Peter would leave me. The truth is that I was a pretty, smart, funny, kind, and confident girl. None of that mattered when it came to matters of the heart.

My first "real boyfriend" was the first man I ever loved, and our relationship altered the course of my life. He was older and already in college when we met. By the time I was enrolled at that same college, he had long since graduated and I had become his personal arts and crafts project. Attaining his acceptance quickly became the primary function of my existence. Any birthday or Christmas gifts were always clothing he wanted me to wear. He criticized my makeup, the way I talked, and the way I carried myself. I was his walking, talking, breathing *Eliza Doolittle*. At least 90 percent of his advice was well-intentioned, with the remaining 10 percent solidly chipping away at any of my nineteen-year-old self-esteem.

After four years of dating, we lived six doors down from one another in campus adjacent apartments. He was always distant, slightly out of my reach; we saw each other when it was convenient for him and went where he wanted to go. I was a friend with only the girls he approved of, even though he never spent time with anyone I knew. He was older, wiser, and I played by his rules. My life was his coloring book, and I always colored within the lines.

One of his many rules was never coming over to his apartment unannounced. I didn't know why and didn't think to ask. This was my first relationship, so I didn't know what the face of infidelity looked like. On a sunny summer afternoon, I went for a run along the trail he told me would be best for improving the shape of my calves. After stretching in the grass in front of my apartment, I kicked into a jog when I noticed his SUV parked outside of his apartment had its lights on. Trying to be the thoughtful girlfriend, I knocked on his door thinking that a headlight/dying car battery situation waived the "never come over uninvited" rule.

Rat-a-tat-tat-tat, my knuckles jingled against his front door.

"Oh heeeeyyyyyy," he said, rubbing his five o'clock shadow with his left hand.

"Hey, boo," I said as I leaned in for our predictable quick-kiss hello we had perfected over four years. He pulled back, way back. I looked into his eyes. The expression looking back at me was a combination of pity, misogyny, and arrogance.

"Yeah, hey," he said.

And then I saw her . . . sitting on his couch . . . wearing a shirt I bought him and nothing else. She was the girl I remember staring at him a few weeks prior, licking a lollipop seductively in his direction. Her ratty bleach blond hair was piled into a messy "just had sex" updo, a defiant look on her face.

I spun around in my discount sneakers and took a detour from my run straight back home, melting into a gooey mess of emotions. Hours later,

HEATHER JOY HAMPTON

I had cried through a whole box of tissues and started to question what I did wrong. In this reality I functioned in, the only person that did wrong was me. I always did anything he asked of me, treated him like a king, and expected nothing in return. I was a mess of snot, emotions, and confusion when he knocked on my door. I burst into tears when I saw him. He hugged me and walked over to my couch where he paced in front of me as I cried into a thick ball of tissues. Barely able to speak, I managed to utter one word: "Why?"

"What am I supposed to say here?" He opened his arms in a "crucify me" pose. Damn, he was the master of body language manipulation.

"Why?" I muttered again, looking up to him standing over me.

He shrugged his shoulders, folded his arms in front of his chest, and said the words that would fuck with my head from then until whenever.

"She had a better body than you."

Nearly a decade later, I still found myself fighting with the shadows in my head, subsequently putting on this façade with Peter because I so desperately wanted Peter to love me. After that incident with my first boyfriend, I always valued myself based on my appearance.

CAMEL STEINER

"Why don't you come over after work tomorrow? I'll fix something, and we can watch a movie."

As casual as the invitation might have sounded, it was never the case. Truth be told, I scoured recipe websites for delicious meals, often collecting the items to prepare dinner from Trader Joe's, Dateway, and Whole Foods. Sometimes, especially on the weekends, I cooked a test run to make sure dinner looked beautiful on the plate.

An hour later, beautified to the max, I wore an apron and fretted over a bouillabaisse on the stove. After living together for many months, I not only knew Zoe's footsteps, but could also predict her mood by the distinct rap of her bare feet on our wood floors when she was walking toward the common living area. I predicted frazzled as I poured more balsamic vinaigrette into my fancy stew.

"Ya know, that guy I went out with a couple days ago? Camel Steiner, the one getting his PhD at Stanford," Zoe said fresh out of the shower, adjusting the towel turban on her head.

"Bad breath, good jeans?" I asked, wiping my hands in my apron. I was resorting to these sorts of descriptions with her dates at this point.

"It's Camel Steiner."

"Ooooooh, you named the puppy!" I squealed.

"Shut up. He had a nice smile. So what . . . Well, he's on his way from Palo Alto with three pounds of king crab legs," Zoe said, her eyes bulging at me.

"No worries, I'm practically done here. Peter and I can hang out in the backyard if you and Camel want the kitchen to yourselves."

"That's the thing. I don't want publicity."

"Privacy?" I said as I turned down the stove.

"Yeah, no, I don't know," Zoe said, tapping her fingers on the granite countertop.

"Maybe it would be fun if Camel and Peter would get along. Peter went to Stanford too," I said, shrugging my shoulders.

"Yeah . . . I think so," Zoe said, fingering a celery stalk.

"What are you going to wear?" I asked, shifting the conversation to a safer topic.

"Good jeans and a top with sassy heels," Zoe said.

I took the lid off the pot of bouillabaisse as the buzzer downstairs rang.

"I'm gonna go let Peter in," I said, taking off my sherbet-colored gingham apron.

"Shit!" Zoe said, making a beeline to her bedroom.

Thirty minutes later, the four of us found ourselves swimming in a big bowl of awkward. Joe Camel Steiner, in his good jeans and button-down shirt, twirled around our kitchen chopping this, rinsing that, and messing with various items boiling on our stove. Joe Camel Steiner was seriously pulling out all the stops with his chef impression, which wasn't working too well on Zoe. She preferred restaurants with white tablecloths over slaving in her kitchen. Zoe's idea of cooking mostly involved the microwave, so she was bewildered by this lean, mean crab-boiling machine taking over her kitchen. Peter sipped his Syrah and winked at me.

"Well, I'm getting hungry for my fancy soup. Babe, you wanna eat?" Peter said, running his knuckles along my forearm.

"Yeah, I'm gonna go grab a sweater real quick so we can eat in the backyard." Zoe needed to be a big grown-up lady and entertain her guest without *publicity*, and frankly, she always acted a little kooky whenever Peter was around. Zoe's voice slipped into a resemblance of some sort of wacky neighbor on a sitcom, finishing sentences with "blah, blah, blue bah." It was grating on my nerves.

At first I thought Zoe might be attracted to Peter because I act similarly kooky when I am inappropriately attracted to a guy, but a few weeks into dating, Peter I realized wasn't exactly her favorite person. Besides exchanging "hi, how-ya-doing" pleasantries and maybe a little small talk that I mediated, neither of them would enjoy being stuck in an elevator together.

Peter was, what is often referred to, as intellectual as in the polite description of the guy in high school with his head stuck in a book. Back then that guy was called a nerd. Tag thirty pounds of solid muscle, a better haircut, six-figure salary, and you've got yourself a sexy intellectual, or at least sexy in my book, but I'm not a good judge. I thought nerdy guys were hot in high school too. Zoe, on the other hand, was a drama club girl. Tag on ten years, a degree or two, better haircut, and you have a creative type whose experiences made excellent stories. Peter read *The Economist* and Joseph Campbell. Zoe read her newsfeed on Facebook, and that was about it.

"Tonight was unusual for me. I've never met anyone like you, and I find myself grasping to comprehend it." Peter stared into his glass of chardonnay on my backyard patio.

"Did my bouillabaisse give you heartburn?" I teased jokingly.

"No, course not. I, well, you are only the second girl I have ever seriously dated."

"Oh," was all I managed to utter while my cheeks blushed. "I dated this one chick for a long time, and it was always a struggle, with you, it is just so easy."

"When did things end, with the girl, I mean?" I asked, tracing the bottom perimeter of my wineglass.

"Five years ago."

"Long time to be single," I said as I rested my wine glass down onto the black iron patio side table.

"Yeah, it was. I guess I was waiting to find you." Peter looked at me sheepishly with a half smile.

"And here I am!" I tossed my hands in the air like one of Bob Barker's *Price Is Right* beauties showcasing a *new washer . . . and dryer*!

"Yes, you definitely are." He smiled and took my hand.

"Are you about ready to go inside, pretty girl? You must be getting cold."

"Little bit." I stood up from the patio chair.

"Let's go inside and get you warmed up." Peter rubbed his hands up and down my upper arms.

The living room was lit by a few candles scattered around. Zoe must have had a change of heart, and Camel Steiner must have brought breath mints I thought, judging by the guilty looks on their faces.

"Oh, Zoe, you didn't need to do all the dishes."

"No worries." Zoe gave me the "I only did the dishes so you two would go to your room," so I gave her the "over and out, but I want all the juicy details tomorrow" look.

Scandal is gossip made tedious by morality.
—Oscar Wilde

Zoe's bedroom door was wide open when Peter and I emerged from my room the next morning. The house was quiet except for the shower running in Zoe's bathroom, and her boudoir was definitely empty of occupants.

"Babe, you better get going. Zoe usually comes out of the bathroom with only a towel on." The front hallway bathroom Zoe shared with Cupcake was definitely occupied. Cupcake always left for work at 6:00 a.m., so it had to be Zoe in there.

"Well, she isn't alone in that bathroom, buttercup. Mr. Crab Legs left his clodhoppers by the couch over there. See." Peter pointed to a pair of black shoes by the couch.

"No, are they, I mean, do you think they are taking a shower together?" I scratched my bed hair.

"Oh yeah," Peter said as he hugged me good-bye.

"We didn't hook up or anything." Zoe said firmly as she folded a pair of jeans in her store that evening.

"So let me get this straight, Camel Steiner works his mojo, gets invited to the bonus round in your bedroom, sleeps next to you all night, then you two take a shower together and *nothing happened*?"

"Well yeah." She said without looking up at me.

"You are so full of shit." I shook my head and laughed.

"I swear, nothing happened, I mean, why would I lie about it?" This was true. Zoe didn't lie or even exaggerate or diminish the truth, which made the situation even more intriguing to me.

"Zoe, you are my hero, I'm too embarrassed to get my hair wet in front of a guy."

"What? Why? That's weird."

"You've seen me with my hair wet. I look like a gremlin."

"Shut up, you do not look like a gremlin. Besides, even if you did, who cares? Peter certainly doesn't."

"I'm confused, why did you take a shower with him?"

"He didn't get *in the shower*, he just wanted to watch me take a shower." Zoe's bathroom had glass shower doors.

"Like a Peep'n' Tom?"

"Something like that, I don't know, it was flattering that he wanted to sit there and watch me."

"I get it." I lied.

CHAPTER SIXTEEN

THE WRATH OF CUPCAKE

A little sincerity is a dangerous thing, and a great deal of it is absolutely fatal.
—**Oscar Wilde**

B EFORE I SAY anything else, I should tell you a few things that were true about my roommate Cupcake.

1. Her sugary sweet nature was often clouded in a superficial veil of judgment. Speaking her mind wasn't what "nice girls" did.
2. Cupcake had a volatile temper that, up until this moment, had been narrated with her high-pitched singsong voice about bar altercations that involved tossing a martini glass into "some ugly bitch's face." Most of these girl fights happened during her wild sorority days, so Zoe and I wrote them off as exaggerated college tales.
3. Zoe and I thought her college antics were funny when told over Two-Buck-Chuck chardonnay as the three of us sat in our house uniforms around the crackling fireplace. Seeing as how we were neither ugly or bitchy, her temper was assumed to never sprout its nasty head around the Princess Palace.

One morning, purple with rage, Cupcake flung her bedroom door violently open, the doorknob loudly hitting the wall. "Mornin', sweetie, did you hear that noise? What was that?" I said to Cupcake, my head stuck in the fridge looking for a Diet Coke. This particular morning, I was summoned for jury duty and fishing for refreshments to sneak into the courthouse.

"I want you to know that I think you are psycho and Zoe is a thief." My head popped out of the fridge like a groundhog. Cupcake was standing with her arms crossed and her jaw locked.

"What exactly did Zoe steal?" I kept my voice calm, taking my Diet Coke out and closing the refrigerator door. I looked Cupcake in the eye, noticing her left eye was slightly twitching. Cupcake complained about her eye twitching a few times when she was stressed-out, but I had not seen it in person.

"For one, my shampoo, she ran out like a week ago, so I know she's been using mine because my shampoo is the only one in the shower. Oh yeah, and she took one of my mugs to her 'little store' and never brought it back." *Whoa, why the need for the finger quotations,* I wondered. Finger quoting Zoe's store was the least of my worries. "And as far as you, you're a bitch and you're psycho."

"Why, um, why would you say that?"

"Last night, when we got home, you know what you said."

"I don't. I really don't."

"It doesn't matter, really. I thought you should know what I think about you." Cupcake swiveled on one zebra print ballet flat and walked out of the kitchen without waiting for a reply, passing Zoe in the hallway. Trying to get my head around the situation, I focus on the trees and greenery I could see through our floor-to-ceiling bay windows that looked out onto Francisco Street.

"What's going on? I heard her yelling," Zoe asked, wrapping her scarf around her neck.

"Not now. I need to get my purse. Wait here," I mouthed to Zoe so Cupcake wouldn't hear me. I quickly walked back to my bedroom, grabbed my purse and jacket.

"C'mon," I mouthed to Zoe and pointed toward the front door with my shoulder.

"What happened?" Zoe hissed as we walked out onto Francisco Street.

"Well"—I took a deep breath—"ya know how she has all these stories about going off on girls in bars?"

"The ugly bitches," Zoe said rhetorically.

"Yeah, the ugly bitches. That's right," I said as we waited for the walk sign at Gough and Lombard.

"So what happened? I was in my room talking to Leticia, so I didn't really hear what she said."

The cars whizzing by on Lombard made it especially nippy that morning. My third summer in San Francisco, and I still couldn't get used to needing a scarf in the summer.

"You ready for this?" I pulled a scarf out of my tote. "So I'm psycho and you're a thief."

"She said you were psycho? Didn't you and her go out last night?"

"Yeah, and apparently, something I said made her decide I'm psycho," I said, throwing my hands in the air.

"What did you say?" Zoe said, looking at me totally confused.

"I don't have a clue. I really don't have a clue," I said, shaking my head, looking down. I was more confused and sad than angry. I thought Cupcake was my friend, practically family, at least that is what I thought until Cupcake ruined the Princess Palace in one PMS-infused rage. But fierce PMS wasn't my problem just then. It was Cupcake. My head in a fog, I went to the San Francisco Courthouse.

Back in Texas, when I was living in the uptown neighborhood known for having Marina-esque girls, most of my friends lived elsewhere and often made comments about my pretentious BMW-driving neighbors who were so vapid and self-indulgent that they turned bourgeois and arrogant. I hadn't seen it personally, but I'd known a few neighbors at various bars to have one too many apple martinis and turn into a pompous loudmouth, which was usually forgotten by the next morning. But in San Francisco, people were more vocal and made it clear that Marina girls were indistinguishable brainless nitwits.

Truth be told, I was mildly excited about the idea of serving on a jury. I served on a jury once in Texas where things were much different. The defense attorney was oh so fine, sort of glistening sweaty and passionate, like Matthew McConaughey circa *A Time to Kill*. He was so good-looking it was almost distracting. It wasn't though. We gave the defendant the death penalty.

After checking in, I sat down in one of those durable plastic metal chairs that reminded me of high school. I looked around the jury pool waiting room and wondered why the DMV or jury duty was always one of those government rest stops that wasn't only depressing because of aesthetics. It was the sad, captive faces of those hoping to pass through as quickly as possible. Not one damn person in that room was mildly pleased to be there, well except for one: the woman sitting the row across from me wearing a brimmed visor and defiant smirk on her lips. She was surrounded by those awful Chinatown pink shopping bags, one of which must've contained some sort of rotting meat judging from the stench trickling into the room.

Three hours later, while my butt was a little sweaty against the plastic seat, my assigned number came up. The jury pool filed into the cramped unventilated courtroom, first filling up the jury box, then the court gallery, with each chair numbered.

"Ladies and gentlemen, I appreciate you taking the time to be a part of the judicial system. I am Judge Franklin. Allow me to introduce you to my bailiff, Hank, and our court reporter, Felicia. We have prosecuting attorneys Frank Kennedy and Allison Watkins with us today. Please raise your hands to show the jury. We are also joined by defense attorneys Jamal Williams and Teresa Chong. Also, please raise your hands. The case that will be tried is second-degree possession of a controlled substance."

"Now, before we get started, let me provide some instructions. The twelve individuals seated in the jury box will be questioned by the defense team first, then the prosecution, then the defense team if they elect to do so. If either legal team chooses to dismiss a juror in the jury box, the individual seated in chair number 13 will take their place. The juror in chair number 14 will then move to chair number 13. All the other potential jurors not seated in the jury box will then change seats accordingly. Does anyone have any questions before we get started? No? Okay, we will proceed, defense, you may begin whenever you are ready."

"Thank you, Your Honor."

"Beginning with Juror Number 1, please state your age, gender you most identify with, occupation, and the age, gender, and occupation of every member of your household."

Juror Number 1: I am forty-four years old. I am female. I am employed by the San Francisco school district. My husband is forty-eight years old and an accountant. We have twin boys that are seven.

Juror Number 2: I am twenty-seven years old. I am female. I am a freelance photographer. My life partner is thirty-one years old, and she is also a photographer.

Juror Number 3: I am fifty-three years old. I am male. I am employed as a janitor. The other member of my household is forty-one years old, male, and an aerial safety and beverage engineer.

"An aerial safety and beverage engineer?"

"A flight attendant, sir. *Do I have to state the obvious?*" he muttered.

"Juror Number 1, are you or anyone in your immediate family a part of the judicial system or in law enforcement?"

"Yes, sir."

"Juror Number 2, are you or anyone in your immediate family a part of the judicial system or in law enforcement?"

"No," she said, rolling her eyes, her bald head catching a reflection from the overhead fluorescent lighting as she resumed picking at her fingernails.

"Juror Number 2, is there any reason you feel that you would not be able to impartially judge the evidence presented in this case?"

"I don't believe in the criminal system, caging humans like animals for years at a time. Jails should be closed."

"Thank you, Juror Number 2."

"Juror Number 3, are you or anyone in your immediate family a part of the judicial system or in law enforcement?"

"Yes, I'm on probation, four felonies within the past three years."

"Juror 4, please state your age, gender you most identify with, occupation, and the age, gender, and occupation of every member of your household."

"'Kay, 'kay?"

"Sir, do you speak English?"

"'Kay, 'kay?"

"The prosecution would like to politely excuse Juror Number 4, Your Honor."

Before Juror 4, who couldn't understand English, mind you, could pretend not to understand, he was up and out of his seat walking out of the courtroom.

"Say, man, you know if they validate parking?" he asked a guy in the back row, who was sound asleep.

The attorney resumed questioning, with the new juror sitting in the number 4 seat.

"I am twenty-four years old, male, live alone, and I am unemployed."

"What was your occupation prior to being unemployed?"

"None, I have a trust fund."

"I see. Is there any reason you would not be able to attend jury duty for up to three consecutive days?"

"I cannot afford to pay for bus fare each day."

"You said you were not employed because you have a trust fund."

"Yes, that's correct."

And then it was my turn . . .

"Please state your age, gender you're most identify with, occupation, and the age, gender, and occupation of every member of your household."

"How y'all doin'? Let's see, I just turned thirty. I'm female, obviously, he-he. I'm an architect. Both of my roommates are female and twenty-eight.

One of them is a second-grade teacher, and my other roommate owns this really cute store on Union Street just a couple blocks from our place. How convenient is that, right?"

"Psshh, typical Marina girl," the unemployed trust fund baby sneered under his breath.

"How long have you resided in the city of San Francisco?"

"Two and a half—wait, gosh, almost three years."

"Approximately three years. Is that correct?"

"You got it."

"Okay, ahem. Prior to living in San Francisco, where did you live?"

"Born and raised in Texas." I smiled.

"Are you fucking kidding me?" Mr. T-Fund muttered.

"Have you ever served on a jury either in San Francisco or in Texas?"

"I sure did, once, six years ago."

"Was it a civil or criminal case?"

"Criminal."

"What was the crime?"

"Capital murder."

"What was the verdict?"

"Death penalty." A gasp let out in the courtroom.

"The defense team would like to politely excuse Juror Number 5, Your Honor."

BOURBON & BRANCH

Across town, I tapped the door outside of Bourbon & Branch, the city's most famous speakeasy. I found the pretentiousness of Bourbon & Branch's speakeasy shtick to be a schmaltzy facade. It was in an unmarked location in the Tenderloin, so the prescribed specific number of knocks and password was silly if you could call ahead and get the buzzword of the day over the phone. I stifled a yawn and adjusted the wool blazer I bought after my dismissal from jury duty. Was it too bland for Bourbon & Branch? No, I decided, not with a cucumber sidecar martini.

"How was jury duty? Did you get selected?" Peter asked as he handed me a sidecar, one of my all-time favorite cocktails, a luscious blend of Cointreau, bourbon, and lemon juice.

"No. I knew I wouldn't be."

"I figured as much. I mean, c'mon, some dude is on death row thanks to you and the other eleven hooligans on the jury."

"Stop teasing. It's not funny." I playfully pushed him. "That guy kidnapped a seven-year-old, raped her for two weeks, then decapitated her, and left her head on her parents' doorstep."

"Damn!"

"Hey, I need to stay at your place tonight. Okay?"

"Mark is out of town." Peter winked and squeezed my knee.

"I really need a Mark-out-of-town night at your place."

"Everything okay?"

"Yeah, I'll tell you about it later." Sitting in jury duty all day only made me over think the situation with Cupcake. Talking about her was the last thing I needed at that moment. What I needed was some Peter, so we downed our sidecars, hopped in a cab, then made the sweet love on every piece of furniture in the living room, dining room, and Peter's bedroom. He was insatiable, and so was I.

"So what's new with the ladies?" Jackson cooed as he brushed my hair.

"The wrath of Cupcake, Jackson, the wrath of Cupcake."

"No shit!" Jackson squealed. "Oops." He covered his mouth and looked around at the room, assessing who he may have offended. The salon was relatively empty that morning, so no harm was done. I raised an eyebrow at Jackson. He often schooled me to let loose since all behavior was acceptable in San Francisco. Why was saying *shit* now unacceptable? "Oh, honey, that is a whole 'nother can o' worms. She Who Must Be Obeyed had a 'talk' with me the other day about being *pro*-fess-ional," he enunciated.

What is up with the finger quotes lately? I thought as I adjusted my black smock.

"I don't give a damn if it's ten a.m. You need champagne. Stat," Jackson diagnosed.

"Here. Now spill." Jackson handed me a glass of champagne with a splash of orange juice.

"So last week, Cupcake randomly tells me that Zoe is a thief and I am a psycho bitch."

"Juicy! What did Zoe steal?" Jackson said, his eyes widening.

"Ummmmm, six squirts of Suave shampoo and she took her mug to Jean Genius like two weeks ago but forgot to bring it back."

"What a petty bitch! That's like twenty-nine cents' worth of shampoo. And why are you a psycho bitch?" Jackson asked as he sprayed hair product in my direction.

"I must have said something to light a fire under her ass. I just don't know what it is." I shrugged.

HEATHER JOY HAMPTON

"Girrrrrrl, that bitch is crazy. I told you, you know I told you, that girl was gonna lose her mind one of these days," Jackson said, tsk-tsking a CHI straightening iron in my direction just like the 1950s homemaker he gave me on my birthday that said, "Honey, it is better to be a year older than a month late."

"Well, it has been totally weird at home the past few days. I've been at Peter's house four or five nights this week, but Zoe said that she will barely speak to her."

"Dubya Tee Efff," Jackson exclaimed.

CHAPTER SEVENTEEN

GEORGE OF THE JUNGLE

Love looks not with the eyes,
But with the mind,
And therefore is winged Cupid,
Painted blind
—William Shakespeare, A Midsummer Night's Dream

PETER AND I had one of (what I refer to as) *our* Saturday nights: dinner at a nice, tucked-away restaurant. Then we talked and smoked cigars on his rooftop overlooking the Marina and Golden Gate Bridge in the distance. "Let's go lie down. I want to love on you," he whispered in my ear just after midnight. He touched me like he was unwrapping a delicate gift with ginger care. Afterward he pulled me close, my chin resting against his chest in a nook made for me. I traced the word *happy* with my finger on his bicep while he slept. The next morning was one of those fantastic Indian summer Sundays. I stretched lazily in bed, savoring the musk of Hampton Court cigars lingering on his skin.

"Want some cereal?"

"Do you have coffee?" I asked as I pulled his button-down shirt from where I flung it onto his nightstand the night before and slipped it around my shoulders.

The view from Peter's living room was dazzling. The sail boats were out in full force with white sails sparkling against the water. The Golden Gate Bridge was wreathed in fog, faraway and mystical. I walked back to the leather club chair and sat on the arm. I sighed internally, partly for the view, mostly for the man I snuggled next to while he munched cereal.

"What are we watching?" I asked as I sipped coffee out of his law school mug.

Peter leaned in and whispered in my ear, "Cartoons," then lightly touched my lips with his.

An hour later while brushing my teeth and doing a horrible job of multitasking, one of my rings fell from his medicine cabinet above the toilet as I attempted to brush and accessorize at the same time.

"Oooh," I said with a mouthful of toothpaste.

"What oooh?" Peter laughed as he kissed my cheek and squeezed around me to grab his own toothbrush in his tiny bathroom. My mouth, full of toothpaste, and eyes wide as saucers looked down into the toilet. He squeezed back the other direction, looked into the toilet, then laughed out loud, and proceeded to fish my $3.99 ring out of the toilet with his hand, just to make me happy. He handed it to me jokingly on one knee, in proposal stance.

"Baby," I stammered, accidentally swallowing a big gulp of toothpaste.

"I would do anything for you." Peter shrugged and nuzzled the back of my neck with his five o'clock shadow and washed his hands. At that moment, I knew I loved him with all my heart.

We walked down to Noah's Bagels later on that morning and picked up a couple of buttered delights and coffee, then strolled hand in hand to the Marina Green.

"Let's go sit over there by the water." I pointed to my favorite spot at the old wooden bench near the water. His hand caressed the back of my neck underneath my wool scarf. I squeezed my Chelsea flavored cup of coffee with both hands and closed my eyes to reduce my sense of sight. The smell of him and the feel of his touch were the only senses I wanted to engage at the moment.

Hordes of shiny ponytails and dewy skin bounced along the Marina Green, running effortlessly, some straight out of *Baywatch*—black Lulemon spandex with the polyurethane blend running along the beach in slow motion. Some girls were Asians wearing elastic-enforced running tops just-barely-belly bearing, a few brunettes; all pretty much completing the typical cardio requirements for underwear models. I looked at these glamazons and their genetically blessed bodies and wondered what the hell Peter was doing with me.

An hour later, we were at our favorite quirky yet quiet coffee shop off on Van Ness. Peter was stabbing the keys of his laptop, ferociously writing, while holding his yellow highlighter between his teeth. I was doing the Sunday morning Sudoku puzzle while trading text messages with Ford about fantasy football. My players were doing horribly that day. On top of the superb people-watching surrounding us—the wacky proprietor, the intoxicated vagrant walking by, and the Marina girls cackling at the next table as they sipped sugar-free soy lattes—I couldn't take my eyes off Peter, leaning back in his chair with his arms crossed while doing his writer's block antsy-knee jiggle, then adjusting his reading glasses before resuming to more keyboard stabbing. And as we sat there, all I could do was react to him—the leaning, knee brushing, glasses adjusting—every moment, adjustment, or gazing my way over his laptop screen was another excuse to look at him.

Hypnotized, I wished time would stand still so I could live in the moment forever. *This is the man I love*, I thought.

That night we stayed up late whispering with our bodies intertwined like pretzels. I fought sleep, watching his chest rise and fall with each breath, burying my nose into his chest hair. Eventually I drifted off to sleep, and when I did, I slept soundly for the first time in two years.

"What are you smiling so big about?" Zoe asked the following morning when I walked into the kitchen.

"I am—" I was too overcome with emotion to talk.

"Yeah, I know, I heard it all night long. That's actually something I've been meaning to talk to you about. I don't have a delicate way to say this, but I can hear you two do *everything*."

"I knew the walls were thin but—"

"I would be more comfortable if he didn't stay over so much."

"Peter's here one, maybe two nights a week."

"His place isn't far. Can't you just stay over there?"

"So let me get this straight, you are telling me that my boyfriend isn't *allowed* to spend the night?"

"Like I said, I would be more comfortable if he didn't stay over so much."

"It isn't like we go into my bedroom and Peter turns into George of the Jungle and I'm swinging from the rafters. Yeah, we were up late *whispering*. I think we are respectful that your bedroom is next to mine and the walls are thin."

"Sleep is very important to me, so as I said before, I would be more comfortable if he didn't stay over so much."

"Why don't you get some ear plugs or I could get one of those noise-cancelling machines?"

"That isn't the point."

"What is your point then? You would be more *comfortable* if he didn't stay over so much?"

"Look, I said what I needed to say, and now I'm done talking about this," Zoe said with her arms crossed.

"If you want us to be less distracting at night, you need to tell me what noises I'm making so I won't make them anymore."

"Your bed makes a creaky noise whenever one of you rolls over, and it wakes me up."

"Zoe, I toss and turn all night. We've talked about this. If anything, I toss and turn less when he's over."

"I know, but when he's over, I hear the creaky noise, then I can hear Peter whispering."

"I didn't know he did that. What is Peter whispering to me?"

"I can't hear what he's saying. I just hear him whispering. I hear the bed creak, then I hear mumble mumble mumble mumble mumble mumble, then silence."

Selfishness is not living as one wishes to live;
it is asking others to live as one wishes to live.

—Oscar Wilde

"So not to get all kinky, but if you are going to continue doing the walk o' shame, we have to get a pair of handcuffs and one of those S&M muzzles," I reluctantly told Peter as he uncorked a bottle of Syrah. Peter took off his glasses. "Okay, now *what?*" He turned his head to the side and laughed out loud.

"I'm only half-joking. Apparently, I roll around in my creaky bed, Zoe finds it distracting when you *whisper* to me, so we're going to have to cuff me down to the bed so I won't roll in my sleep and put a muzzle on you in the off chance I manage to break free and you want to whisper about it."

"Hearing noises in the other room is part of having roommates."

"I know. I got pretty pissed. I think I even referred to you as George of the Jungle."

"George, George, George of the jungle, strong as he can be. Watch for that tree!" Peter sang as he tickled me.

IMPINGES

Zoe and her cackling friends ordered takeout and gossiped at the Princess Palace at least twice a month. Mostly I popped in and out, carefully trying to allow my roommate time with friends in the common area of our home. Zoe always filled me in on the juicy details later anyways.

"So I'm facedown doggie style, and she ripped out the hair from my vagessica like that!" Janice snapped her fingers while giving an encore performance of her recent Brazilian wax done at Spa Lab.

"Didn't that hurt, sweetie?" I asked, pouring a glass of Trader Joe's finest Two-Buck-Chuck.

"Well yeah, it hurt, but the hair didn't grow back for like three weeks!"

"Hmmm, I've been thinking about getting one."

"She's got a Pacific Heights Gentleman now, you know . . .," Zoe said. I noticed that her eyes rolled a bit, and I mentally rolodexed that look to overanalyze later.

"Okay, ladies, y'all let me know if things get really rowdy." I tried to stay upbeat in front of Zoe's friends even though I was already beginning the over-analysis of her eye rolling in my head.

I woke up the next morning with a slight headache to the thumping beat of techno music, Zoe's "get ready" music of choice. The clock on my nightstand blinked 9:30 a.m., too late to bitch about noise on a Saturday morning. I washed two aspirin down with mouthwash after I brushed my teeth. Caffeine was needed ASAP, so I put on a pair of jeans and a wool sweater. "Wool in the summertime, only in San Francisco," I said under my breath to myself.

HEATHER JOY HAMPTON

"Headed to Isaac's barbeque?" I said to Zoe as she buckled the strap of her latest pair of espadrilles.

"Yeah, Janice is picking me up in like two minutes. You wanna come?"

"No no no, I just woke up. I'm not fancy-Jew-BBQ ready," I said, pointing to my makeup-free face.

"You're going to leave the apartment like that?" Zoe said, with one eyebrow raised. The Marina was nothing more than a preppy Petri dish. Looking like shit was a guarantee you would run into someone you knew, like some guy that never called back for a third date.

"I got my sunnies," I pulled my oversized sunglasses out of my purse as evidence.

"Oh okay. I should be back sometime this afternoon. We still on to go shopping later?" Zoe asked.

"Def," I said as the buzzer went off downstairs.

"That's Janice. Gotta run!"

WAR IN JUNE

"Oh my goodness, is that what I think it is?" I asked Zoe, and I braced myself against the living room wall.

"Oh that? Just some War in June football I won in a raffle at the BBQ," Zoe said, waving her hand in the direction of the ball as she dismissed it as some trivial detail about her day. A raffle drawing was held for several prizes like spa treatments at Bliss Day Spa or dinner at Morton's Steakhouse. She crossed her manicured fingers for the Y & I Boutique gift certificate, which was won by none other than Where's Waldo Stanley Sorrenstein.

The last two prizes were a massage at Spa Lab and an autographed football from some player she had never heard of. Football was not Zoe's forte. She once walked in on Peter watching Monday night football and asked what inning it was.

When her name was called for the football, Zoe yelled, "Oh, I loooove War in June."

"You see, *Warren Moon* is one of the all-time best quarterbacks ever to play the game," I explained over enunciating his name.

"Quarterbacks are the guys that throw the ball, right?"

"Yes, something like that. "Did anyone notice that you called him War in June?"

"That's his name, right?"

"No, Zoe, his name is Warren Moon."

"Whatever."

WINCHESTER MYSTERY CASTLE

"What do you want to do tomorrow?" Peter swiveled around to face me from the leather chair in his bedroom. I was sitting on his bed reading a book wearing his button down shirt and my glasses flipping through a magazine.

"Ummm, ever been to Winchester Mystery Castle? It is supposed to be totally haunted and creepy," I said as nonchalantly as possible. My secret hobby was researching date ideas.

"Nah, but I've always wanted to. It's in San Jose. There's a cool shopping area next to it with a bunch of restaurants. We should make a day of it."

The next morning, I stood in front of my closet, dumbfounded. What could I concoct that would be casually effortless, sexy but not overtly, could transition from day to night if we went somewhere nice for dinner? There would also be a lot of walking through the Winchester Mystery Castle, so shoe selection would be challenging as well. I settled on my favorite jeans, wooden sandals with the gold rivets, teal T-shirt that brought out my eyes, and a tan lightweight jacket. Add a sassy gold purse I found in the 75 percent-off bin at the Coach Outlet in Petaluma, chunky bracelet, and earrings. I was double thinking my choice in jewelry when Peter buzzed the door downstairs.

"I'll get it," Cupcake chimed from the kitchen, shuffling her fuzzy slippers across the wooden floors.

I buckled my shoe and clippety-clopped toward the front door. "Hey," I smiled.

"Hey, babe, ready?"

"Yep."

"Let's go check out some hauntedness."

Winchester Mystery House was supposedly haunted but seemed like it was haunted by a broken, lonely heart more than anything else. All the twisting hallways, spider web-patterned stained glass, dusty passageways. Sarah Winchester's eccentricity about ghosts and bad spirits seemed like an explanation for what was haunting her. If you have nothing to live for, then why would you spend your life running from death, or bad spirits?

My mind wandered as the tour guide explained Sarah Winchester's fascination with the number 13. What if I end up like Sarah Winchester?

Old. Alone. Half-crazy. Loaded. Having more money than sense would certainly be nice, but spending my golden years wandering around a rickety mansion bossing around construction workers paled in comparison to what I aspired to become when I was old: Southern, well mannered, well coiffed, spirited, and a little bit slutty à la Blanche from *The Golden Girls*.

I took Peter's arm as we walked into the buzzing afternoon crowd of Santana Row's hip weekend scene, fortifying myself with his warmth. Peter wanted to breeze through a book store in search of a book about how superheroes were the modern-day mythology. I was never one to read comic books as a child, so the books he purchased were incredibly entertaining for me to flip through as he ordered coffees at a sidewalk café.

"You're sort of like Lois Lane," Peter said as we sipped cappuccinos at a café table outside of Cocola Bakery.

"That's funny. You sort of remind me of Clark Kent."

CHAPTER EIGHTEEN

THE APPLE SEED

Guard well within yourself that treasure, kindness. Know how to give without hesitation, how to lose without regret, how to acquire without meanness.
—George Sand

ONE OF THE sparks of validation I pined for in elementary school was shiny metallic stars for a job well done. Homework turned in on time, getting an A, or whatever incentive program they give third graders. I loved those damn little stars.

As a big grown-up lady, I awarded myself those same stars whenever I saw fit. Sure, sometimes I got a little carried away with tagging my planner with silver and gold stars, but the green and red stars served specific purposes. Green stars were for money stuff (paydays, bill due dates, etc.). The red stars were, of course, for when my crimson tide rolled in. Somehow sticking those little red stars onto my calendar made up for the bloating, cramps, and moodiness.

I flipped back to last month's calendar and the shiny red star. Tracing my finger down the day squares on the calendar as I counted: week 1, week 2, week 3, week 4, week 5, fuck. I closed the leather-bound planner and tightened the belt of my robe as I slowly scooted away from it and went back to finish my makeup.

The mascara wand trembled as it scraped through my lashes.

Don't freak out.
Don't freak out.
Don't freak out.

Simmer down now, Olivia. No reason to freak out unless I know it to be true, right?

Picking up a pregnancy test at the drug store before I grabbed my morning coffee would be an easy solution to stop doing the menstruation math of adding the number of weeks since my last period. The assortment of pregnancy test options was daunting, their bright pink lettering lurching out from the drugstore shelf: "Get results six days before your missed period!" or "Most effective brand!" After a few minutes of deliberation, I picked the cheapest test off the shelf and an economy-sized bag of Skittles on my way to the cash register, creating a hot dog bun of sorts covering up my test in case Bragasaurus or Cameron happened to cruise by the drug store for headache or heartburn meds before work. I paid the gum-chomping cashier and dropped the test into my tote.

It amazed me that nearly every corner in the FiDi had one of the Middle America-loving Starbucks that San Francisco despised, yet each location had a line every morning. What was far more interesting was how baristas memorized your name and drink preference as if you were an old friend. "Here ya go, Olivia, see you tomorrow!" my favorite barista smiled as I grabbed a handful of sugar packets and my fat-free latte.

My eyes ticked like the secondhand arm of a clock as I anxiously waited for the WALK light to beam green at the corner of Mission and Beale Street. Maybe it was the nerves. Maybe it was my new platform heels. Maybe it was the slickness of the fresh rain on the slick asphalt. My left ankle lost its footing, and I fell to the ground. It was one of those moments where time slips into slow motion. My first thought was, *Save the coffee!* and my second, *Oh, God, please don't let the pregnancy test fall out of my tote!* Neither of which happened. I landed like a pro with my coffee safely inside the 100 percent recycled paper cup. Crowds of pin-striped suits stepped over and around me as I struggled to stand up. Whatever happened to manners? Oh yeah, this was San Francisco.

I went to the break room after everyone else left for lunch, stuffed a Styrofoam cup into my tote, and went to the lavatory. The instructions were simple enough as I read through them. Tinkle in the cup, dip the test in the tinkle, and then get back to my desk to finish up that spreadsheet. The pregnancy test turned vivid blue in a matter of seconds. I was pregnant.

Knocked up.
With child.
Future baby mama.
Sperminated.
Preggo.
Shit.

My hands started to tremble. Like they do when I haven't eaten all day. The crystallized memory of my precious Peter holding both my hands the night we met, his hand on the back of my neck while we sat at the happily ever after bench, encircling his fingers between mine when we made love, and apparently an offspring. I squeezed my eyes shut and pressed my knuckles against my eyelids until I saw stars instead of a disapproving scowl from my parents at the news that I had a bastard in my belly.

After some time, my shoulder blades became stiff, and my elbows created perfect red circles against the top of my thighs. I tucked the test neatly back into the packaging and gave myself a pep talk before going back to real life.

"Henry is looking for you." Cameron appeared at my office door with a sympathetic look on his face. I quickly glanced down at my blouse to check if I was wearing a "Just took a pregnancy test" sign.

"Thanks, Cameron."

"Hey, O?" Cameron asked.

"Hmmm." I realized I was making eye contact but not blinking.

"You have a piece of toilet paper stuck to your shoe."

BABY DADDY

OLIVIA: When do you get back in town?
PETER: 9ish
OLIVIA: Can you stop by my place on your way home?
PETER: Everything okay?
OLIVIA: Yeah, just need to talk to you in person

I worked late that night, walked from my office to Union Square, stopping by a bookstore. I didn't see a book titled *I'm Knocked Up. What Do I Tell My Boyfriend?*, so I opted for a couple of other books about pregnancy. My ear buds stayed firmly in my ears as I smiled at tourists waiting in line at the cable car turnaround, posing for pictures before climbing onto the oldest moving national monument in America. It was windy as usual, and the city lights sparkled as the bell of the cable car rang over the tunes in my ears.

PETER: flight delayed, back in town after 11
OLIVIA: I'm sorry babe
PETER: talk in the AM, around 6:30? I'll stop by b4 work
OLIVIA: 'M'kay

I hopped off at the last stop near the Wharf and walked up the steep Bay Street hill back to the Princess Palace, thankful that my roommates had retired to their bedrooms. I was too overwhelmed to muster enough energy to wipe the panic off my face. As much as I adored Zoe and Cupcake, this was a little too much reality for those two. I climbed into bed and flipped through the pregnancy books, wondering what I would tell Peter.

"Will you be my baby daddy?"
"I'm knocked up."
"Remember when I said my birth control was 99.7 percent effective? Yeah, that 0.03 percent happens sometimes."
"Your swimmers and my eggos got me preggos."
"There's a half-Armenian growing inside me."

I woke up at 6:00 a.m. and brushed my teeth, fluffed my hair, patted concealer over the dark circles, and slipped on a long-sleeve pink sundress. A slight upgrade, I guess. *This is your moment, baby mama, choose your words carefully. Lead up to it, and don't terrify Peter.*

"Hey." My voice went hoarse and turned raspy.

"What's wrong?" Peter asked as he clicked the Lock button of his sedan.

"I'm pregnant," I quivered, tearing up. This was way harder than I thought it would be.

"Hey, hey, don't freak out," he said, taking both my hands and swinging them outward and inward. He was so much calmer than I was, yet he was deeply breathing in through his chest and exhaling slowly in a controlled manner.

"I'm not freaking out," I said, shaking my head, wiping away a tear.

"When did you find out?" Peter asked, making a second swab at the damp spot of my cheek with his thumb.

"Yesterday," I said, looking down at my fuzzy slipper feet.

"Honey, why didn't you call me?"

"I wanted to tell you in person," I responded, cocking my head to the side.

"Damn, I wish we could have found this out together."

"I didn't want to tell you unless I knew for sure."

"I tell you what. I'm not going to spinning class tonight, and I'll leave work a little early so we can spend some time together tonight," he said, brushing a wayward lock of hair out of my eyes.

"Okay," I nodded, reluctantly.

"Baby, look at me." Peter tipped my chin up to look him in his eyes. "Everything is going to be fine." Then he pulled me into a soft, smushy hug. It was one of those hugs where arms go to places they normally don't in a regular hug. His right hand was behind my neck, his left hand in the small of my back. I wrapped my arms around his waist and buried my head against his neck.

"I'll be over at six to pick you up, okay?" Peter whispered into my ear.

"Okay," I whispered, my mouth muffled into his neck.

I walked back into the Princess Palace and leaned against the door after I shut it closed. Could I seriously transition from Marina girl to mama? What about my work schedule? What about Peter's work schedule? Could my Pacific Heights Gentleman be a proud papa by next summer?

PETER: No matter what happens, this won't be easy, but we'll get through it
OLIVIA: Telling you was one of the hardest things I have ever done

I walked over to my favorite boutique at lunchtime. There was a three-inch-thick pile of paperwork on my desk, but my mind was too cloudy to concentrate on on-site renderings; instead, I focused on my belly. When would my belly start to show? How big would my ass get? Could I lose the baby weight afterward? Well, this size 2 eyelet corset top was out of the question. I ventured over to the size-medium section of the 50 percent-off rack and picked out a beautiful lilac empire-waist blouse and burgundy wrap dress. Standing in front of the three-way mirror in the dressing room, I tried to envision what my body would look like in four months.

"How do you feel about it?" Peter asked as we walked into his bedroom and shut the door.

I sat down on his bed and tucked my legs under. "Well, getting pregnant like this isn't the best of circumstances, but you know, I've always wanted to be a mom. I'm just not so sure how I feel about it happening now."

"You would be an amazing mother." Peter squeezed my shoulder. I looked at him gratefully and sighed. "This is your choice, and I want you to do whatever you feel is right. I'm going to support whatever decision you make about this," Peter said, sitting next to me and putting his arm around me.

"I don't really see it that way. I mean, being a father is just as important as being a mother. This baby is just as much mine as it is yours."

"So what's the next step? What do we do?" His usage of the word *we* was comforting.

"Well, I need to go to the doctor to confirm that I'm pregnant, and we can talk about our options when we're there."

A few hours later, I collapsed and fainted in his kitchen, holding a bowl of my favorite non-meal dinner of canned tuna fish mixed with crumbled crackers and Tabasco. He caught me as I fell, better than Valentino in a silent film.

"I don't know what came over me . . ."

"I have that effect on women," he said sheepishly. Beads of sweat had broken out on his forehead in a matter of nanoseconds, adding an extra shine to his gorgeous brown ringlets.

He always knew what to say to make everything better.

THE APPOINTMENT

The wallpaper in the doctor's waiting room was a yellow rosette pattern that an expectant mother would decorate a nursery without knowing the sex of her baby. I flipped through a three-year-old issue of *Ladies Home Journal* magazine as Peter tapped his sneaker resting on top of his knee while he read over my shoulder.

"Olivia Michaels."

"I'm Olivia."

"The doctor is ready for you."

I quickly kissed Peter and walked back into the check-in area. Weight, blood pressure, step into the lavatory for a pee test, strip, then I found myself sitting on top of the examination table staring at a chart of the female anatomy, a bulletin board on the other side of the room with countless photos of babies Dr. Leslie Chang delivered. I smiled to myself and thought about what our baby would look like.

"Hi there, sorry to keep you waiting, I'm Dr. Chang," the friendly yet serene doctor said as she sat down on the rolling stool and looked over my chart.

"So your last period was nine weeks ago, which puts conception at seven weeks, but by standards, you are nine weeks pregnant. Congratulations, Mommy." She patted my knee and stood up to put on rubber gloves. No one had ever called me Mommy before.

"Let's do your first ultrasound. Whaddya say?" she asked as if I had a choice.

"Yeah, sure." I looked down at my baby blue paper gown, then up to the fluorescent light fixture above my head. I always thought ultrasounds were like sonar equipment or something, at least TV told me so. No, this was silence, a long, thick, pregnant pause, the irony.

"Looks good, everything looks good." Dr. Chang smiled with her warm brown eyes sparkling.

"This wasn't a planned pregnancy," I said to Dr. Chang as she pulled off her gloves, then washed her hands.

"Most of them aren't, Olivia, but you'll do just fine. I would recommend that you don't drink or smoke, avoid sushi, unpasteurized cheeses, get enough sleep, and avoid stressful situations," she said with a hint of encouragement in her voice.

"So if I didn't want to go through with the pregnancy, is that a procedure you can do?"

"No no, absolutely not," she said as the encouragement disappeared from her demeanor. "Well, you're nine weeks along in your pregnancy. Should you choose to terminate, you have three more weeks to do so before your second trimester begins."

"Okay, that gives me something to think about."

"It was lovely to meet you, and hopefully, I will see you again." Dr. Chang shook my hand, looking me squarely in the eye. "The receptionist can schedule your next appointment."

"Thanks. It was nice to meet you too."

I climbed off the exam table and pulled off the itchy paper gown. Could I go through with this? Am I ready to be a mom? I pulled my thong out of the pocket of my jeans and slipped them back on. Bra, jeans, and T-shirt followed. I slipped my feet into my loafers and zipped up my hoodie. What will Peter say if I tell him that I want to have the baby?

I walked back into the waiting room, and Peter looked up from the *Wall Street Journal* he brought to read. One of those half-smiles that never reach the eyes formed across his face. It felt manufactured. "How did it go?"

"Fine, normal, doctor did an ultrasound. I'm nine weeks along. I'm not supposed to eat sushi or unpasteurized cheese. I don't even know what unpasteurized cheese is," I said as we walked toward the elevator.

"I think cheese like Brie isn't pasteurized." He punched the ground floor elevator button.

"How do you feel about everything?" He rubbed the back of my neck with his thumb as we walked out of the elevator.

"I'm confused. I want my children to be raised under the best circumstances."

"Well, here's the way I see it." Peter unlocked his car and opened the passenger door for me. "It goes without saying that you know I love you, and yeah, I see myself marrying you sometime in the future. I see us being a family someday down the road. I just, I don't know O, I don't think I'm at a point where I'm ready to be a father."

I looked down at my hands. Then I did it. I lied. I lied to Peter. I lied to myself. "So if one or both of us aren't ready for this, maybe we should look at some alternatives."

"If we have a baby, I won't be able to accomplish everything I have planned. I mean, I feel like an ass for saying this."

"I understand." Then my lie got bigger. "Honestly, I'm not ready for this either. C'mon, I live with two roommates in the Marina. Not exactly a stroller-friendly situation." This was total bullshit. I/we would have figured a living situation out sometime in the next nine months. I lied to please him. I lied to keep him. In a twisted way, I sacrificed the little apple seed growing inside of me for him, for what he wanted. I loved Peter more than I loved myself.

"We'll have kids at some point. I just don't know if the best time is right now."

"Yeah, I guess you're right." And the biggest lie of my life grew a little bit more.

A week later, we found ourselves sitting in another waiting room. I tightened the wrap sweater I was wearing around my waist, crossed my arms, and put my head on Peter's shoulder. The door opened, and they called my name. Peter whispered, "I love you," and kissed my forehead.

The nurse ushered me into a cramped tiny room just outside of the waiting room where she went over the procedure. I stared down at my fidgeting hands and began to cry.

"You obviously have some apprehension about this, so I'm going to give you a moment to process everything. Would you like me to bring your boyfriend back?"

"Yeah, if you don't mind."

"Hey, hey, what's going on?" Peter shut the door and sat down in the chair next to me.

"I don't know if I can do this."

"Well, I support you with whatever you want to do."

"What if we have a baby? Would that be the worst thing in the world?"

"Yeah, probably, it would be career suicide for me."

"Why?" I asked, staring down at my fingers trembling in my lap.

"I'm supposed to be someone people at the firm admire. No one will respect me if I have some illegitimate child running around."

"I don't really think that's the case. Besides, this baby could change everything."

"That's what I'm afraid of." The look in his eyes terrified me. It was distant, recluse, tired.

"Yeah," I whispered.

"Babe, look, we need more time, time to be us, be together, just the two of us."

Afterward, we went on about our life, and I pretended to forget about it.

Every morning I slept at his house, Peter's alarm on his phone squealed and vibrated like a toddler's annoying toy at 5:00 a.m. against the faux mahogany nightstand he bought on sale at a shady furniture store south of Market Street. Peter, being the good boyfriend he was, usually silenced the alarm and dressed for his workout without rousing more of a "Mornin', babe" out of me and was out the door in thirty seconds flat to run the Lyon Street Steps.

I was usually awakened by the soothing sound of him showering afterward, pulling his pillow to my nose and inhaling his smell, one of my favorite things about him. Peter always emerged from the shower in a crisp white towel, with a bit of steam following in his wake. By 6:15 a.m., we were driving down Gough through the early-morning fog to Francisco Street. We went on about our days after one of Peter's soft and endearing kisses where our foreheads and lips touch.

THE CRASH

"Sorry I didn't get back to ya. O, let's reschedule our appointment to go over the atrium renderings next week."

DATE: October 17
TO: Olivia Michaels
FROM: Paul Rogers
SUBJECT: RE: Friday Appt

Thanks for sending your floor plans to the bank. We're waiting to find out what's going on with the bridge loan before moving forward with the rehab work. Probably doesn't make sense to get together until then.

Cheers,
Paul

DATE: October 23
TO: Paul Rogers
FROM: Olivia Michaels
SUBJECT: Mission Street Update

Paul,

Just wanted to follow up again on the Mission Street project.

Sorry to hear your lender has put the financing on the back burner. I've prepared a few cost effective approaches to the redesign in the event you would consider completing the rehab work with other funds.

Regards,
Olivia Michaels

"Look, it's really no use coming into work today. The Orange County guys cancelled all of our existing deals."

"What's going to happen?"

"I don't know what to tell you. I really don't." And he didn't. No one really knew in fact.

The $50K millionaire lifestyle bloated home real estate prices for years, especially in California, causing the value of surrounding homes to drop like a guy's tighty whities the night he loses his cherry when home owners who frequently bit off more than they could chew lost their grip on the balancing act of juggling credit card minimum payments, interest-rate-only home loans, and leased cars.

The economic earthquake shook the home mortgage market first, shaking financial futures of thousands of families to the ground, leaving their lenders with the rubble. The aftershock quickly rippled through many other industries indirectly affected. Architects create structures. Creating structures costs moola. Who had the moola? Banks, or at least they used to. Pretentious posers living higher than their means and the predator financial chop shops who sold their mortgages fucked the banks over, and we all got monetary STDs in the process.

DATE: November 15
TO: San Francisco Team
FROM: Corporate Communications
SUBJECT: Company Memo

Due to the current economic conditions adversely affecting our organization as well as others across the nation, senior management has elected to be proactive and reassess our business model.

Direct contact will be made to all employees affected by the end of the week. We thank you in advance for your cooperation during this difficult time.

THE INTERVIEW

Two weeks later, Cameron and I flew to Los Angeles to interview for our current jobs.

"How did it go?" Bragasaurus asked me the following morning.

"I think it went well. I'm crossing my fingers. Have you reconsidered interviewing?"

"Oh, hell no, honey, Whore-hey is my little sugar daddy. I'm going to sit at home and be fat and happy. Hopefully, either you or Cameron will get the job."

"Wait, did you say either?" I asked as I repositioned my laptop on the living room coffee table.

"Oh, I didn't tell you that?"

"No, you didn't tell me that."

"Oops, well, I wouldn't worry about it. The job probably won't be in San Francisco anyways."

"I didn't know that either. Thanks for the heads-up."

CHAPTER NINETEEN

SMUG ALERT

Procrastination is the art of keeping up with yesterday
—Don Marquis

" **B** IG PLANS FOR the weekend?" Bragasaurus asked after we wrapped up a conference call with yet another one of our developers going under.

"Peter and I were planning on going to Napa. Other than that, hanging out with the girls."

"While Peter's probably playing Dungeons & Dragons." Cameron snorted and rolled his eyes. "Look, I'm going to go back to my desk."

"Oh yeah, sure, thanks, Cameron." I occasionally wondered if Bragasaurus nursed a mild crush on Cameron.

"You know, he googled your boyfriend, don't you?" Bragasaurus admitted as he twirled a pen between his fingers, his ruby ring catching the sun.

"What are you talking about?"

"Oh, I figured they would have told you last week when you were in Los Angeles."

"You thought they told me what?"

"Cameron knows someone who works for Peter. I guess Cameron's friend said Peter was reclusive and a little—what's a good word I can use—eccentric. I don't know the whole story."

"Cameron is spreading rumors about my boyfriend?"

"Apparently." Bragasaurus turned to his computer screen, signaling this conversation was over.

"Great," I huffed. "Thanks for the heads-up." I walked out of his office and shut the door. I was stunned and p-i-s-s-e-d off.

I knocked on Cameron's opened office door loudly. "Yeah?" he sighed, without looking up from his monitor.

"Hey," but in my mind I was thinking, *Fuck you.* I closed the door, squeezing the knob, took a deep breath. Cameron was the poster child for everything wrong with my life that day.

"Let me tell you something. My personal life is not your business and should certainly not be mentioned in an interview for that matter. I've worked my ass off, and I deserve to keep my job, and you know it. You have no right to spread rumors about me or who I am dating *especially* given the circumstances. I need this job. I want this job, even if it does mean relocating. But I'll be *damned* if I'm going to start a mudslinging contest with you. If you want to play dirty, you are going to be sitting in the mud all by yourself, mister. Furthermore, Cameron, you are an engaged man. You should be helping your fiancée with wedding planning instead of trolling the Internet looking for dirt about my boyfriend, or how about this, do your damn job! If you want to let everyone know you are *that* interested in who I am dating, then you might want to consider what other people think of you, because frankly, it's a little creepy to google Peter. How do you think that makes you look? I'll tell you how it makes you look—childish and a little creepy."

Damn, that was a lot of yelling without breathing. Cameron just stared at his keyboard.

"Sorry," he mumbled under his breath, shrugging his shoulders.

"I appreciate that. I'm sure that took a lot for you to say that. Have a great weekend." His door made a loud whack as I slammed it shut, my despise for Cameron permeated out of my cashmere sweater like an air shaft full of polluted smoke. I knew, even as the words spewed from my mouth, that I was wrong. Shouldn't have gotten so upset with Cameron.

That night Peter and I found ourselves celebrating his roommate's birthday at the starkly modern German restaurant Suppenkuche in Hayes Valley. While sipping beers out of boot-shaped pint glasses, Mark's co-worker waxed on about his pregnant wife. I bit my bottom lip and smiled as Peter leaned over, rubbed my empty belly and whispered in my ear, "Someday, babe."

The truth is rarely pure and never simple.

—Oscar Wilde

"Have fun last night?" Zoe inquired as she tapped the keys of her laptop sitting on her pajama-covered thighs.

"Yeah, I did," I said, smiling inwardly. "Guess who I saw last night?"

"He's everywhere, I swear." Zoe smiled, shaking her head.

"Yeah, I thought Stanley Sorrenstein only Where's Waldo'd in the Marina."

"Where were you at?"

"The German place in Hayes Valley for Mark's birthday. Saw your buddy, Stanley Sorrenstein, on a date with a Haight-Ashbury-esque chick."

"Who is Mark?"

"You know Mark, Peter's roommate."

"Oh yeah, I guess I do. Things are going good with Peter?" she inquired matter-of-factly without looking up from her laptop.

"Sure, things are going amazing," I said curiously. Zoe was irritated with my smugness, and frankly, I didn't care.

"What's new with you?" I asked as I sat down next to her.

"This came in the mail." Zoe flung a velvet-covered envelope to me.

"What's this? I love this envelope! Mucho luxurious!"

"Becky's wedding invitation," she clucked.

"Wait, you didn't tell me she set a date!" I said, defensively. Bridesmaid demands were mandatory reporting requirements at the Princess Palace. Hell, Cupcake had been a bridesmaid four times in the past year.

"That's because she didn't tell me." Zoe stared at the screen of her laptop, avoiding eye contact.

"The wedding is in three weeks."

"Wow! That's quick. You're going, aren't you?"

"It is black tie at the Westin downtown."

"I can go with you if you want." I looked up and tried to make eye contact with Zoe but couldn't.

"Nah, I can go to it alone. The invite didn't have the option of a plus one. Everyone is in *love* these days." I didn't know how to feel. All I felt was distance, similar to when you realize you can't find your car in a parking garage. You know your ride is right there, somewhere, but you can't find it. Zoe was sitting ten feet from me, but I couldn't find her.

Things at the Princess Palace were changing. Good news was met with smiles that didn't show any teeth. I was becoming smugger by the day with Peter, Zoe more distant. I was happy. No, I take that back, I was smug. Smug may have been a better description. I was smuggy wuggy driving a buggy.

I started avoiding Zoe and Cupcake, working too late on purpose or taking paperwork to the hole-in-the-wall sushi place on Lombard Street and Van Ness. It was the perfect hiding spot. Barely anyone ate there. Tuesdays and Thursdays were half-off sake night, so I could drink and be alone. I often drowned my thoughts about the baby I should have been pregnant with. Problems and regrets float like Styrofoam unfortunately.

In an ocean of desperation, Peter was my lighthouse. I loved with the intensity of a child coated in scars; as if by loving him without abandonment, I was allowing all those scars to heal. My heart hurt sometimes just thinking of him. Every time I saw him, I grew intense butterflies the moments before he would walk through the door. His face would light up and glow with the burning confirmation that my emotions were not only justified but also returned. I learned the hard way that he never meant to apply for my lighthouse keeper position. Loved me, he surely did, but he could have never loved me enough—that was my job.

CHAPTER TWENTY

CUPCAKE'S SHE-MERGENCY KIT

Nobody has ever measured, not even poets, how much the heart can hold.
—Zelda Fitzgerald

"HI," CUPCAKE SAID quietly, leaning against my bedroom door frame. We had barely spoken in weeks, except for a brief conversation about the electric bill.

"Hey," I cautiously responded as I patted the tusk of the big pink elephant in the room.

"So Felix is hosting a wine-tasting benefit next Friday at eight o'clock in SoMa, and he wanted to see if you could make it. Feel free to bring Peter if you want."

Exhale. "Yeah, okay, sure," I mumbled, nodding my head.

"Great, should be fun, have a good night." Cupcake smiled and closed my bedroom door.

OLIVIA: Are you going to Felix's wine tasting?
ZOE: Wasn't invited.
OLIVIA: Katie didn't invite you?
ZOE: Prob a couple event.
OLIVIA: if I go, u go.
ZOE: is P going?
OLIVIA: Yeah.
ZOE: not gonna b a 3rd wheel.
OLIVIA: Plz come.
ZOE: K.

"You should sit up front with Peter. I'll sit in the back. I need to get room to get my boots on," I said to Zoe as I ran on tippy toes down our bedroom hallway after Peter buzzed downstairs. Honestly, I used my boots as an excuse for Zoe to sit in the front seat since I knew she would only sit in the front seat if I insisted and had an excuse. I was determined for Zoe to warm up to Peter.

"Zoe is sitting up front. I need room to put my boots on," I said to Peter as I quickly pecked him on the lips. He nodded, knowing I would explain the whys later.

"Ready to be my copilot?" Peter asked Zoe as she fastened the seat belt. I cocked my head to the side and inwardly smiled that he understood I needed him to make Zoe feel included.

The wine tasting was held at one of those work/live loft spaces either owned by creative types or Palo Alto commuters desiring a hip address close to Cal Train.

"I'm glad you came." Cupcake beamed, pulling my shoulder in for a half hug two hours into the party.

"Hi, Peter. How are you?"

"I'm good. This is a fun party. I thought about moving into one of these spaces."

"You should! You totally should!" Dr. Party Girl purred, touching Peter's arm.

"We'll see. Depends on what we decide on." Peter winked at me. Zoe rolled her eyes at both of us.

"Olivia, can I talk to you for a second?" Dr. Party girl half-slurred.

"Sure, hold my glass." I turned to Peter as he brushed a lock of hair behind my ear and took my glass of Syrah. I followed Cupcake up the seven steps toward the living area of the loft where a line of five people had formed near the restroom.

"Shit, a line. That's okay. We can talk out there." Cupcake walked outside to the balcony, wobbling a bit in her stilettos. I followed behind her.

"What's up, Katie?"

"Not much, I just wanted to apologize and clear the air."

"There's really no need to apologize. You said what you feel, and I respect your honesty."

"That's the thing. I don't think those things about you"—Cupcake lowered her voice to a loud breathy whisper in case any of the either waiting-to-tinkle people were listening in—"and I apologize if what I said hurt your feelings."

"I appreciate that, I really do," I lied. The sentiment was lovely, but the conversation should have occurred at home, in private, sober.

"Everything okay?" Peter asked, giving me a once-over and handing my wineglass back. I never told him the details about that morning with Cupcake.

"Oh yeah, everything's perfect." I took a big gulp and looked across the room.

"You're sexy when you lie." Peter laughed, grabbing me around the waist and kissing my cheek.

"I wanna go home." I looked up at Peter. "Let me go see if Zoe is ready."

I walked over to Zoe who was in a heated discussion with Felix. "Hey, I'm exhausted. We were thinking about heading home."

"No worries. You two leave. I'll go back home with Katie." Zoe barely looked at me.

"You sure?"

"Ummm, yeah, I'm a big girl. I don't need you and What's His Face to be my chaperones."

I stared blankly at Zoe, waiting for the punch line. It didn't come.

"Well, okay then, it was lovely to see you, Felix. Y'all have a great night."

CUPCAKE MEETS HER PASTRY CHEF

Any Marina guy, or straight guy in San Francisco for that matter, can be the gateway to a magical detour of life that you never imagined possible. The guy in the pin-striped suit when the 30Sexpress hurdles past a stop sign on Broadway, the muscular sweaty guy fresh from 24 hour fitness standing in front of me at Dateway's checkout stand, the intellectual loudmouth with a popped collar in the Bermuda Triangle, the hipster wearing a white studded belt and skinny jeans making ironical conversation in a noisy Mission bar.

Shortly after the wrath of Cupcake reared its ugly head, our bunny-slippered, reality TV—watching companion curiously disappeared from the scenery of our living room exactly three weeks after meeting a twenty-eight-year-old accountant from Kansas City.

Zoe and I giggled and brainstormed when (or if) our Cupcake would come home one Monday night while watching *The Bachelorette*.

"She was carrying a purse way too big for a no-nooky fifth date." I mentally high-fived myself for my expert detective skills, sometimes my over-analysis of everything paid off when it came to solving the dating patterns of my home girls.

"How big was it?" Zoe asked, raising one Elizabeth Taylor-esque eyebrow while doing her "tell me" bobble head.

"Like stripper-size, ya know, like one of those bags strippers carry into the club with all of their gear, definitely big enough to hold a she-mergency kit, well at least the first sleepover she-mergency kit." I clucked with a decisive lip pucker and head nod. Cameron's drunken monologue about identifying which girls walking down Broadway were heading to work their money makers one Wednesday night while we got drunk on the patio at Cantina two years prior was coming in handy.

"I swear, you over think everything," Zoe tsk-tsked.

"For starters, she loves that teeny-tiny Coach clutch she always carries when she goes out," I said triumphantly.

"So what is a 'she-mergency kit' anyways?" Zoe asked.

I had to put my librarian glasses back on for this explanation. "Well, the first time overnight version of the she-mergency kit would be a toothbrush, deod for your overnight BO, body spray to freshen up downstairs, makeup remover towelettes, hairbrush, maybe bobby pins or a ponytail holder, sexy panties to slip into if you've been wearing SPANX under your outfit so you don't have a Bridget Jones 'Hello, Mummy' moment."

I was terrified for Katie, and a bit envious of her ferocious commitment to this new man in her life. Pastry Chef wasn't a Peter Pan. He was serious about her from day one, and it didn't take long for her to put all her eggs in his basket, hoping he would whisk them into a wedding cake one day.

Cupcake and her Pastry Chef took the engagement expressway, doing ninety miles an hour. I was careful with my words when I mentioned their engagement to Peter.

There are many things that we would throw away if we were not afraid that others might pick them up.

—Oscar Wilde

"Not surprised, babe. Is she moving out?" Peter asked as we walked hand in hand down Polk Street on a lazy Sunday afternoon.

"She wants to wait until they set a date before moving in with him."

"That should buy you enough time."

"Time to find another roommate?" I asked, cupping my hands over my eyes to block the sun and staring at a freckle on Peter's ear.

"Let's see what happens. My roommate is moving out in six months when he takes that sabbatical to Costa Rica. Ya know, the word *sabbatical* is so bourgeois Bohemian, but let's face it, a sabbatical isn't much more than an extended vacation." Peter commented as we waited at the corner of Union and Polk for the walk sign to turn green.

CHAPTER TWENTY-ONE

ZOE'S PACIFIC HEIGHTS GENTLEMAN

Two men look out through the same bars: One sees the mud and one the stars.
-Frederick Langbridge

Z OE KNOCKED ON my door early one Tuesday morning after she spent the night with her Pacific Heights Gentleman for the first time and was eager to divulge details.

"How was last night?" I mumbled as Zoe climbed onto my bed.

"Ya know my jeans that make my butt look juicy that I can wear with heels or flip-flops and have enough stretch to hide any food babies when my monthly crimson tide rolls in?" Zoe said, glowing as she fiddled with the ruffle of one of my decorative bed pillows.

"Your magic jeans with the dark rinse?" I said, sitting up in anticipation.

"Yeah yeah yeah, those jeans I bought for practically a dollar last summer, not the pair I bought last week. Well, I might like him more than those jeans."

Oh, Zoe, my soldier of cautious optimism.

For the first time, both of us were smitten simultaneously. Our friendship was renewed that morning as we giggled about our good-looking, successful, intelligent, adoring boyfriends. Peter and I were off to see a play at the American Conservatory Theater that Saturday while Zoe and her Pacific Heights Gentleman were going snowboarding in Tahoe.

"Do these ski pants make me look butchy?" Zoe shouted, lumbering down the hallway from her bedroom with a *swoosh-swoosh* sound as her thighs rubbed together.

I glanced up, then back down to my laptop. "Nah, just wear a lot of eyeliner in Tahoe and my fuchsia scarf."

The Lyon Street Steps glared back at me, menacingly. The narrow steps glistening with morning-dew sheen held slight promise that I might slip and fall during my descent back down. Back down wasn't my problem at the moment; it was climbing back up from the courier-delivered walking papers I received the afternoon before. No closed-door conversation, no overly apologetic conference call with corporate in Los Angeles, simply a signature-required confirmation that my career was officially over. Cameron, and his wisecracks about Peter, got the job and would be relocating to LA immediately. I, on the other hand, was put in charge of "dismantling" the San Francisco branch. That is the fucking word they used: *dismantling*.

I hadn't seen Peter in nearly a week, which wasn't totally out of the ordinary. What was out of the ordinary was my new hobby of thumb twiddling and, apparently, ass kicking I thought as I turned up the volume of my ear buds and charged up the Lyon Street Steps.

> *Everything is meant to be let go of so that the*
> *soul may stand in unhampered nothingness*
> —**Meister Eckhart**

"My dad could sit on that bench for hours, people-watching while my mom shops." Peter motioned to a bench in front of Macy's where most of the street performers set up shop every afternoon. My personal favorite was the guy that spray-painted himself silver from head to toe and pretended to be a robot.

"Never seen sidewalk performers at a wedding before," I said as a bride emerged from a limo and walked toward a pop-up white tent sitting in the middle of Union Square.

"Hopefully all that fluffy fabric, I don't know what you call it, at the bottom of her dress will hide the urine stains from the cement."

"Ruching," I said, squeezing his hand.

"Is the ruching what makes her dress look wrinkled at the bottom?"

"It is pronounced *roo-shing*, and her dress isn't wrinkled, that's how the dress is designed." I sort of loved it when Peter didn't know about something since, most of the time, he was a human encyclopedia.

"All right, rooooshwooshing it is," Peter over enunciated. "So you're going to help me pick out my mom's birthday present because that's why I keep you around, ya know."

"Hmmm, what's my budget?" I was both flattered and terrified of this game.

"I don't really care, just no commas in the price tag, okay?"

"What about a Hermes scarf? I think she would like that. They have a store a block or so away."

"I knew I kept you around for a good reason." He winked at me. After Hermes we had dinner, then walked over to the American Conservatory Theatre. There is something a little magical about seeing a play at the ACT. The walls must be gilded with both history and gold.

"You are the prettiest girl in the lobby."

"Nice try compared to this crowd," I said under my breath. "I think I see my seventh-grade science teacher over there." I was pointing to a woman wearing a prairie skirt and Crocs with wild curly blond hair that resembled Einstein's hairdo.

"You are the prettiest girl in any room," he said, taking my hand as we walked to our seats.

"You know, you're pretty cute for a liar." I gave Peter a quick kiss as the lights came down as Tom Stoppard's *Rock 'n' Roll* play began. The performance was stocked with top-rated actors and rich with story lines. Although I do have to admit that grabbing a drink in the lobby before the play started was nearly as entertaining as the actual performance.

Zoe's ski-mance could not have gone better, so she made the grand gesture sitting in her Pacific Heights Gentleman's SUV somewhere outside of Sacramento on the way back to the city.

"So, me and the girls are having a Thanksgiving party the weekend before for all our friends. Think you can make it?"

"Tsk, I think so. Who all is coming anyways?"

"Olivia's friends, Katie and her fiancé, a few of her friends, Janice that you met and a few other friends, my cousin might stop by if she gets in town."

"Whoa, wait a sec, do you want me to meet your family *already*?"

"Uhhh, I didn't think it was a big deal, just my cousin. Besides, you don't even have to be introduced as my boyfriend."

"I just don't feel the fire. I don't think it's a good idea if I come."

Bursting through the door with Charles Manson crazy eyes, Zoe yelled, "He said he didn't feel the fire!"

Peter peeked out from a comic book he was reading on the couch while I baked cookies. "You can get a cream for that, ya know."

Peter and I very much needed a weekend to spend relaxing and decompressing after he spent two months working eighty-plus hours a week finishing an extremely important case. Our relationship had been compressed into two days a week: Friday night romantic date and one other night during the week. Peter's way of showing love was by giving his time, and he gave me everything he had available. I had never felt more loved or as much a priority as Peter made me.

This would be our first weekend away together, and I spent more time researching where to go, what to do, etc., than I care to admit. I discovered a boutique inn in Bodega Bay with luxurious accommodations including oversized whirlpool jetted tubs, cedar wood-burning fireplaces in each room, and spa treatments. We laughed after checking in how we would become an old married couple this weekend. I would be obligated to ask him ridiculous questions that he would answer "Yes, dear" or grunt a no.

"Okay, I'm ready to go eat," I said as I emerged from the bathroom fluffing my hair.

"Well, you are too damn pretty to ever be my old married wife." Peter winked at me as he buckled his belt. "You'll just have to settle with being my new bride then."

We drove a mile up the road to the Rocker Oysterfeller's restaurant where we had a big meal of home-style pulled pork (Peter) and fresh scallops (me).

"When was the last time you took a bubble bath?" I asked as I walked into the bathroom and turned on the jetted tub after we got back from dinner.

"Ummmm, third grade." Peter grinned as he slipped off his shoes and socks.

"Twenty-plus years without a bubble bath? Long time, my dear."

"Well, I guess you will have to show me how it is done then." I unbuttoned Peter's shirt, and he lifted my dress over my head. I stepped out of my heels and undid the hooks of my bra.

"I always forget how short you are without your stilts on." In heels, I was only two or three inches shorter than Peter. Once I took them off, my head barely scraped his shoulders.

We climbed into the tub together and turned into kindergarteners playing with the bubbles. Peter pulled my back against his chest and squeezed me tightly.

"Olivia, I need to tell you something."

"I'm listening."

"This has been the best night of my life. I want you to know that." Peter ran his hand over my wet hair. I turned around and stared into those brown eyes of his; my chin began to quiver in anticipation.

"I can't believe how lucky I am to have you, Olivia."

"Please don't do this, not now, not in the soapy nekkidness."

"Yeah, not a PG story to tell the grandkids, huh?" Peter laughed.

My insides ached with love for Peter, but in a mellow, excited way I hadn't ever experienced.

"I don't care if you ever marry me. I just want to be with you. You know that, right?"

"I do, but what if I want to marry you?"

"Do you?"

"Of course, at some point."

"I like that. I like at some point."

We spent the weekend reading books in front of a crackling fireplace with our ankles intertwined. My boyfriend, the fastidious athlete and always meticulously dressed, let his beard grow and left his running shoes at home.

As Saturday afternoon crept by, I sat on the edge of the king-size bed and lovingly watched him sleep the afternoon away with my hand gently fingering the curls against his forehead. I was able to admire my favorite part of Peter: the perfect brown freckle on his left earlobe for hours without worrying where the time would go.

Our room was so grand and cozy; we couldn't even be bothered to leave it for dinner, which worked out perfectly since the inn catered a lovely three-course dinner in our room. We smoked cigars and talked for nearly two hours on our private patio about everything, and nothing, at the same time.

Bodega is a quiet, rustic town located on the coast. There were kite shops, gift shops, crab shacks, and a few restaurants scattered along the "main drag." We discovered it when we came up for air Sunday morning. We stopped in the Gourmet au Bay shop to check out the eclectic gifts and whatnots. The shop featured wine stoppers made out of doorknobs, coasters shaped like flip-flops, and unusual containers to hold spices, etc. Our initial Sunday idea was to go wine tasting, but we decided to drive the scenic Highway 1 back home instead, about a four-hour drive along the coast. With the Rolling Stones or Gipsy Kings playing on Peter's car stereo, we held hands and took the long way home.

I finally found my purpose in life: to love this man. I had never been so certain of anything in my entire life. We were both better people together than separately. He made my anxieties float away. I polished and made his rough edges soft. Peter wasn't who I thought he would be: less all-American and more peculiar, which made him all the more enchanting to me. He articulated his fascination with comic book heroes and Star Wars and Indiana Jones as if he was discussing the merits of Franklin Roosevelt's New

Deal. He was deliciously unfamiliar and exquisitely endearing. He never hid his peccadilloes. He let me know exactly who and what he was, which I could never do. I was too busy trying to be the super girlfriend. I could never let him into my weird little world. I feared what he would find.

TURKEY DAY

"Whatcha doin'?" I asked as I dropped three bags of groceries from Trader Joe's onto the kitchen floor.

"Trying to make a pumpkin-spiced martini," Zoe said without looking up from a cocktail recipe book. She looked like an angelic mad scientist mixing various fluids and spices with one of her magnificent eyebrows raised as she concentrated. "Try it. Whaddya think?"

"I think we're going to have a bunch of drunkety drunk friends over tonight."

"Yeah, we are!"

Five hours later, the Princess Palace was stocked full of friends and a traditional Thanksgiving feast in the kitchen: candied yams, stuffing, green beans, pies of all kinds, cranberries from a can, a big-ass turkey courtesy of me and my man.

"Olivia, I would like for you to meet my new friend Miles." Jackson beamed, smiling bigger than I've ever seen him smile before.

I smiled from the inside out as I scanned across the living room and saw Peter deep in conversation with Ford and Isaac.

"What up?" Man Child said, already drunk.

"Same old, same old, how are you?"

"I'm all right. Still dating What's His Face?" he slurred.

"Yeah, I am still dating What's His Face." I looked down at my gray patent leather spectator heels, then over to Peter who winked at me.

"Are you fucking blushing?" Man Child asked, becoming belligerent.

"Probably."

"So let me ask you this . . . Is he better than me?"

During a brief three-month lapse in judgment, I dated the Man Child shortly after Cupcake's altercation with his buddy, Mr. Apple. We kissed for the first time at the Mumm Winery in Napa. I was drunk on Mumm's latest sparkling vintage. The sun was setting and some tourists from Poughkeepsie snapped a photo of us. The powder-blue sky of the valley had softened into a deep mauve as the sun set. Man Child in his black pullover, me with my Burberry scarf and jeans tucked into tall boots. Sadly, our just-add-water relationship quickly turned sour. He threw tantrums when he didn't get his way and complained more about having fat thighs than any woman I know. I often felt like I was dating a toddler trapped in the body of an Abercrombie model. It ended badly at 21st Amendment over Watermelon Wheat beers.

"He's different than you."

"How so?" he slurred.

"He's better for me."

"Well, when you're done with him . . . Whaddya say about coming back to me?"

"I don't think that is going to happen. This is *the guy* . . . I'm sorry." I softly smiled and walked away, for good, back to Peter in the middle of a heated debate with Isaac and Ford about small business laws in San Francisco.

I decided to take advantage of having the place all to myself, so I stayed at the Princess Palace alone for Thanksgiving. The Marina was quieter Thanksgiving afternoon, probably since so many people were home for the holidays. Midwest, Texas, East Coast, LA, or any other place Marina people come. I ran the Golden Gate Bridge. I watched TV. I read. I wrote. I counted my blessings for all the good fortune I received that year. I counted Peter twice. Cupcake was right after all. This was the year it would happen.

I finished adding all the deliciously sparkly ornaments to the Christmas tree as the teapot on the stove started to whistle. I stood back and admired my handiwork: my first Christmas tree completely decorated in robin's egg blue-and-silver ornaments. The silver snowflakes twinkled from the glow of the tree lights. I went to the kitchen, plopped a packet of ginger-spiced tea into a mug with the Dallas skyline motif, and poured hot water, inhaling steam from the mug, letting my eyes close and face absorb the warmth.

My mind started to reminisce about those first few months living in San Francisco. I often wandered down nearby Columbus Avenue into North Beach, a bona fide destination for authentic Italian cuisine, passing L'Osteria del Forno, a tiny romantic bistro between Union and Columbus. Surrounded in luckiness and manufactured thankfulness, I desperately searched for a piece of the wonderfulness San Francisco possessed.

There was a lot to do with my free time that year without one true friend to spend my free time with. I was exhausted from the long workweek most Friday nights and cooked dinner at home alone while watching mindless television. Saturday nights were the hardest. The rest of San Francisco was bustling with nightlife antics, and I was at home desperately wishing for integration into society.

Every night I stood on the balcony and looked east out onto the Bay Bridge. Sometimes the fog covered it completely, but I gazed out onto that portion of the sky. At times, I felt an emotion akin to contentment, but going weeks without socializing of any sort, or the touch of another human being, caused me to cry myself to sleep many nights.

I took my tea into the living room and climbed into Cupcake's overstuffed chair. Even though I was all alone that Thanksgiving, I felt content, basking in the glow of having all my "boxes" in life checked off.

Peter picked me up on his way home from his parents' house after Thanksgiving. There were three cupcakes shaped like monkeys from his nephew's first birthday sitting in the passenger seat.

"I kept the passenger seat on the Coolant setting the whole drive back so the monkey face on the cupcakes wouldn't deflate." He smiled.

"You're a monkey face." I took his face in my hands and kissed him firmly on the lips.

"Probably, I didn't shave the whole time I was at my parents' house." He grinned at me with that look he gave when he wanted me to say something sarcastic back. I didn't. He looked adorable. He had never looked anything less than adorable, or maybe he had, but I didn't notice because I was madly in love with him, so all I did was smile back at him.

"What are we doing tonight, babe?" he asked, turning onto Broadway Street.

"Wanna go look at Christmas trees in Fort Mason?"

"Anything to make you happy." He smiled. Three hours later, we were loaded on spiked hot chocolates, thanks to the Rotary Club's Christmas tree farm/benefit, which was really an excuse to drink too much and buy an overpriced tree.

We spent the next weekend at Peter's apartment. It was one of those perfectly lazy weekends: brunch, lazy afternoon watching episodes of *Curb Your Enthusiasm* Peter DVR'ed, nice dinner out, spent all day Sunday napping and canoodling. We talked a little about our future: what we would do for New Year's Eve, Peter told me, while smoking cigars on his rooftop patio how he wanted to take a road trip with me down the coast on Highway 1 stopping in Carmel, Big Sur, then Santa Barbara. He gave me his fleece North Face pullover to wear home since I had run out of clean clothes. It smelled like his man soap and my shampoo.

THE ASTROLOGER

"Hey, guys, what's going on?" Cupcake waltzed into the kitchen. Her bunny slippers may as well have been Cinderella's glass pumps. My eyes locked with Zoe and her perfectly arched right eyebrow heightened a bit.

"Well, aren't you chipper?" Zoe said to Cupcake.

"Mmmmhmmmm," Cupcake purred.

"So dish, sweetie! How is it going with Mr. Wonderful?"

"He's great. He's really great," Cupcake said as she took a sip of soy milk, then paused and looked down at her hands. "Okay, ladies, I gotta get going. See ya!" Cupcake said, bouncing out of the room.

"Wait a sec, I need to talk to you. Do you have a minute?" Zoe said to Cupcake.

"Oh yeah, sure, what's up?" Cupcake said.

"So I met with Davidicka at Asia SF."

"Couldn't your astrologer come up with a better transgender name, maybe Vidalia," I said, thinking of a type of onion that sounded like a girl name. "Ya know, feminine, multifaceted, complicated."

"Well, he did have on a lovely corset," Zoe said.

"Wow, that must have taken a lot of effort getting into that contraption," Cupcake said.

"Anyways Davidicka suggested I close the store and maybe move to LA."

"Do you have any peanut butter? I wanna make a sandwich?" I said.

"Yeah, but it's that organic kind from Trader Joe's. You probably won't like it, but you can have some. It's in the freezer." Zoe put everything in the freezer—bread, milk, cereal, and apparently peanut butter.

"How am I supposed to put it on the bread if it is frozen?" I was more concerned with creating a delicious PB&J than hearing about an astrology reading from a transvestite on their lunch break.

"And maybe get a place in Santa Monica."

"Whoa, wait a second. Are you seriously thinking about moving to LA?" I was stunned. Partly for her reasoning, partly for the timing, partly because are Princess Palace would be changing.

CHAPTER TWENTY-TWO

SEE-YA-LATERADE

Words have no power to impress the mind without the exquisite horror of their reality.

—**Edgar Allan Poe**

I PULLED BOUDREAUX INTO a parking spot as the afternoon rain started to fall. *The Golden Gate Bridge looked sweaty in front of Dateway,* I thought as I grabbed three reusable shopping bags from the passenger seat and jumped out of my truck. The Mayor with the Mousse outlawed grocery stores from providing plastic bags a few months prior, probably to cancel out the aerosol from all the hair spray he used. Good green move on his part. I slipped five bucks to the Salvation Army Santa ringing his bell for donations and wiped a bit of Golden Gate mist from my face as I pulled a grocery list out of my Gucci belt bag to peruse the list of ingredients for tonight's dinner with Peter.

A couple of months after I moved to San Francisco, I had foot surgery, which initially exposed me to the intense self-involvement of my newly acquired acquaintances that could not be bothered to help me get home from the hospital post surgery, or check on me. After that experience, I got my first taste of homesickness, which left a permanent stain on my impression of San Francisco. The week I spent at home on bed rest was entertaining, thanks to catching up on trashy TV and online shopping, planning for how I could independently get around once I went back to work. I purchased a Gucci belt bag online to carry my wallet, keys, and lipstick while I hobbled around the Financial District for six weeks. The Gucci belt bag was simply too trendy and adorable to be labeled a tourist fanny pack, plus was convenient for ventures to Dateway or keeping my arms free at wine tastings in Napa.

Shiny red and green bell peppers, yellow onion, lettuce, jalapenos, fresh garlic, and lime were tossed into my wobbly shopping cart. I checked those five items off my list as I heard a familiar voice. "Hey, sexy, wanna rub my melons?"

"Jackson! What are you doing on this side of town?!?" I grabbed my friend for a tight hug. He looked and smelled amazing, as always, rocking a new do and fresh faux tan.

"Oh, honey, you know I get around," Jackson said as he surveyed the Dateway specimens scouring the produce section. "I stopped by Zoe's store on Union Street to pick up some skinnys and figured the eye candy was worth it to do my groceries at the hetero Dateway. Love the Gucci, dahling, so urban of you. What are you up to this evening? Going Mexicana with the girls tonight?" Jackson guesstimated my plans for the evening based on my produce collection thus far.

"I'm headed over to Peter's house for some fah-ji-tahs and fun timez-ahs tonight. He's going out of town this weekend, so I wanted to cook something festive."

"Well, with all of those jalapenos, it better be hawt and festive, honey!"

"Thanks, T. I'll see you on Saturday for my trim."

"I want all the dirty details about your night of romance with Mr. Wonderful." He wagged his long finger at me.

A package of tortillas, chicken breast, and fajita seasoning mix later, I scanned the wine aisle searching for a memorable bottle of Syrah. Peter started collecting wine corks from our nights together and wrote the date on each of them before lining them up on the windowsill in his bedroom.

OLIVIA: Dateway packed, B there in 15
PETER: K, just got home

"Okay, Shortcake, put me to work. Whaddya want me to do?" Peter massaged my shoulders as I set the grocery bags onto his kitchen counter.

"Keep that up, and I'll put you to work doing something else." I winked at him as I pulled the groceries out of the cotton reusable grocery bag.

"Petey need nourishment to show woman real love later," Peter said in his Mr. T à la caveman voice.

"How about you put on some Gipsy Kings and open that bottle of wine over there?"

Gipsy Kings had become "our music" ever since we went to Bodega Bay for the weekend. We were inseparable as we cooked dinner together earlier that night. It felt as if he was trying to absorb as much of me as possible before leaving the next day. Ninety minutes later, we climbed up his rooftop patio into the chilly December night.

"You excited to see your buddies this weekend?" I said as I blew warm air into my cupped hands.

"Yeah, I mean, I haven't seen everyone for a while, but I'm not looking forward to the drive though."

"How long does it take to get to Malibu anyways?"

"I dunno, seven maybe eight hours, depending on traffic . . . Have you thought anymore about what you want to do after next month?" he said, changing the subject.

"Yeah, I've already updated my résumé and everything. I'm scared I won't be able to find anything else." That damn job, and all the hoops I jumped through, would soon be history.

"We'll be fine. Don't stress about it," Peter said, hugging me tightly. His *we* made everything right with the world. I buried the worry about my professional future in his nook. When I left the next morning, we hugged each other in one of those embraces where you nuzzle and spoon vertically. The next day Peter drove to Malibu for the weekend. Not seeing him for three days felt like eternity. Had I known what would transpire, I would have held on longer that morning.

THE MALIBU IMPASSE

Peter drove down to Malibu, pulling into his buddy Joe's driveway just before dinner time.

"What up, bro? C'mon in!" Joe said as he pulled Peter in for a bro hug.

"How ya doin' man?" Peter said as he swung his duffel bag off his shoulder, sitting it down on the Mexican tile inside Joe's foyer.

"All right, I guess, just getting ready for the party tomorrow."

"I like the new place. Looks great!" Peter said as he looked around the foyer that opened up into a great room living area.

"I can't take any of the credit, really. Mallory did all of the decorating. I just write the checks, ya know?" Joe said as he playfully slapped Peter's back. "Grab your junk, I'll show you where you're sleeping for the weekend."

Peter followed Joe through the enormous living area, saying hello and waving hi to Joe's aunt and uncle. He used to go with Joe to their cabin in Tahoe every February. Uncle Frank was getting older and wasn't as up for snowboarding anymore.

"So, yeah, sorry I gotta put you in the back bedroom. Bruce and the wife are bringing the baby so they are taking the bigger guest bedroom."

"Hey, no worries, this is great." Peter looked around at all of Joe's old stuff: the replica Eddie Van Halen guitar, his records neatly stacked, that impossible to find framed Joe Namath football jersey he saved up for nine months to buy.

"Yeah, I come in here sometimes to get away." Joe said, shoving his hands in his pockets.

"You still play the guitar?"

"Nah, well sometimes I guess. I haven't really done much with it since the baby. Yeah . . . anyways, how's Olivia doing?"

"She's great. She's really great."

"Tell Olivia I said hello."

'Yeah, yeah, I will, definitely. So, ah, how ya been lately? How is work going?"

"Good, good, everything is going good I guess." Joe shifted his way from leg to leg, rubbing his five o'clock shadow. "I mean, ya know, ah, never mind. Let's go downstairs and grab a beer."

"Sure, bro, sure." Peter followed Joe back downstairs. He looked different, beat down, bloated, not himself at all, like a puffy melancholy version of the guy that used to have all the girls chasing after him back in the day.

"P!!! You made it! How are you?" Mallory squealed and clapped her hands together above her head since the baby was firmly strapped to her in a baby carrier across her chest.

Peter leaned him for a half hug. "I'm good. I'm good. How's everything going?"

"Oh, so stressful! I just got off the phone with the bouncy house people. Get this—they want to charge fifty bucks just to rent a filter for the generator. Can you believe that?"

"Filter for what?" Joe asked, handing Peter a bottle of Corona and the beer opener.

"Honey, those houses are like breeding grounds for all sorts of germs and bacteria and the chemicals the generator pumps into them all day." Mallory was slicing strawberries and cooing to the baby and checking her blackberry and carrying on a conversation all at once. Peter was dizzy just watching her.

"Then why are we renting one?" Joe said, taking a long swig of his bottled beer.

Mallory took a loud deep breath, "because the city wouldn't give us a permit for the pony ride corral," she said as she rolled her eyes in Joe's direction then turning to Peter.

"So, how's Olivia doing?" Mallory said as she dumped all of the strawberry stems into the compost bin.

"She's great. She's really great."

"Ya know, your Mom told my Mom about Olivia's steak recipe she made for you guys." Mallory said, winking at Peter.

"What?" Peter looked at Mallory then at Joe then at Mallory. "I didn't say anything!" Mallory laughed and went back to cooing at the baby.

"She's just messing with you bro. You know we're just happy to see you've finally found your girl. Cheers, man."

"Cheers." Peter and Joe clinked their bottles together.

What amazed me was that on the day that my life went awry, I woke up in the most fabulous mood. The December sunlight crept into my bedroom that morning, awaking me as if a grandmother's paper-thin-skin-covered hand lightly tapped my shoulder. I gazed through the bay windows of my bedroom out to my backyard and snuggled under the covers for a few minutes longer. Listening to the leaves rustle and the distant sound of a foghorn from the bay, I closed my eyes and smiled inwardly.

A few minutes later, after I dragged my lazy ass out of bed, I walked into my closet as I brushed my teeth, admiring the New Year's Eve dress I picked up the weekend prior at Ambiance on Union Street. It was a sexy gray sweater dress. The five-inch heels I planned to wear made me almost as tall as Peter, perfect for our New Year's kiss I decided as I spit into the sink and rinsed my toothbrush off.

This would be the last night Peter and I would see each other for two weeks, the longest we've ever been apart. I was headed back to Texas for an extended Christmas vacation, much needed after scurrying in and out of town every holiday season since I moved to San Francisco. Now that my job no longer demanded my time like a temperamental two-year-old, I could take a vacation to relax with my family for a change.

My furry slippers padded down the long hallway into the living room as I wiped crunchy sleep boogers from my eyes. I put on a pot of coffee and flipped on the television as Willard Scott exclaimed that Gertrude Simons from Pine Bluff Arkansas was the Smuckers over one-hundred-year-old person of the day. Wise old Gertie enjoyed backgammon and Slurpees on warm summer days. *Good for her*, I thought to myself as I pressed the

Start button of my laptop. The weatherman reported it would be a high of fifty-eight degrees again today. That overly tanned dude had the easiest job on the planet. It was always a high of fifty-eight degrees in San Francisco. E-mail from Bragasaurus. Sale at Paper Source. Oh look, an e-mail from Peter. What a sweetie. He must be just as excited to see me today.

I might have felt a quiver of concern from the subject line had Peter ever once expressed concerns about us. I became light-headed as I clicked on the e-mail, and the hits just kept on rolling. Clearly Peter had more of a flair for drama than I would have guessed.

FROM: Peter
TO: Olivia
TIME: December 18, 11:17 p.m.
SUBJECT: I'm Sorry

I am truly sorry, but things need to end here for me. You are a wonderful person, and I could never say anything bad about you. But I've learned about myself that I'm not ready for this—I may never be ready for this. I just cannot give the things that a real relationship deserves. I hope you can understand that, and I also hope for nothing but good things for you.

Always,
Peter

I read, reread, re-reread his e-mail attempting to unscramble the words so somehow they would make sense. I read it so many times that I accidentally memorized them, choking on the unladylike bile coming up from my throat. The words reflecting back from my computer screen appeared to be excuses etched in a tombstone: vague, canned, and perhaps a little too much of the truth.

Katie pranced into the living room wearing the new dress she purchased to wear in her engagement photos; the hem of the dress swung as she walked, catching light from the bay window behind me. Her hair was swept into a whimsical chignon with every hair in place creating a look of romantic playful elegance.

"Oh, what do you think?" Cupcake beamed at me, practicing her photogenic smile.

I felt myself gasping and coughing as I fought to regain acceptable behavior.

"You okay?" she innocently asked, confused by my reaction.

"Be right back, sweetie." My jaw throbbed as I clenched my teeth. I walked to the bathroom and turned the faucet to cold, grabbing a washcloth. I ran it underneath the tap and pressed my face hard with both hands. I tried to breathe. I thought breathing was an unconscious act.

My instinct was to call or text him, to write back, if only to prolong our contact. Waiting on a response from him, and knife in the heart as painful as it may have been, would at least add a glimmer of hope. I doubted the value of my words, so I couldn't bring myself to write the words that could bring him back to me.

"Olivia, are you okay?" Cupcake frowned in concern as I walked back into the living room.

"You look stunning, Katie, you really do." I cleared my throat and trying my damnedest to curl the edges of my mouth into a smile.

"What's wrong?"

"Peter, ahem, Peter." I stared at my laptop screen as if the machine was the culprit, not Peter. I couldn't get the words to come out of my mouth. If I told her, that would make it a reality.

"Peter, what?"

I shook my head and shrugged my shoulders, dismissing my panic from the conversation. "I'm going to go for a walk. Have fun today with your photo shoot." I hugged Katie, tightly. She looked like an angel, an absolute angel.

I walked down into Fort Mason near the water. It was a desolate area where I could have myself a good cry without Zoe or Cupcake knowing, but I couldn't. I didn't feel sadness, really, just panic and confusion. After I sat there for a while stewing, I got mad, girl-power style. I stomped all over San Francisco, angrily switching tunes in my ear buds to any angry song by a female artist. *How dare he do this?* I tried as hard as I could to hang on to the frustration. Anger is a much more poetic emotion to dive into than self-disgust or self-realization that the imaginary bubble I built my life around just popped. Truth be told, how could I honestly have thought Peter intended to spend the rest of his life with me? Fuck, I didn't even want to. How can I get mad at Peter for choosing to say good-bye to someone that I wasn't even sure I wanted to be around?

CHAPTER TWENTY-THREE

UPHEAVAL

The place where optimism most flourishes is the lunatic asylum.
—Havelock Ellis

"YOU LOOK AWFUL, Pun'kin," my dad said as he hugged me and took my suitcase. His voice was gravely, and concerned.

Over the next few days, family time formed a hazy fog around my head. Mom kept me busy with last-minute Christmas shopping, cookie baking, gift wrapping, and I threw myself into each task. I slipped in and out of visible misery, depending on what varying degree I was able to keep up a charade of normalcy. Some days I faked it better than others, actually laughing at my brother's off-color jokes or pushing my niece on the swing set, until inevitably I wound up crying uncontrollably in the spare bathroom with the faucet running.

"Calm down," Zoe counseled as I wiped one of my tears from the phone. That was just it. I couldn't. It was as if my relationship with Peter and all the future memories we were creating vanished with the click of his Send button. The unthinkable happened. Peter was slipping through my fingers with each passing day. The long, cold, thick silence of granite indifference was debilitating. I questioned my self-worth. I doubted all my abilities. I criticized every ounce of my physical appearance. I wanted to cut open my chest to make sure my heart was beating. I wanted to be hit by oncoming traffic to break my exterior to match my insides.

For everything you have missed, you have gained something else,
and for everything you gain, you lose something else.
—Ralph Waldo Emerson

I doubled over in pain as tears, once again, enveloped my soul the night before I left to fly back to San Francisco. My father held my head in his hands. "Honey, you need to be strong. You need to tell him, 'I stand behind you' no matter what."

"I . . . don't understand . . . why he doesn't . . . love me . . . anymore." I hiccupped into a tissue.

"Baby, he does. I promise. Just let this work itself out." My father wiped a tear-dripped lock of hair out of my face.

The combination of exhaustion, dehydration, and anxiety developed into a squishy head cold that last night in Texas. I barely slept and unsuccessfully attempted to blame it on the sneezing. Early the next morning, before the sun came rose, both my parents drove me to DFW airport. Two big hugs were better than one that morning. My boarding pass read "Please see ticket counter" instead of a seat assignment. It was as if the universe were too uncertain of my future to bother committing a seat to me on the plane. My life had never been so upturned.

I glanced around the other travelers waiting in line for the ticket counter. While I surveyed the room, I glanced down at myself and assessed the damages: $1,200 Burberry bag, $330 True Religion jeans, $95 cashmere sweater covering a $10K boob job underneath a $500 buttery leather jacket and $425 Hermes scarf. My hair was nearly $250 per month to maintain the cut and color. I easily had $300 in makeup alone inside of my designer suitcase. I was a prima donna spoiled brat crying over problems that basically didn't exist.

A wave of shame passed over me. The darkest moments experienced in my life were entirely self-created. A six-figure job should have created a significant savings account, but it only added designer labels to my wardrobe. My focus on the here and now left me depleted, depressed, and disappointed by my choices in life. I should have been battling with covering a baby bump instead of fighting with the shadows in my head.

"Excuse me, I'm scheduled to fly back to San Francisco this morning, but when I checked in online last night, it said to see the ticket counter."

"Oh yes, your flight was cancelled," the airline agent said smartly. Her lipstick bled into the sides of her mouth, creating a joker-like effect.

"When is the next flight?" I said.

"Not until tomorrow afternoon at three o' clock, unfortunately," she said as her acrylic nails clipped the ticket counter keyboard.

"No no no, I need to get back home today."

"I understand, miss. Let me see what options we have for you. You can fly into Orange County and then transfer to SFO."

"Fine," I mumbled blowing my nose.

The secret of life is to appreciate the
pleasure of being terribly, terribly deceived.

—Oscar Wilde

I got home mid afternoon. Silence rushed through the house as if the volume had been turned down off news footage of a nuclear explosion as I wheeled my suitcase into my bedroom.

OLIVIA: I am home. Can we have a do-over? This has been a huge misunderstanding.

I anxiously stabbed the message into my phone, closed my eyes as my thumb hovered over the green Send button. I tried to talk myself out of sending the message. I knew it wasn't a good idea, but I did, then set the phone down on my nightstand.

Must stay busy, must stay busy, must stay busy, I thought to myself as I grabbed my purse and left the apartment. I couldn't look at the damn phone one moment longer, so I walked, and I walked, and I walked—up and down Marina Boulevard, then to the Embarcadero, and back to my house. Two and a half hours. That was long enough, right? Long enough to finish doing whatever he could have possibly been doing and read my text message.

I twisted my key into the door, jiggling it a bit. It had always been a sticky son of a bitch. We even had the landlord come over once because Cupcake swore the lock was broken. I walked down the long hallway into my bedroom, kicking off my shoes as I made my way around the field of dreams. Now, what a joke that scheme turned out to be! *If you build it, he will come.* Yeah, he came all right, and now he was gone.

I sat at the edge of the bed staring at the phone. No light blinking. What do I do now? This moment? This week? Forever? I simply had no plans. All my plans revolved around Peter, and he was the last straw.

Must stay busy.
Must stay busy.
Must stay busy.

HEATHER JOY HAMPTON

What can I do now? Take a shower, yes, that is a good idea. I'm sure he is planning a warm and witty response. We'll see each other later, right? Scrubbing the stink off me was the best plan I came up with, so I showered, letting the hot water run down my back as I cried until the hot water ran cold. I unwrapped the soggy towel turban around my head and crawled into my bed with my phone at my chest. Four hours later, all my faith and confidence in the future evaporated. Peter exposed my heart so big and gaping that now it felt like a heavy, lifeless appendage.

I felt trapped inside a heart incapable of beating on its own.

I had no idea I had been living on the surface of a bubble until it popped. I met my fate of becoming an old spinster with bloodshot eyes stained from crying, shaking hands, wringing a soggy tissue, and a shirt soaked with salty tears.

I couldn't function. I could only cry.

Big, wet, hot tears.

The kind that have a matching wounded-animal groan.

A deep, hollow moan coming from my gut.

I cried out of frustration.

I cried because I no longer had control of my life.

I cried in desperation.

Most of all, I cried because I lost hope.

Have you ever broken an object and watched the pieces fall neatly to the floor? A big piece flies here, a bigger piece flies over there, a few pieces go who knows where? If you are lucky, you might even be able to glue the pieces back together again, into an object stronger because of the break.

A shattered heart is another story, similar to a delicate glass vase slipping out of your grasp and shattering. You immediately know the aftermath. Teeny tiny, itty-bitty pieces, scattered every which way, so many tiny pieces that the idea of being able to put all the tiny pieces back together again seems absurd. Your best bet is to collect all the shattered glass and hopefully no one will step onto a tiny piece. Those shattered pieces of glass were my heart.

I wasn't brokenhearted. I was shattered-hearted.

The next morning, I woke up to the sound of my bedroom windows creaking open. I opened my eyes and squinted at the bright sunlight. For a moment, I didn't know where I was. I could see the tan-colored walls against bright white crown molding, chocolate-colored comforter, and oatmeal-colored carpet. I was at home. In my bed. Alone. My sheets smelled slightly moldy from sleeping with a damp towel. Someone must have opened the window. I didn't really care who opened the window, maybe a burglar that would shoot me and put me out of my misery. If it was a robber climbing through my window, he better not take my shoes. He would have to kill me before he took my shoes.

"Honey, you are going to have to get out of bed at some point," Zoe said, standing in front of my bedroom window. I could only see her silhouette. "Seriously, you'll feel better if you get up."

"What time is it?" I said, scratching the eye boogers that accumulated from crying in my sleep.

"It's ten o'clock," Zoe said as she walked around to the other side of my bed, picking up tear-soaked tissues. "I knocked on your door all night long. Why didn't you answer? I was worried about you." I hated the guilt tactic. This was my pain, my situation.

"I locked the door," I said flatly. I appreciated her concern, but it wasn't helping. I just wanted to be left alone, maybe even for good.

"I know. Isaac and I took the knob off." Zoe sat down next to me, wiping sweaty hair out of my face.

"Y'all took the knob off?"

"We found your toolbox in the hall closet," Zoe softly said. "I think you should come out with us tonight. We'll have fun. I promise."

"I can't," I mouthed, unable to speak. I began to cry again realizing I was too upset to be around other people.

The hardest thing to learn in life is which bridge to cross and which to burn.
—David Russell

"I can't handle this . . . I . . . don't . . . know . . . what . . . to . . . do." I half-hiccupped/half-cried into the phone. My head, congested from crying and blowing my nose, made my voice barely understandable.

"Baby, you have to pick yourself up and move on from this. Are your roommates around? Can they sit with you?" my mom asked.

"Zoe is going out for the night. It is New Year's Eve, Mom."

"I can't handle this, Mom," my voice trailing into a soft whisper. I felt as if the life was being sucked out of me, breath by breath.

"How about I come out and stay with you for a few weeks?" my mom pleaded with me.

"You don't need to do that," I said, while mentally trying to Scotch-tape my future back together as I furrowed my brow at the mounds of snotty tissues in my bedroom. Maybe I could become a hoarder of used tissue boxes or a crazy bag lady.

"No, sweetie, I think I do," she said firmly. "Let me talk to Zoe for a minute."

"Hey, sweetie, it's Olivia's mom."

"Hi, Mrs. Michaels, I'm really worried about Olivia. She's not eating."

"When was the last time she ate?"

"I don't know. I haven't seen her eat or leave her room since she got back from Texas."

"Dear Lord, okay, Zoe, here's what I need you to do. Take her to the emergency room in the morning and make sure she's not dehydrated. I'm booking a flight out there right now."

Zoe paced in front of baggage claim with her lavender cashmere-covered arms folded across her chest and head hung low as she waited with me for my mom. I sat on the floor against the baggage turnstile with my head buried between my arms wrapped around my knees. I literally could not stop crying, even enough to get in the car and pick up my mom from the airport alone.

She was the first person from her flight to enter the baggage claim area and ran toward me, dropping her purse and carry-on as she grabbed me like I was a wedding ring slipping down the garbage disposal. She squeezed me tight, and I felt one of her hot tears hit my cheek.

"We're gonna get through this, baby. We're gonna get through this." She brushed my hair out of my tear-stained face and forced herself to smile. God bless her for trying. I looked over to Zoe holding my mom's purse and carry-on suitcase. Zoe also had tears in her eyes. Peter broke a lot of hearts that week, broke my heart and the hearts of the people that matter the most to me.

Mom took care of me as if I were a child.

She made sure I got out of bed every morning.

She made sure I ate, at least breakfast. I cried in my egg omelets.

She made sure I traded my pajamas for regular clothes. I cried changing from my flannel pajamas into long-sleeved T-shirts and jeans.

She made sure I went outside at least once a day. I cried walking around the Marina, hiding behind big sunglasses even when it rained.

She made sure I survived my last day of work, riding the 30Sexpress with me to collect my belongings. Her strong hand pulling my head to her shoulder, she cooed a little bit to me like she did when I was in kindergarten and fell from the jungle gym. The Gap girl sitting across from us scowled, probably from the May/December romance she thought was sitting in front of her. I told my mom that as we got off the bus. We laughed together, and for a moment, I forgot about Peter.

My office had the stale smell of cardboard and packing tape. I opened the top drawer of my desk and stared at the paper clips, stapler refills, scattered rubber bands, and dust. *What am I supposed to do with all of this?* I thought to myself. "Baby, let's get the rest of your stuff," my mom said, taking down a vintage TWA advertisement of a cable car rolling up California Street. I bought it in Texas at Z Gallerie a few days before I moved to San Francisco. The sales clerk gushed how she was an army brat and lived all over the world, and San Francisco was the coolest city on the planet.

"Yoo-hoo! Is anyone here?" I peered out of my office door and saw Bragasaurus, wearing dark jeans and a black leather barn coat with Ray-Ban aviators. He looked ten years younger than the last time I saw him. I wondered if he sold his soul to the devil in exchange for an open tab at the fountain of youth.

"Well now, who do we have here?"

"Henri, this is my mother. Mom, this is, Henri."

"Pleased to meet you." My mom smiled.

"Honey, why isn't that hot man of yours helping you clean out your office?"

"They are not together anymore," my mom said before I had a chance to whitewash an explanation for Bragasaurus.

"Olivia! What happened?!"

"They broke up, that's what happened," my mom said in her "end of discussion" tone. A bloated pause for comment moment floated into the room, as if we were friends, and he expected me to provide details. Did he seriously think I was going to sit down and tell him my sad story? If I did, could I keep my job?

Cameron was already working out of the Los Angeles office while encouraging Emily that LA was where she wanted to live, knowing she would never actually move. Truth be told, his new position was simply a layover between marrying Emily and moving into her parent's three-story Philadelphia mansion.

HALF MOON BAY

Mom went back to Texas the next afternoon, and there was no longer anyone to "make sure" for me. I opened up the refrigerator and stared into it. What was mine? What belonged to Zoe and Cupcake? I fished out a microwavable Salisbury steak patty dinner from the freezer. It was beef and fatty, therefore didn't belong to either of them. I read the container's ingredients, four minutes in the microwave, then let cool for two minutes. I normally don't bother reading the directions. This time I did because that is what adults do.

A marathon of reality TV shows sucked me into its gullet. The rejection of contestants was mildly soothing. I felt like an asshole for enjoying watching thick streams of black mascara and eyeliner drip down a former stripper's face after being rejected by a washed-up rock star. I tried to find attributes about Peter that were washed-up and pathetic. My mind was a blank. Peter found nothing right with me, yet I couldn't find anything wrong with him.

That night I pulled his shirt out of a drawer and contemplated wearing it to sleep. It smelled just like him—man soap and fresh laundry, so I slept with it directly under my nose instead. His scent had faded a bit, but if I put my cheek to the fabric his body once touched, I could almost feel him. I closed my eyes and drifted off to sleep.

I awoke early the next morning after my mom left with no real plan for the day. I showered, tracing my fingers over my tummy and hips Peter once did as the warm water rushed over my body. I put the nightgown I wore so often at Peter's house and his undershirt in my tote just in case I decided to stay somewhere overnight. I wanted to escape the city, go away for a day or two, and more than anything—not run into him.

I drove down Highway 1 to Santa Cruz. The whimsical beach atmosphere, wooden roller coaster, and convertible cars driven by college students openly smoking marijuana felt inexplicably wrong. I was weary with a heavy heart, and the carefree laissez-faire town did not mirror my melancholy mood.

On the way back to San Francisco, right before Davenport near the Bonny Doon winery, were these cliffs with spiky edges and sharp drops into a navy blue-colored sea. They beckoned me. I pulled over and walked down a small path lined with tiny yellow flowers to the edge of a cliff. There was a young father with his toddler daughter picking flowers who smiled as I walked past them.

For weeks I stood on the edge, losing any desire to live. My thoughts overflowed with Peter, my mind was as jagged and rocky as the cliff above the water's edge. I wanted the water below to wash me away for good. The damp bottom of my sneaker lost its footing beneath me, and I slipped for a second, only a foot or two away from the cliff. In that definitive moment in time, I could have let myself "accidentally" slip off the cliff and end my life. The father nearby would attest that it was an accident. I realized I had the desire to find some way to get out of this thing. I just didn't know how.

CHAPTER TWENTY-FOUR

THE LIST

Hope is necessary in every condition.
—Samuel Johnson

I N ORDER TO achieve anything, you must have both the desire and the ability. The week prior, I realized I had the desire, so now I needed to find the ability. At the suggestion of Missy, I made an appointment with a life coach. Much different than a therapist, a life coach dealt with life's immediate problems by providing solutions.

Teresa Anderson's office was tucked away in a three-story building across the street from the cute Italian restaurant Jason McAllister took me to on our first date. I walked past the building twice before figuring out her "office" was in an apartment building. I didn't realize the address on her business card would be an apartment instead of an office.

"C'mon in, you must be Olivia." She smiled and waved me to come inside. "I'm Teresa, so pleased to meet you." She had the kind of glossy straight hair I aspired to have. Her thick brunette hair framed deep-set hazel eyes and a big toothy smile.

"Have a seat. Sit down. Make yourself at home." She motioned as we walked into the second bedroom of her apartment/office. Teresa neatly arranged herself in a lime green leather club chair motioning for me to sit on the tan velvet love seat in front of the bay window looking out onto Chestnut Street. I dropped my purse onto her hardwood floor and clasped my hands tightly in my lap after I sat down.

Picking up a pen and notepad, Teresa the life coach smiled at me for a moment, I assumed to assess the damage she's dealing with. "So this is totally informal. We're going to talk about whatever you want to talk about. We're going to work on whatever you want to work on. My job is to help you create the tools to fix whatever isn't working in your life. Does that make sense?"

I nodded, sucking back a bit of pain between my lips.

"So tell me what prompted you to seek out a life coach?" she asked with eyebrows raised like commas. Her face was perfectly made up, completely void of judgment at my disheveled appearance and swollen, puffy eyes.

"I'm broken." I closed my eyes to pause the now all too familiar tears. Sometimes only a drop or two, sometimes I cried for hours. The tears were always there waiting to flow out.

"Just had your heart broken?"

"Yeah . . . yeah." I hiccupped and nodded.

"Tell me about it." She lowered her commas and put her pen down onto the polka dot notepad. Is that a Kate Spade notepad? I didn't even know they made those. Okay, circle back ADD, girl.

"I was madly in love, and he broke my heart."

"What did he say when he ended the relationship?"

"He said he wasn't ready for this. He may never be ready for this."

"How did you respond to his feelings?" Teresa began to scribble notes while maintaining eye contact.

"I didn't have a chance to. He broke up with me over e-mail."

"Let's put him aside for a moment. Is there anything else in your life that is difficult for you right now?"

Shit, lady, if I could put him aside, I wouldn't be sitting here jonesing for your notepad.

"Sure, I lost my job, and I'm an architect, so there aren't exactly a million jobs out there to design new buildings right now. Both my roommates are moving away, so in a month I will have no place to live."

"That is a lot to deal with at once," Teresa commented as she made notes.

"There's more. I accidentally became pregnant last year. *We* decided it wasn't the right time for us to start a family, so I had an abortion, and it is the biggest mistake I have ever made in my life."

"You are a strong girl for getting through all of that." I looked up at her and glared. *You don't know me from a can of paint, and no, I'm not "getting through it." I'm knee-deep stuck in it, and I don't know where to begin to get out.*

"I was. I used to be a strong girl. Now I am barely hanging on," I said, putting my sweaty clenched right hand onto my chest.

"I went through something similar once seven years ago. I was at the airport in Brazil flying back to the US because my father had a stroke and got a phone call from my boyfriend, who was also my boss, by the way. He told me I was being replaced. When I got back home, he wouldn't return my phone calls—at all. Turns out he replaced me in more ways than one. He married her three months later."

"How long did it take you to get over it?"

"I'll let you know." She winked at me and jotted down a note. "I can't guarantee you will get over him, or get back to the way you were before all of this happened, but it does get easier with time."

"I hope so."

"Here's what I would like for you to do for next time: make a list."

This lady is good, I thought to myself. Lists made on cute notepads, like her adorable polka-dot notepad, lists with little boxes that I can check. Maybe that isn't Kate Spade. I think I saw her notepad at FranklinCovey last month.

"It could be anything, everything. Take a cooking class. Go to Thailand. Buy a necklace you were hoping he would get you. Run a marathon. Just make a list of as many tangibles you would like to accomplish, learn, try, do, buy, achieve."

"Tangible?"

"What I mean by tangible is being able to complete that item on the list. Happiness, for example, being happy isn't tangible. It is an emotion you feel at a certain moment. Happiness is fluid. Make sense?"

"Makes sense." And I smiled for the first time that day.

"You're going to get through this. You might not believe that now, but you will," she said as she walked me to the door and gave me a side hug of reassurance. I walked over to my favorite stationary store on Union Street after I left her apartment/office to pick out my own cute notepad and matching pen.

"Anybody home?" Guess not. I walked into my bedroom, kicked off my shoes, and climbed onto my bed, pulling the notepad and pen out of the shopping bag.

Tangibles. Tangibles. Let's see . . .

Change my phone number
Learn to sew
Get another job
Buy a right hand ring
Get a tattoo
Buy the locket Peter was going to give me for Christmas
Learn how to play the guitar
Run a marathon
Get rid of everything that reminds me of Peter

It wasn't much, but it was a starting point at least. Like most nights, I couldn't sleep. I went for a run around 5:30 a.m. while it was still dark outside. The mist falling that morning made the sidewalks more slippery than usual. I pulled my phone out from the booty pocket of my running pants and tucked it safely between my two jog bras so it wouldn't get wet. As I picked up speed crossing Pacific Street, Peter's car passed me headed south down Gough Street. I guess he had not been able to sleep that night either. I stopped and watched the tail lights of his car as he sat at a stoplight a few streets ahead well after the light turned green as cars swerved out of his lane and sped past him. This is too much. Being this close was too much.

Another item was scribbled on the list that morning:

Move back to Texas

"What's all this?" Zoe said after opening the door of my bedroom.

"Things I can't have anymore," I said, neatly folding the periwinkle blouse I wore on my second date with Peter and placing it into a Trader Joe's plastic reusable grocery bag.

"But you love all these clothes . . . Why are you getting rid of them?" Zoe pleaded, hopping onto my bed with a bounce of frustration in her step.

"They served their purpose," I said in a voice much deeper than normal as I pulled a cashmere sweater off the hanger and folded it on top of the second-date blouse, a pile of sentimentality.

"Why are you getting rid of things you love?" Zoe said, neatly tucking her legs behind each other and staring at me with her big brown eyes.

"You tell me. Why does anyone get rid of anything? Peter loved me, and then he got rid of me!" I screamed back at her, bursting into tears.

I sank down onto the beige Berber carpet of my bedroom as Zoe rushed over to hug me tightly. I felt like a tube of toothpaste she was trying to squeeze the hurt out of. There was no use, but I loved her for trying. I whispered to my best friend as she hugged me, "I'm moving back to Texas." She pulled away from her Colgate embrace and stared into my eyes, so red from crying that the jagged red lines resembled a road map.

"Are you sure you want to do that?" Zoe asked, her eyes narrowing in concern.

"Yeah . . . I have to. I love it here, but I can't stay in San Francisco. My life here is over," I said with yet another chubby hot tear streaming down my face.

Choosing to flee San Francisco was extreme, but painfully necessary. At a critical time in my life, it pushed me to take responsibility—to stop waiting for the elusive someone or something to mend and define my purpose in this world. Sometimes letting things go is an act of far greater power than defending or hanging on. So that's what I did. I let go—of all of it.

I would have willingly turned myself inside out for him. Instead, I was forced to turn my world inside out to save myself. Could I survive knowing that the world I so desperately wanted to create with him could only come to fruition in my mind? I asked myself the hard questions. I fell apart over and over again. I wanted to be broken open, to sit in the dark of my heart. I trusted myself and had the humility to climb down into the bottomless pit that had left me voraciously hunger for more. Peter had been able to fill that pit up. It wasn't bottomless I decided. It was just a really deep vortex that desperately needed to be investigated.

So I discarded things that reminded me of him: clothing, photos, keepsakes, mementos, belongings big and small that would be a constant reminder, keeping only a few small mementos packed in a moving box labeled with his initials.

Afterward, I packed up all my belongings and everything I learned while living in San Francisco and set out to change a few things.

They say time changes everything,
but you actually have to change them yourself.
—Andy Warhol

The rhythmic lull of packing leaves little time for idle thoughts. It is remarkable the energy having a purpose produces. I spent twenty-four hours on the floor of my bedroom carefully folding and packing, until my eyes were glazed over and every fold of my skin sprinkled with beads of sweat behind the bend of my arms, the crooks behind my knees, crevice between my breasts. I did not think about Peter.

Instead, I felt a heavy blank space between my ears, where the memories of us were forced out through my eyeballs in the form of juicy thick tears. My bedroom felt like a blank space too, a growing expansion between the romantic homeyness we created and the dull emptiness of silence. His extra toothbrush was thrown away. His pillow was no longer indented. The few mementos I couldn't bear to throw away were safely packed in the big box near the door.

"I'm all out of packing tape," Zoe said, standing in the doorway of my bedroom, which was now stocked floor to ceiling with moving boxes.

"There's some over there, I think," I said, pointing to an area by the bay window of my bedroom.

"Well, my movers are coming on Friday. I just talked to Katie, and she said her fiancé and some of his buddies could handle moving her stuff out, so I guess they will do that sometime this weekend," Zoe said, climbing on top of my bed, grabbing one of my throw pillows.

"You okay?" I asked.

"I'm sad I won't be here in the morning."

"It's no big deal. We can do the whole good-bye thing tonight, okay?"

"Let's have a good-bye drink at Notte, like we did when we moved in," Zoe said, tracing the edges of the velvet throw pillow on my bed.

"I don't really want to go to a bar tonight. I need to finish packing, and well, frankly, look at me," I pointed to my dusty cargo pants and college sweatshirt.

"Let's stay here instead! Only on one condition, no tears tonight, I'm serious. This is a crying-prohibited zone tonight." I smiled and hugged Zoe.

"We should totally burn the man chart in the fireplace!" Cupcake proclaimed after a few glasses of wine. So we did. Tearing up the poster board into eight smaller sections, then tossing them into the fireplace was symbolic.

For a few hours that night, I was able to push Peter out of my mind enough to enjoy my roommates one last time. Zoe and I stayed up and talked after Cupcake went to bed.

"It felt good to burn that damn thing," Zoe said.

"I need to do the same thing to Peter's stuff."

"Go get the box."

"I can't. I can't."

"C'mon, you'll feel better!"

"Here, open," Zoe said, handing me the kitchen scissors. The sharp blade of the knife cut into the moving tape, separating it to each side of the cardboard flaps. These were things I didn't want to see, but decided they were too precious to discard. I can always buy another periwinkle top like the one I wore on our second date. This box contained mementos I could never replace. My keys to his apartment were on top of everything else in the box in a preaddressed red envelope, just in case he ever asked for them back, so I took a deep breath and tossed the envelope into the fireplace followed by:

Movie tickets
Baseball game tickets
Program from the play he took me to for my birthday eve
Program from the ACT play we saw
Thank-you note from his mom
Receipt from breakfast after the first time I spent the night with him
Barbie toothbrush he bought so she could guard my bathroom like Batman guarded his bathroom
Notepad from our hotel room in Bodega Bay
Paper place mat from the weird hookah place
Wine corks we saved and wrote the date on
Boarding passes for every time he picked me up at the airport
His Christmas present that he never received: basketball game tickets
Recipes for all of the meals we, okay I, cooked
Photos I took with his family

One by one, I tossed each item into the fireplace. Zoe, my cheerleader, encouraged me like a labor and delivery nurse, "Okay, only a few more items to go! You're almost there! I can see the bottom of the box!"

I quickly tossed the positive pregnancy test into the fireplace as Zoe jumped and said,

"Hey, wait a second, was that a—"

"I'm not talking about it," I said while my chin quivered. Zoe never knew I was pregnant. Even though she would have been a supportive friend, I couldn't tell her. She knew how badly I wanted to be a mother. We played the "what will our babies look like" game at least three times.

"Feel better?"

"No, I don't feel better. I feel same. Tonight isn't about Peter. Let's talk about something else," I said, shaking my head.

"It's getting late, and you need to be up in a few hours, gimme one last hug," I said as I peeled my butt and body off the floor.

"I hate now," she sniffed.

"No tears tonight, remember?"

"Yeah, I remember. Are you going to bed?"

"Nah, I'm going to stay up for a little bit."

"Don't forget to turn the fireplace off."

"Hey, Zoe, thank you for being such a good friend."

"Traveled down the road and back again," Zoe belted out.

"If you threw a party," I joined in, "invited everyone you knew, you would see the biggest gift would be from me, and the card attached would say 'Thank you for being a friend'!"

I walked into the kitchen and committed it to memory. All the good times and girl talk we shared in that kitchen. I thought about my dad doing his kitchen autopsy before we moved in, learning how to cook my first turkey in the oven at our Thanksgiving party, the cabinets with shock absorbers so they couldn't be slammed, the refrigerator that beeped when it was open for longer than thirty seconds, picking out which wine to drink from the built in cubbyholes.

"Good-bye, kitchen," I whispered to no one but myself. I flipped off the lights in the kitchen and turned off the fireplace. There they were—Peter's keys. Everything else burned in the fireplace but those damn keys. I went back into the kitchen, grabbed a skewer, then pulled them out and went to bed.

CHAPTER TWENTY-FIVE

THE MUG SHOT

We must be our own before we can be another's.
—Ralph Waldo Emerson

I WAS HOLDING THE soot-covered keys in my clenched sweat-covered fist when I woke up the next morning, still wearing a sweatshirt and cargo pants on my field of dreams stripped of sheets and all the trimmings. Instead of being as dreamy as a chocolate bar, the mattress looked bare and exposed. I showered, using travel-sized shampoo and hotel soap from the W hotel in Seattle. I shaved my legs and tossed the razor and hotel products into the trash as I toweled off, then stuffed the towel into the trash too. I sifted through my suitcase and pulled out a bra, pair of socks, and underwear avoiding the full-length mirror in my bedroom wrapped in bubble tape at the corners. I didn't want to look at the body Peter decided he was no longer interested in seeking naked. I put on the cargo pants I slept in and slipped on a long-sleeved shirt. I twirled my wet hair into a messy bun, causing a big fat bead of water to trickle down my neck and into my shirt. It felt cold. At least temperature was a sense I was capable of feeling.

I plodded into the kitchen and found Cupcake stirring her coffee in the only mug either she or Zoe owned. "We're gonna miss that big nice Dallas mug of yours," Cupcake said softly. "When are your movers coming?"

"In a little bit," I said, staring down at the hardwood floors. Their auburn color often reminded me of my natural hair color.

"Really?!" Cupcake squealed. *Yes, really, dumb ass,* I thought to myself. I only told her four times the movers were coming at 9:00 a.m. "Well, I guess this is good-bye then!" Cupcake pulled me into a bony hug. It was one of those airport good-bye moments, only dramatic given the circumstances, with lots of squeezing and promises that we would talk soon. It felt phony, bittersweet, painful, and taxing. For me and Cupcake, this was the end of our friendship. Adios, à **b**ientôt, arrivederci. Saying good-bye to Katie was easier than I thought. In the end, Katie was exactly what I thought she was: a cupcake, sugary sweet without a lot of substance.

I struggled with saying good-bye to Peter. Various situations played out in my head while I shampooed my hair, or stirred my coffee, or stood at a stoplight waiting for the walk sign. Every situation resulted in an unfortunate ending. Even if he begged me to stay, and even if I did, I would always wonder if he changed his mind because he loved me or because he didn't want me to leave. He discarded me as if I was distraction, someone who "got in his way." Why should he get the courtesy of a good-bye?

With a steady hand, and a makeshift plan, I closed the door to my home in San Francisco for the final time, February 2, 2009, with nowhere to be for over a week. I was relieved to be done with the city, to be able to loosen the knot tying me to the struggle to maintain my sense of self while still meshed with San Francisco society.

I drove down Gough Street to Broadway and made a left so I could pass Peter's building for the final time. The art deco entry, with its sharp-edged arch above the heavy door that I could never manage to get my key to work, called my name.

I begged to be on the other side of that door, just one more time.

To see him walk out of the elevator bank and make a silly face back at me, just one more time.

I said good-bye to the building aloud and continued on my way to Van Ness Avenue and out of the city by the bay.

HEATHER JOY HAMPTON

I drove down Highway 1 south for hours along the coast. It was so beautiful and so romantic, all the more emphasizing his disappearance from my life. This was supposed to have been "our trip" down the coast. Now that our romantic getaway would never come to fruition, I thought that by taking this trip despite losing him I could reclaim some sense of self. Nope, all I felt was emptiness. I was in the driver's seat, not Peter. I hated every minute of it.

My ties to California were bound tighter than ever despite the distance I gained the first day on the road. I spent one night in Carmel and the next night in Santa Barbara, where Peter went to undergrad. The next morning I was completely off the beaten path that I thought I would once share with the man I loved. This had become my own journey to travel, my own path to find. Reminders of the moments we shared were many miles behind me. The road back home had diverted onto a path I never thought I would take: through the Mojave Desert. The topography of the desert matched the desolate hopelessness in my heart. I forced myself to come to my final conclusion that all the pain I felt inside was self-inflicted. The person causing all my tears took stock in me, and all the wonderful moments we shared, and then decided he no longer was in need of my company.

After several days driving, all my music had been played, and the radio wouldn't pick up any channels, so I tuned into the melody of my own internal song. I became a coward in my own mind. I was bound by all the threads of my personal tapestry.

It was dusk when I slammed Boudreaux's door and walked toward the observation rail of the Grand Canyon. The striped layers of colored sediment were breathtaking, partly for the sheer magnitude and natural beauty, mostly because it looked like my personal mug shot. The hole inside me was too deep to see the bottom, the jagged edges and rocky cliffs complicated.

After the sun went down, I checked into my hotel room at the Holiday Inn Express outside the entrance to the canyon. I put on my thickest sweater, piled my hair on top of my head, plugged in my ear buds, and went in search of dinner at one of the handful of restaurants scattered along the wide boulevard. I decided on saltine crackers for dinner at the kitschy gift shop/general store at the end of the road. I perused the office supplies aisle, took a gander at the tacky tourist memorabilia, and flipped through a book dedicated to all the people that died at the Grand Canyon. It was getting late, and I was the only person in the store, so I guess that is why the cashier decided to chitchat.

"This your first trip here?"

"Yeah, it is."

"How long you here for?"

"Just for a couple of days."

"We don't get that many visitors this time of year."

"I can imagine. I didn't realize it would be this cold."

"So, uh, what's going on here?" she said, looking down at my peculiar compilation of purchases: index cards, Kleenex, packet of highlighters, interior decorating magazine, and bottled water. I lost my appetite walking down the boulevard as well as my ability to bullshit, so I told the cashier my sad little story.

"Listen here, some day there's gonna be some guy who's gonna be real happy your boyfriend turned out to be such a jackass."

THE END

EPILOGUE

I became insane, with long intervals of horrible sanity.
—Edgar Allan Poe

I STOOD IN THE drug store soap aisle of one Saturday night. Which one was it? They all looked so similar? The names and descriptions of soaps designed to attract men are so funny to me . . . Should I click the tops and test them? I was a sad case altogether in my cargo pants that now barely hung onto my hips and basketball T-shirt I purchased to wear to a game with Peter. A full-blown crying fit didn't need to go down in the drug store, and I wasn't certain I could retain control of my capacities once I danced with the scent of Satan.

"Awhh, don't worry, hunneee. He'll still luv yew if you bring home tha wrong one." I smiled sheepishly at the blue-haired woman, grabbed a 24 oz. bottle of man soap described as smelling of ice, wind, and freedom then walked directly to the checkout stand.

I thought I would never scratch my itch for his scent when I moved 1,800 miles away from Peter, but the moment I shut the door of my apartment, I collapsed onto the kitchen floor. I was used to smelling the musky, peppery man-soap aroma floating out of the plastic soap bottle when we cuddled with my head in the crook of his chest. Now I appeased my sense of smell from a plastic soap bottle, making it all the more clear how much I longed for him. My sense of touch yearned to rest my face on his chest . . . to taste the sweet and saltiness of his kisses after he went running . . . the soothing deep tenor of his voice.

The sharp pain and jagged edges of his rejection stabbed my heart with a steely dullness. My heart hurt in ways I never imagined it could. I missed Peter terribly. The questions I asked myself were horrid and rancid.

What if I was prettier?

What if I had acted differently? Would he have loved me then?

How is it possible to love someone more than you love yourself when they never loved you at all?

I changed my address. I changed my phone number. But I couldn't change my mind. It was filled with missing him. The absence of his mark only made it more obvious how much I desperately missed him. For months, I fell off the grid, falling apart over and over again.

A dark place in my heart took over when I was exhausted from searching for meaning or explanations or answers to the questions that encircled my brain like the sweaty clenched hands of fifth graders playing Red Rover. I wanted so badly to spend time with my friends and family, maybe even have a boyfriend. They always saw through my bullshit eventually and were left feeling confused and exhausted. It was humiliating and easier to be all by myself. The wear and tear sunk into my eyeball sockets and the lines of my hands. A lot of my hair had also fallen out, which would have been a cause for concern if I bothered to comb it; most days it went from wet ponytail straight out of the shower to dry and flat fly-a-ways. My hair grew six inches before I noticed much less bothered to cut it.

Every breath of me was consumed. The heartache and the pain became an entity all its own, grown as organically as our love affair. I never meant to eschew the torment. It was like a heavy appendage that I carried daily, attached to my soul, attached to my mind, attached to everything around me. I grew fond of the burden over time. For all its grotesque and masochist symbolism, that entity was the closest connection I had to him, and I couldn't bear to let it go.

I was homesick for San Francisco too. I missed Zoe. I still couldn't manage to sit on the middle cushion of my couch. In my imagination, Zoe's butt impression was permanently there from all the nights she spent sitting Indian style with her laptop trolling for free dinners online.

I dote on his very absence.

—William Shakespeare

I had a chicken dumpling-sized lump in my throat as the flight attendant ripped my DFW/SFO boarding pass. For months the idea of going back to San Francisco felt like vacationing at the scene of a crime. Those seven by seven miles contained so many fabulous friends I missed dearly . . . and the man that I cried myself to sleep about nightly. The idea of seeing him, even being within a one-mile radius of him, terrified me to the core. Sometimes you have to look fear in the eye and say, "I don't care." In this particular

HEATHER JOY HAMPTON

situation, I was facing my fear of San Francisco for the sake of Jackson. He was getting married in two days, Zoe and I were bridesmaids, so this trip to the land of Cabernet and heartbreak was out of necessity.

Instead of the pint-size cabbie with the newsboy cap, I was picked up by Jackson. The warmth of his bear hug and cologne that smelled like pine trees brought me to reality. I was back to be there for my dear friend and to spend time with the people that helped make San Francisco home.

"Get in the damn car, Jessica Depressica! We've got some work to do," he said, running his hand through my hair. Frankly, it was a hot shitty mess. I hadn't cut or colored my hair since I left, and my hair was definitely showing much need of his artful handiwork.

"Spill!" Jackson said as he lowered my head into the salon shampoo sink. I closed my eyes and felt the heat of the water against my scalp as Jackson's hands ran shampoo through my hair. I wanted to avoid the question altogether. There wasn't anything to say, really.

"Well, if you won't, I will. You probably won't like this since I know how much you like being a blonde, but I don't give a shit. We're dying your hair back red." Jackson said, switching the water to ice cold as he rinsed shampoo out of my hair.

I nodded in approval as Jackson wrapped a towel around my head and we walked back to his salon station. I plunked into the cushy salon chair and watched Jackson pull the towel off and comb through my hair, still half blonde on the bottom. Sort of ironic how our appearances emulate how we feel inside. I felt embarrassed and exposed allowing my friend to see just how much (or how little) I gave a shit about how I looked.

Two hours later, my hair was back to its natural color with a new glamorous haircut. Jackson spun me around in the salon chair and leaned over, his cheek touching mine. "Honey, look at yourself, I know how you are because you are a Leo like me, overly critical and the tiniest bit dramatic," Jackson said, winking at me. He stood up and brushed my hair with his hands. "Promise me you will say this a thousand times a day until you believe it to be true: the woman looking back at me in the mirror is someone worthy of love." I looked at myself in the mirror, and although I could always find faults with my reflection, his comment was exactly what I saw: a woman worth loving. Tears spilled over onto my black salon smock.

"Girl, you better cry it out now because your eye makeup better be fierce tonight!" Jackson said, winking at me.

A few hours later, I buckled the strap of my heels, then smoothed the skirt of my taffeta bridesmaid dress, and sat for a moment on the pillow top bench seat in a Sonoma winery overlooking a bluff in the Russian River Valley.

"Awhhh yeah!" Zoe squealed as she walked into the room. Her dress was identical to mine, but a deep purple compared to my sour apple green dress. Each of the bridesmaids wore dresses the same color as their birthstones.

"My ladies are all semiprecious stones today!"

"Semiprecious, huh?" piped a burly cousin that Jackson's mom forced into the wedding party. She resembled a lumberjack squeezed into a two sizes too small bridesmaid dress like boudin sausage.

"Well, except for you, Martha. You are totally precious today," Jackson said, rolling his eyes at the Brawny advertisement ruining his wedding.

The ceremony was intimate and lovely. Jackson exchanged vows with Patrick, the love of his life, he met nine months prior. They both wore pale gray suits with lavender ties and looked like love personified. After the ceremony, the other groomsmen and bridesmaids were all set to dance the night away. I, however, was feeling altogether melancholy.

"Jackson made me promise to say an affirmation in front of the mirror," I said as to Zoe as we drove across the Golden Gate Bridge in her new convertible after the ceremony.

"Yeah, he did! What was the affirmation? I promise never to cut my bangs?"

"He made me promise to say 'the woman looking back at me in the mirror is someone worthy of love' a thousand times a day."

"That's a big-time commitment. What are you supposed to do with the rest of your free time?" Zoe and I laughed.

"It isn't bad advice, you know," Zoe said as she leaned over and squeezed my knee.

"I know," I said, "I'm going to try."

"Promise?"

"Promise," I said, nodding my head.

"You sure you're going to be okay staying all by yourself?" Zoe asked as she pulled in front of my hotel in Union Square.

"Yeah yeah yeah. I'll be fine. I just need some alone time in San Francisco for the night. Seriously Zoe, I'll be just fine. We'll talk soon." I leaned over and hugged her. She didn't understand what I was going through and I didn't know where to begin to explain it to her.

I hopped out of her car, pulled my bag out of her trunk, and waved good-bye.

Barn's burnt down, now I can see the moon.
　　　　　　　　　　　　　—Mizuta Masahide

I switched my wedding heels for knee high boots, pulled a denim jacket on, and twirled a scarf around my neck as I walked out of my hotel still wearing my bridesmaid dress. Truth be told, it was a fantastic dress and looked adorably trendy paired with casual accessories.

I stood at the corner of Mason and Market waiting for the walk sign to light up, remembering how I once followed a blind man after watching him navigate through thick hordes of street traffic. Frankly, Union Square is an urban assault to your five senses. I was curious how the other four were experienced by a person without sight. The cacophony of multiple languages and conversations at any given cross walk combined with street performers playing on the sidewalk, beggars, protestors, the unique smell of old sneakers, leftovers, and expensive perfume. I became mesmerized watching his walking stick with a yellow fuzzy tennis ball attached swivel back and forth in a semi-circle across the sidewalk.

Life goes on in a city so full of history, story after story woven together, creating a tapestry of overlapping circumstances. It was then that I realized just how lost I had been living in San Francisco. Confused. Unappreciative. Fragmented. Desperate to hang onto my roots while discovering who I was in the process. The heartbreak, the pain, the loss, was never 100 percent about Peter. That heartbreak, that pain, that loss, was simply the catalyst, which forced me to deal with pain buried so deep inside me even I had forgotten it existed. Peter was the one who was supposed to save me from all that pain, forever. It took me a year to realize that he couldn't/wouldn't save me from anything. I had to be my own hero. I had to save myself. The blind man couldn't see the big picture. Neither could I living my grand adventure outside of my comfort zone without the best of intentions. Hindsight has 20/20 vision sometimes. I missed my life in San Francisco. I missed my friends. Hell, I even missed being a Marina girl.

CONTRIBUTORS

Cover art and illustrations were drawn by Livia Hajovsky. She has experience in a wide variety of artistic mediums spanning over three decades. Livia lives in Fort Worth, Texas with her husband. Her other works can be found at *http://livia-theartjunkie.blogspot.com/*.

Author's photograph is courtesy of Sal Sessa. His photography experience includes corporate events, professional head shots, meetings, conventions, and trade shows. His portfolio can be found at www.salsessa.com

Edwards Brothers, Inc.
Thorofare, NJ USA
June 22, 2011